JOIN MY BOOK CUB

If you enjoy this book, you can join my book club to find out more about my writing, to receive stories set in the world of this book and to read the opening chapters of my next book before it comes out.

Please see the end of this book for full details.

Thanks,
Rachel McLean

PART I
OCTOBER 2019 TO OCTOBER 2020. LONDON AND BIRMINGHAM.

OCTOBER 2019. LONDON

HAYLEY PRICE WAS DEAD, AND JENNIFER SINCLAIR WAS going to get the blame.

Never mind that Hayley took her own life. Never mind that someone in Bronzefield Prison had provided her with the tool. And never mind that the prison staff had taken their eyes off a woman on suicide watch.

As far as the media was concerned, Hayley's death was the fault of Jennifer Sinclair, Prisons Minister.

Today Jennifer would be making a statement in the House of Commons, explaining why Hayley had been allowed to die. And it needed to be good. The prison governor's job was at stake – of course – but so was her own.

It was five am, and Jennifer was up early, taking advantage of the quiet of her London flat. Little disturbed her from outside: the milkman making his way along the street below, a couple of late night revellers ending yesterday instead of beginning today. Inside, all was quiet. Her husband Yusuf hadn't stirred when she'd slipped out of bed and her two sons were fast asleep in sleeping bags on the living room floor, staying in London for a special occasion.

She sat on the floor of the kitchen, the only uninhabited room, and stared at the sheet of paper. Her civil servants had insisted on drafting a full speech, but she knew she'd do better with notes. Thinking on her feet had got her this far; hopefully it wouldn't fail her now.

She glanced at the oven clock. Not long before Hassan would wake to realise it was his tenth birthday. She didn't want him to find her sitting on the floor.

She pushed herself up, rubbing her cramped legs, and crept towards the bedroom. It was a treat having the whole family here - normally they'd be at home in her Birmingham constituency - but the timing of this crisis was far from ideal.

She reached the door to the bedroom and heard movement behind her.

"Mummy?"

She looked round. Hassan was sitting up, rubbing his eyes. His older brother Samir was still snoring.

She pushed the speech from her mind. "Morning, darling. Happy birthday."

His eyes widened and he let out a shriek. He threw off the sleeping bag and jumped up, pushing past her to wake his dad.

"Daddy! Wake up!" he cried. Jennifer followed him into the bedroom.

Yusuf sat up in bed and feigned a yawn.

"Hello? Why would anyone want to get up this early on a Wednesday?"

"Daddy!" Hassan repeated, and jumped on him. Grunts came from beneath the duvet. Jennifer sat on the end of the bed and gave Hassan a hug.

Yusuf leaned in and wrapped his arms round both of

4

them. "Anyone would think it was a special day," he groaned, pulling back and throwing Jennifer a wink.

Hassan shrieked. "Daddy! It's my birthday!"

Yusuf threw back the quilt, grabbing Hassan in one swift movement and tickling him. Hassan shrieked with delight.

Yusuf laughed. "Go and get your brother, Mr Early Waker."

Hassan nodded and sprang for the door, confident in the knowledge that when he returned, there would be presents.

Five minutes later he dragged Samir into the room.

"Alright, alright, I'm coming," Samir moaned, yawning.

"You can't sleep in on my birthday," Hassan replied.

Samir shrugged. Four years older than his brother, he was becoming skinny, gangly even. His skin was pale with fatigue and he had dark circles under his eyes. He would have been up late watching YouTube videos on his phone, Jennifer knew. He tried to hide it but the glow from beneath his duvet – or sleeping bag – was a dead giveaway.

"Hello, love," she said, reaching out towards him. "Come and sit with us while Hassan trashes the place."

She shifted into the middle of the bed, making room. Samir glanced at her then perched on the edge of the mattress. He pulled his sleeping bag around his shoulders.

Jennifer pushed aside the stab of rejection and shifted her attention to Hassan, who was scrabbling under the bed for presents. Samir dived onto his brother, pretending to grab the presents first. Hassan pushed him off.

"Come on Samir," said Yusuf. "It's Hassan's day."

Samir scowled and Hassan emerged from under the bed, his face flushed. He passed a present to his brother. "It's OK. He can help me."

Jennifer threw Yusuf a smile. That was just like Hassan, always wanting to share with his brother.

"Go on then," she laughed. "Get ripping." Yusuf lifted her hand to his lips and kissed her fingertips, his eyes fixed on her face. The boys ignored them, intent on tearing open wrapping paper. Yusuf squeezed her hand, then dropped it and joined in with the boys, pushing wrapping paper to the floor. Jennifer sat back and watched, smiling to herself. Seeing her boys enjoy moments she'd never had as a child felt like an accomplishment.

Then her eyes glazed over and she turned away, the boys' cries fading.

She couldn't stop thinking about that damn speech.

～

Four hours later, Jennifer stepped into St Stephens' lobby, the high, vaulted space between the Commons Chamber and the rest of the House of Commons. MPs hurried in from their offices and staff dashed between meetings, clutching sheafs of paper and mobile phones. Against this backdrop, reporters threw questions to passing ministers or else talked intently to camera. The noise was overwhelming. As Jennifer ducked past a TV crew, she overheard her name. The reporter – Gillian Wakefield, from the BBC – had her hand up to her ear, listening to her anchor in the studio. She was nodding, a smile playing on her lips. Jennifer paused to listen, stepping out of the reporter's eyeline.

The reporter dropped her hand and straightened up.

"Well, Mark," she said, "Nothing official of course, but several sources indicate that the minister's position could well be at stake."

Jennifer stiffened. She pinched her fingers together, grinding a fingernail into the ball of her thumb.

She started moving again, regretting that she'd stopped. She was happy to face down the cameras – relished it, even – but right now she didn't need to be distracted from her speech. Later, she would do all the interviews they wanted and prove to the world that she wasn't going anywhere. But for now... she needed to focus on surviving.

"Ms Sinclair!" cried a voice. "I wonder if I could have a quick—"

They'd spotted her.

"Sorry." Jennifer slipped between the other MPs and disappeared into the chamber.

As she reached the double doors she felt a hand on her shoulder. She willed the irritation from her face and turned round, ready to face down the reporter. But it was John Hunter, Home Secretary. Her boss.

"John. Thank goodness."

He raised an eyebrow.

"Nothing. Just..." She shook her head. "Press attention."

"Not surprising."

No, not surprising at all, she thought.

His grey eyes were cold. "We need to talk." He glanced around. "Not here."

"But I was just—"

He pulled her to one side, towards the Strangers' Gallery. They huddled next to the wall, their heads close together. Jennifer leaned on the wood panelling.

"This needs to be good," he said.

She nodded. "It will be. You know it will."

His normally ruddy cheeks were pale. "Michael's got his eye on you."

Michael Stuart was the Prime Minister. Jennifer didn't

know whether he would be present for her statement, but she knew he would be watching.

"Of course," she replied. "He should do."

John allowed himself a laugh. "Confident, are we?"

She pulled back her shoulders. "Yes. I won't let you down. You know that."

"Right then. Let's see what you've got, eh?" He placed a hand in the small of her back and guided her to the chamber. As she pushed the doors open, he whispered in her ear.

"Meet me for lunch, afterwards. Members' Dining Room."

She frowned. Normally they spoke in his office, or sometimes hers. Why the Members' Dining Room?

He slipped past and she watched him work his way between their colleagues, shaking hands and slapping shoulders. She wished she had his ease.

She shuffled along the front bench, taking her place next to her boss. She looked sideways at him; he was twisted round in his seat, laughing with two backbenchers behind them. She watched, trying to work out how he did it. How he performed so well in public.

The dining room. It's a public space, she realised.

If the Home Secretary was going to sack her, she wouldn't be able to make a fuss.

2

OCTOBER 2019. LONDON

JENNIFER SMOOTHED HER PALMS ON HER SKIRT AND
stood up, taking a deep breath.

Across the Chamber, the Opposition bristled with
contempt. Order papers waved in the air and voices rose to
the vaulted ceiling. She focused on the dispatch box in front
of her, trying to drown out the nagging voice inside
her head.

Behind her, it wasn't much quieter. MPs cupped their
hands to their mouths and hooted across the chamber. The
wooden benches reverberated with hands slapped on their
backs, and air gusted towards her as people leaned forwards
in their places.

Beside her, John was quiet.

She waited for the noise to subside. It didn't.

"Order!" the Speaker cried, reddening.

The shouts were replaced by whispers. She took
another breath and glanced at her notes. She didn't
need them.

She pulled back her shoulders. Time to perform.

"I have a statement to make about recent events at Bronzefield Prison," she began.

The noise started up again.

"This House is aware of the unfortunate and tragic death of Hayley Price, one of Bronzefield's inmates."

More shouting. *What must we look like to the outside world?* she thought. This was nothing to get excited about. A woman was dead.

Hayley had been just nineteen years old, arrested for stealing from a pharmacy. She'd wanted the drugs to abort an unwanted pregnancy. On remand at Bronzefield, she'd somehow got hold of a coat hanger. The results – Jennifer had seen the photos – hadn't been pretty.

Poor girl. Only five years older than Samir. She wondered what Hayley's mother was going through.

She looked at the Speaker, who was calling for order. When the noise calmed, she kept her voice low.

"Thank you, Mr Speaker. I would like to ask my honourable friends to join me in showing respect for Hayley's memory and sympathy for her family at what must be a dreadful time for them.

"Hayley Price was a vulnerable young woman imprisoned when she should have been helped."

Muttering from behind her. She lifted her chin higher.

"At nineteen years of age, Hayley found herself pregnant." She paused to look around her colleagues. John was still, staring ahead. She sniffed and raised her voice, aware of the impact of her words. "She tried to end that pregnancy, but found herself on the wrong side of the law. Which is how she ended up at Bronzefield."

Just out of her line of vision, she sensed John turn towards her. She licked her lips.

They want me to apologise, she thought. *They want me to make excuses.*

That wasn't going to happen. She continued.

"Hayley tried again to end her pregnancy, but instead she died. In the most brutal, bleak and lonely circumstances we can imagine any young person dying in." She paused, allowing the words to sink in. "We must never allow that to happen again. As a civilised society, we have a duty to protect all of our citizens. Even those who break the law. And especially those who are most vulnerable."

She looked around her colleagues. *I'm not going anywhere*, she thought. "I will work to ensure that our prisons are not only places of security but places of safety too. Where offenders will receive the sentence they have been handed down, but no more."

She looked up and across the chamber. Her hands were still together but loosely now. No-one was shouting, or jeering, or even muttering. The chamber was quiet.

None of the MPs surrounding her had the slightest idea what it would be like to be Hayley Price. Raised by a mother who'd never held down a job, pregnant at nineteen, a criminal.

Jennifer knew more about it than most of them. Left alone with her mother at six years old, after her father had walked out. She still didn't know why. If she hadn't found Yusuf, who knows where she might have ended up?

She looked at the Speaker. "Mr Speaker, if you would permit me an indulgence on Hayley's behalf."

He nodded.

"I would like the House to join me in a minute's silence so we can remember Hayley and consider how we can prevent another tragic death like hers."

There was rustling as people looked around, then

bowed their heads or placed their hands in their laps. Jennifer stayed standing for the minute, listing to the faint tick of her wristwatch. At last the Speaker coughed.

"Thank you," she said, and sat down. She felt John's hand on her shoulder and turned to see him nod.

~

S he arrived in the Members' Dining Room at a quarter past twelve.

As she passed between the tables, she sensed a hush descend over the MPs. A few people got up to congratulate her. She thanked them as graciously as she could, but felt awkward and undeserving. She'd rescued her career, but it hadn't helped Hayley.

John was late. After choosing some fish and salad from the buffet, she chose a quiet corner table and took the seat facing the room. Then she bent to her bag and grabbed her phone.

She soon exhausted her inbox and picked up a fork, looking around the room. Her gaze rested on a white-haired man sitting at a window table with three expensively suited companions. As his companions talked, his gaze was fixed on the room. His eyes flickered around, registering each of the other diners as they arrived or departed, taking them in with a curled lip. The white hair framed a copper-coloured face, the forehead a touch too smooth and shiny. Botox, she suspected. His bright blue eyes and the thin line of his lips were barely visible against his perma-tanned skin. Looking at him always made Jennifer think of cheap American soap operas.

The man was Leonard Trask, Leader of the Opposition. On TV, that smirk looked like a smile, and the tan became a healthy glow. But in person, the effect was different.

Jennifer stared at him despite herself, regretting it when his eye caught hers. He smiled. She held his gaze for a moment, then pretended to be answering a call.

She kept her head down until John arrived, scrolling through Twitter as she ate. She was trending.

John hurried in, exchanging greetings and pausing for brief conversations. He threw her a nod before helping himself to a salad and making his way to their table.

Jennifer looked at his plate and raised an eyebrow. John laughed. "Surprised? Got to do something about this, eh?" He rubbed his belly. A hard-won belly, acquired through years of socialising in the dining rooms and bars of this place.

Jennifer settled into her chair, waiting. John leaned back and surveyed her.

"Well done," he said.

She smiled, relieved. "Thank you."

"I think you saved the day."

She shrugged; it wouldn't do to crow.

"So," he continued. "What's happening at the prison?"

"I've spoken to Sandra Phipps. The governor," she said. "I'm going tomorrow."

He cocked his head. "You haven't already been?"

"It only happened yesterday morning."

"Or the night before."

"I know." She sighed. "But I only found out yesterday morning."

"Before or after the press?"

She closed her eyes for a moment. The previous day she had been woken at six am by a call from the office. Quickly followed by a call from the Daily Telegraph.

"That's hardly the issue."

"It makes us look bloody incompetent, you know. If you hadn't—"

"Yes, but I did."

He sighed. "You're right." He held up his hands in defeat. "I know, I know. You did well. Michael's pleased."

She wasn't sure how to respond; she and Michael had never exactly clicked. "Good."

"Indeed. Anyway, let's get these bloody salads down us and back to work."

She let herself relax. "Did I tell you it's Hassan's birthday?"

"Hmm?"

She smiled. "Yusuf's brought him and Samir down to London for a couple of days. A treat."

"Oh. Good, good." John knew her family; Yusuf had worked for him as a researcher in John's first term as an MP. Back then it was Yusuf who was the ambitious one, the future MP. But fatherhood had changed him, and now he was more than content running a homeless shelter in Birmingham city centre. Jennifer admired his skill with people, the way he made those at their most desperate feel better about themselves, and the relationships he'd built locally. And he admired her ability to talk her way out of corners, like she had this morning. She'd learned to stand up for herself as a child, realising no-one else was going to do it for her.

"They're on the London Eye, this afternoon." She frowned. "Or maybe getting a pizza, I can't remember which was first."

"Nice," John replied, glancing at his watch. He started to push himself up, but then something in the mirror behind her caught his eye. He sat down again.

She looked over his shoulder to see a uniformed security guard weaving between the tables, heading for them. John's eyes were trained on her face; he looked worried. What was going on?

John stood and turned as the man reached them. There was a whispered conversation between them. John's features clouded as he listened.

He turned to her.

"We'll have to continue this later," he said. "I'm needed. And you've got to go to Committee Room 14. Right now."

Around the dining room there was a flurry of movement: people pulling phones out of pockets, bending to retrieve them from bags and briefcases. Jennifer's own phone buzzed on the table.

"Why?" she asked.

Ministers were rising from their tables. Backbench MPs watched them, confused. Jennifer saw one of the ministers shake his head at a junior colleague. Their gazes shifted to John.

John shook his head. "Can't tell you. Not yet. Just go."

He marched out of the room, looking straight ahead.

3

OCTOBER 2019. LONDON

THE COMMITTEE ROOM WAS FILLING UP WITH LABOUR MPs by the time she arrived, the crush of bodies making the room feel damp with sweat.

She scanned the room for clues as to why they'd been summoned here. Officials darted in and out, searching the crowd and making notes but not stopping for long enough to speak to anyone. Groups came together then broke apart, new huddles forming in a kind of dance. The room was filled with the hum of low conversation; rumours, questions, speculation. *Facts?*

It was as full as a controversial meeting of the Parliamentary Labour Party, and almost as deafening. But no one was sitting on the long wooden benches: instead, they all shifted around the outer edges of the room, newcomers holding their breath to squeeze past colleagues.

She pushed through, muttering the occasional hello. People weren't interested in her now; she was old news. She wanted to know who was here. It didn't take her long to realise that there wasn't a single Cabinet member and not many of her own rank. It was mainly backbenchers.

She had a moment of panic, then pushed it away. John had sent her here, and he knew – even if no one else did – that she hadn't been relegated to the backbenches. Besides, after her reception in the chamber this morning, surely no one would expect...

She leaned against the wood panelled wall. Her palms were dry and her feet ached in her stiff new shoes. A vicarious birthday present from Yusuf.

She felt a hand on her shoulder and looked up, tensing. It was someone from the Serjeant at Arms office, the team that administered the building.

He smiled. "Minister, would you like to take a seat? We could be here for a while."

She opened her mouth to ask a question. But he was gone, weaving his way through the crush and tapping the occasional junior ministerial shoulder.

She looked at the benches. They were all but empty, with only a few elderly and one pregnant MP sitting down. Each of them sat alone, staring ahead in silence or jabbing at their phones for news.

She fished her own phone out of her bag, scrolling through Twitter. She was still trending, although the attention was starting to dip. But there was nothing to explain what was happening here, why they'd all been summoned. No one had leaked it, yet.

A group of men drifted towards her, pushed by the swelling crowd. She pretended to stare at her phone's screen while she listened in to their conversation.

"Tony from The Times says there's a terror threat. Nothing confirmed yet."

"I've seen pictures of police vans at Waterloo."

Waterloo?

She looked towards the tall windows. People were

crowding towards them, maybe hearing the same rumours. She fought her way through the wall of suits, ignoring people's muttered complaints, until she emerged beside the window.

She pressed the palm of her hand against the window, the mullioned lead cold to the touch. Outside, the city looked much as it ever did. Tourist boats made their way up and down the Thames, windows glinting in the sunshine. On the opposite bank, runners and idle strollers wove around each other. And beyond that, in the direction of Waterloo station and her own flat, dark buildings rose up, the skyscrapers of the City looming behind them.

The crowd had tightened behind her; she couldn't have moved if she'd wanted to. People jabbed their elbows into each other and tripped over each other's feet in an effort to stay upright.

A rumble came from outside and she felt the weight of the crowd as people leaned to see out. She threw out an arm to steady herself, her breathing short. Another rumble: this time the crowd stilled, staring out and across the river.

Beyond the water, beyond the tourists and the London Eye, smoke gushed up and over the rooftops, spreading and billowing as the wind caught it. She stared as it thickened and rose. Behind her was silence, the Parliamentary Labour Party collectively holding its breath.

The cloud cleared the rooftops and the breeze pulled it in their direction. The buildings surrounding Waterloo station disappeared from view, followed by County Hall and the pods of the London Eye.

She felt her chest hollow out. The London Eye!

She fell back into the crowd, clutching her throat.

What had Yusuf told her this morning? The Eye and then a pizza. *Maybe you can join us later?*

She stared at the oversized Ferris wheel. Tiny figures moved inside the highest pod, the one at the very apex of the wheel. She lost sight of it as the cloud rose to envelop it, pitching it and the other pods in a grey-brown haze.

She stared at it for a few moments, blinking. She span round and clawed her way through the crowd. "Get out of my way!" She didn't care whose feet she trampled, felt no concern about bodies stumbling as she pushed them aside. She had to get out of here – get to her children.

She stumbled into the back of a bench, her knuckles grazing on the worn wood. She caught herself and managed to take a shaky breath, massaging her temples, willing the images out of her head. Images of Yusuf and the boys in that pod, staring into the dark cloud. *Stay calm*, she told herself. *You're no use to them like this.* Samir clutching Yusuf's hand despite his maturity and Hassan's little fingers pulsing in his dad's. So easy to lose their grip in the darkness and the panic...

She shook the images from her head, gasping. She fumbled her bag open and delved inside for her phone. Trembling, she brought up her favourites and jabbed at Yusuf's name. It took two attempts to hit the right key.

She clutched the phone to her ear, eyes darting around the room. Even the elderly MPs had left their seats and were standing at the back of the throng, trying to see what was going on. Just Mary Boulding, eight months pregnant and barely mobile, sat alone in the centre of the room.

The phone was silent. She pulled it from her ear and looked at the display. No service. She screwed up her face and tried again. Her breaths were shortening, becoming little more than gasps.

A woman passed her, floral perfume wafting in her wake. Jennifer gagged.

She bent over, willing the nausea to subside.

When she'd regained control of her breathing and felt she could move again, she looked on the floor for her phone. There it lay, next to her foot, the white light on its side blinking.

She grabbed it. Yusuf?

No. It was an email from 10 Downing Street, an automated circular with details of tomorrow's events. The wifi was still working, then.

She opened WhatsApp and barked out a quick note to Yusuf. *Are you OK? Call or message me. I'm at work.* She stared at the screen, waiting for a response. She considered for a moment then forwarded it to Samir. He never picked up her messages but it was worth a try.

She lowered herself onto a bench, throwing her head back and her gaze up to the ceiling. Overhead, the ornate carvings stared impassively down at her. This room – this building – had seen other days like this.

The crowd had shifted to one end of the room and was facing the raised platform at the front where committee chairs and witnesses or guest speakers normally sat. Once again she was faced with a wall of backs.

She approached it, puzzled. Then she heard a familiar voice.

"Good afternoon, everyone."

John.

She squeezed through the crush. *I'm a Home Office minister*, she thought. *I need to be up there.*

John coughed then took a long swig from a bottle someone passed up to him. His tie was askew and his shirt had damp patches under the arms.

He whistled out a breath and passed the water to an

advisor. There was a sheet of paper in his hand but he didn't look at it.

"Sorry to keep you in here, everyone."

Murmurs surrounded her.

He looked around his audience, his eyes alighting on Jennifer. He allowed his gaze to rest on her face for a few beats too long, then looked away.

He looked towards the window. The muttering stopped. "There's been an explosion," he said. "In Waterloo tube station."

Jennifer felt her legs go weak. She tried to pull her phone out of her pocket but couldn't move her arms in the crush.

"We don't know the details yet," John said, taking another swig of water. "And we couldn't tell you all of it if we did."

Gasps ran through the crowd. John raised a hand to ask for quiet.

"That's not all," he said, his voice turning grave. He looked at Jennifer again, his eyes searching her face. "There's been another one. Roughly the same time." His eyes were drilling into Jennifer now. She shifted her weight, hearing a tut as her heel spiked someone's shoe.

"Spaghetti Junction," John managed to say. Jennifer stared back at him, her pulse throbbing behind her eyes.

Spaghetti Junction.

Gravelly Hill Interchange.

In her Birmingham constituency.

John watched her as he spoke. It was as if they were the only people in the room. She gave him a single nod. *Go on. Tell me more.*

He didn't break eye contact. "Before the explosion at Waterloo there was one at Spaghetti Junction. Not as big as the one here in London," he nodded towards the window, "but it's chaos."

She closed her eyes. Around her people were talking in whispers, gasps and murmurs. She opened her eyes to see John looking away, deep in conversation with a man she didn't recognise. One of his political advisors was at his back, trying to get him out of the room.

John reached behind, batting the hand away. He turned back to the crowd.

"You all need to stay here until we can give you clearance to leave." He looked around at the gathered faces, the people who trusted him. "Everyone. The building's in lockdown. "

4

OCTOBER 2019. LONDON

As John disappeared into the corridor, Jennifer found a burst of energy. She pushed towards the doors, only to be blocked by a security guard.

"Sorry ma'am."

She sprinted towards the door at the other end of the room and heaved it open before anyone could stop her. She slipped out, her heart racing.

Two guards stood along the corridor outside the main door. She had to get past them; she pressed herself against the wall and glanced up and down the corridor.

Beyond the two guards, a group was moving away from her. John and his team. They were almost at the top of the stairs. She'd never catch him.

Thinking quickly, she ran for the flight of stairs at the opposite end of the corridor.

She emerged from the stairwell into the corridor below, running along the back of the building. If John was heading for the Home Office, as she thought he was, he'd be down here, too. She turned and raced past the canteen. It was eerily quiet.

Normally this corridor would be full of members, staff, press and visitors. Making their way to the chamber after lunch or heading in the opposite direction for afternoon tea on the terrace. But it was empty.

Her footsteps thudded on the heavy carpet, her breathing filling the empty space. She skidded into a turn.

She gasped. Heading straight for her was John and his entourage.

She flung out a hand to the wall, using it as a brake. She skidded to a halt in front of John.

He broke off his conversation and stared at her.

"Jennifer. Thank God."

She took a few deep breaths; she must look terrible.

"I need your help," she gasped.

He nodded. "Your constituency, of course. I'll get someone to brief you."

"No," she said. Her voice was coming back. "It's not that."

He frowned. "But—?"

"Yusuf. Yusuf and the boys."

John took a breath, as though forcing himself to be patient. "What about them?"

"Hassan's birthday, remember? They're in London. Pizza and the Eye."

She wondered how much he'd been listening to earlier. Their lunch seemed like a lifetime ago.

"I've been trying to get hold of Yusuf and I can't," she said. "Samir, too."

John blanched. He motioned towards the security advisor who leaned in close to him. John said something in his ear.

He looked back at Jennifer. She stared at him. *Hurry up, dammit.*

"Come with us," he said.

Jennifer followed John and the other men along the corridor, passing the canteen and the members' tea room. They headed along corridors Jennifer hadn't had cause to venture down before. Finally, they arrived at a door where the advisor stopped and looked at John.

"Seriously?" he said.

Jennifer scowled at him. Why was this taking so long?

John nodded. "Yes."

The man sighed. He knocked and opened the door without waiting for a response. John and Jennifer followed him inside, John closing the door behind them.

They found themselves in a poky office lined with computer monitors and CCTV screens. A woman flitted between these, jabbing at keyboards and pressing buttons. Jennifer stared at the screens. One of them showed a mass of smoke. Ambulances and police cars littered the foreground, but there was little human movement.

The woman looked up and glared at Jennifer.

"Home Secretary," she said, reaching for a mouse and clicking it. Immediately, the screen Jennifer had been looking at went black. What didn't she want them to see?

"Calm down, Andrea," John said. "This is Jennifer Sinclair. Prisons Minister." He shot Jennifer a look.

Jennifer pinched her thumb; her nervous tic. "Yusuf?" she croaked.

"Of course. Sorry." John turned to the woman. "Ms Sinclair's husband is out there somewhere. Waterloo or the Eye. She can't get hold of him."

Andrea stared at him, her face tight.

"Well, get on with it!" he snapped.

She blushed and picked up a mobile that was lying on a

desk. She jabbed some digits in then after a pause, she spoke discreetly into it, half-turning away from them.

There was a pause. All eyes were on Andrea. Jennifer took a few whistling breaths, desperate to stay composed.

Finally the woman looked at her and held out the phone. Jennifer blinked. The woman pushed the phone at her, shaking it.

"Take it," she said.

Jennifer grabbed the phone and fumbled it to her ear. She closed her eyes and forced her mouth open to speak.

"Hello?" she croaked.

"Jen!"

"Yusuf?"

"Yes, of course! Where are you? Whose phone is this? I thought—"

Her legs were buckling. John grabbed a chair, sliding it behind her. She sank into it.

"Are you OK?" she whispered. The two agents had returned to their work but John was watching her. A nervous, guilty smile played on his lips. She smiled back at him.

"We're fine," came the reply. "We're at the flat. Hassan was tired so we came back early."

She bit her knuckle, pinching her skin between her teeth. She thanked the heavens that Hassan had woken so early.

"Wait there," she said. "I'll come home."

John frowned. "What about your constituency?" he hissed. "What about Spaghetti Junction?"

She bit her lip. "I'll be an hour or so," she told Yusuf. John gave her a terse nod.

Yusuf's voice sounded tense. "Why the wait?"

"Turn on the news."

There was silence on the other end of the phone. Then: "Shit."

"What are you seeing?"

"Waterloo. And Spaghetti Junction."

She closed her eyes. She needed to get to a TV. She needed to know what was happening back at home.

"Don't let the boys watch it. I need to find out what's happening."

Silence. She imagined him nodding, staring at the TV. Where were the boys? She hoped Hassan was asleep in the bedroom.

"What do I do, Yusuf? I haven't got a clue."

He cleared his throat. "I don't know. But you'll figure something out. People are going to need you."

She swallowed. *I need you*, she thought.

"OK. I'll talk to John."

"Be quick. The boys want you."

The line went dead.

5

OCTOBER 2019. BIRMINGHAM

THE LAND BENEATH THE RAISED MOTORWAY OF Spaghetti Junction was a strange mixture of canal towpaths, junk yards, litter-strewn paths and what were probably the least picturesque canal-side flats in the city.

Jennifer climbed out of her car, taking in the carnage that had destroyed this corner of her constituency.

Five hundred metres from where she stood, a pile of concrete and mangled steel rose up. In the shadow of the silent motorway overhead, mechanical diggers added more rubble to it.

Police cars and fire service vehicles were parked haphazardly on a patch of grass studded with occasional piles of dog mess. Beyond that, a police cordon stirred in the breeze, shuddering each time another crash of collapsing rubble sent reverberations across the site.

Behind her, clear of the motorway's structure, were two hastily erected Portacabins. People paced in and out of them, voices raised against the sound of machinery.

A uniformed police officer approached her, holding out his hand. Brett Sanders, Assistant Chief Constable. She shook his hand, still looking past him to the motorway beyond. He turned to Yusuf and shook his hand too, placing a familiar hand on his arm. Jennifer knew how much contact Yusuf had with the police from his work at the shelter.

"Thanks for coming," Brett said.

"No problem," she replied. "Tell me what's happening."

The Chief Constable put his fingers to his lips and blew a loud whistle. She flinched, surprised and impressed in equal measure.

The diggers fell quiet. Workers climbed out of them, scurrying towards the safety of the Portacabins.

Jennifer looked up. Towering above them, beyond the diggers and the rubble, were two cranes. They plucked at the jagged edges of the overpass, picking out loose metal and concrete and lowering it to the ground. After a moment, they stopped too.

The only sounds were the distant hum of traffic and the trill of birdsong. She was familiar with this spot, had often walked along the towpath. The roar of the motorway was a constant fact of life to anyone living near it, but today the silence was deafening.

Born and raised in this part of Birmingham, Jennifer was used to the background notes of the M6 and Aston Expressway as a constant fact of life, as something that rumbled through your bones and became a part of you. Now, it was as if the heart of the city had been ripped out.

The quiet was broken by the thwack of a helicopter overhead. She looked up, shielding her eyes against the low October sun. Police or media, she couldn't tell.

She took a deep breath and turned to her police escort, which had grown to include the Chief Superintendent for the area and a plain clothes officer. They gestured towards the Portacabins and she followed.

As they picked their way across the grass she spotted movement from the corner of her eye. A small crowd had gathered, whether to ogle the wreckage or to see what she had to offer, she couldn't tell. She gave a tight wave, knowing better than to smile.

Yusuf was walking beside her. She grabbed his hand and squeezed, but got nothing back. He hated the public eye, something he'd realised when standing for election in an unwinnable seat a year after they'd met.

They were almost at the Portacabins now. They'd had to fight their way through vehicles, squeezing between cars. The bulky Chief Constable sweated in his heavy uniform, grimacing his way through the gaps, muttering under his breath.

Jennifer turned to wait for him just as a man stepped forward from the crowd, dipping under the police cordon. She resisted the urge to shrink back: these were her constituents, after all. But the police were less reticent. Two officers stepped in and each put a hand on his shoulder, guiding him backwards. He glowered at them and spat at the ground.

He raised a finger and pointed at Yusuf.

"Your bloody lot!" he shouted. His voice was high and ragged. "This is your fault! Go home, the lot of you!"

Yusuf's hand dropped. The police officers dived on the man, pushing him to the ground. Another appeared in front of Jennifer, ushering her into the Portacabin.

"No," she snapped. "Let me go. I'm not hiding."

She approached the crowd. Someone was holding a phone up, filming the man. He was being bundled into a car now, his head pushed down as he ducked into the back seat.

She turned to Brett. "Wait," she said. "Why are you arresting him? He hasn't hurt anyone."

"Threatening behaviour, ma'am. We can't be too careful."

He was close to her, his arm almost touching hers. She spun round, looking for Yusuf.

"Where's my husband?" The policeman pointed to where Yusuf was already being ushered into one of the Portacabins.

"Excuse me." She hurried after him.

A young woman sat at a desk inside, talking into a mobile phone. She glanced up and hurried out, still talking into the phone.

Jennifer's mind was racing. She had no idea how it felt to be talked to like that.

"I'm sorry, love."

"It's not your fault."

She shrugged, feeling inadequate. "I shouldn't have made you come."

He slumped into the chair and rubbed his forehead. "I can handle *that*. Racist abuse is nothing new."

She nodded, looking back out of the window. The police car was driving away with the man inside. She needed to get back out there.

Somewhere outside there was a splintering sound, as another building collapsed. Jennifer shot her head up. "Shall we go back out?"

Outside, she could hear voices. Their welcoming party must be wondering what was going on. Not to mention the onlookers with their phones.

He put a hand to his neat beard and looked past her.

"Course. Sorry, love. I shouldn't have let them bundle me away like that. *You* didn't."

She shrugged and he came over to her. She leaned against him and he ran a hand through her hair.

"You're tougher than me," he said.

She snorted. "I pretend to be."

"No, you don't."

"Maybe half the time."

"Well, it's pretty convincing." He kissed her forehead. "Let's get back out there. Reassure people."

"Thanks." She opened the door. The cranes had starting inching into life again and she heard one of the diggers start its engine. This was bigger than her.

"I hate this," she whispered. "Seeing what they've done to our city. That poor woman we had to visit this morning, her daughter dead. And tomorrow I've got Bronzefield again, a meeting with the governor."

He stood behind her, his body warm against hers. "I'm sorry. I know it's hard."

She turned and held out her hand. "That woman this morning. Mrs Jacobs. I kept thinking about Waterloo. About the bomb, and how I felt when I couldn't get hold of you."

She could feel the rise and fall of his chest behind her, reassuring. She paused, listening to the noises of machinery and distant voices.

"I couldn't do this without you, you know," she said.

She felt his body tense. "Me too," he whispered.

6

NOVEMBER 2019. LONDON

J<small>ENNIFER PAUSED ON THE THRESHOLD OF THE</small> C<small>ABINET</small> Room, watching John Hunter. He was deep in thought, a frown creasing his brow. He gazed at the back of his free hand resting on the table in front of him, his mouth half-open in a sigh and his face a patchy grey. He glanced at the door, spotting her, and he forced a smile.

"Morning John."

He grunted before turning back to the paperwork spread out in front of him. He'd taken advantage of having the Cabinet Room table to himself by strewing papers across the green cloth. Jennifer wondered what Michael would think when he arrived.

She took a chair next to him, placing her own red box on the carpet by her feet. She was still made a little nervous by this room, and by her own ambitions to be a member of the Cabinet one day. She was struck by the way the dense carpet and heavy curtains absorbed the top-notes of her voice.

She lifted her red box onto the table and took out some papers. As always a pre-briefing had come first and her civil servants had updated her on the situation at Bronzefield. She was in regular phone contact with the governor, making sure the prison was putting the agreed measures in place to prevent another death. She'd only managed one visit to the prison so far; every minute she wasn't in the House she was at home, reassuring her scared constituents.

The fear was tipping over into anger. An Islamist group had posted a video on YouTube claiming responsibility for the attacks; within hours, the scapegoating of Muslims had begun. Two days earlier Yusuf had been on the bus when a man had started goading a woman in a hijab, tugging at her headscarf and telling her to take it off. Yusuf had intervened, sitting next to the woman and providing a barrier between her and the man, who enjoyed the opportunity to turn his vitriol on a Muslim man.

John pushed the sheet he'd been reading across the table, sending it into the empty space reserved for the Prime Minister. He leaned back in his chair and turned to Jennifer.

"So how are things?"

She sighed. "Constituency or prisons?"

"Both."

"Under control. The inmates at Bronzefield seem to be reassured by the new measures we're putting in place."

"The Governor there owes you her job."

She frowned. "Maybe. She's doing her bit, too. It's not easy."

He nodded. "How are your boys? How's Yusuf?"

Her chest sank. "Scared. Samir's school's about ten per cent Muslim and there's a lot of racist bullying going on. It's been getting to him."

He raised an eyebrow. "The school not deal with it?"

"Not really, no." She frowned. "It's happening all over Birmingham. Not just the kids either. Yusuf told me—"

John coughed as Michael Stuart entered. He was in a hurry, pulling the angled Prime Ministerial chair out and sweeping John's papers back across the broad table. He looked healthier and less crumpled than John. His neat dark hair showed no signs of grey and his skin was an even tone with few lines or shadows. He plucked an invisible fleck of dirt from the sleeve of his slim-fitting blue suit, placed his elbows on the table and leaned towards her.

"Jennifer, good to have you here. What's that about Yusuf?"

Sometimes she wondered if they were interested in her more for her Muslim husband than herself. She thought about Yusuf, and the way the attack had invaded his life: now he had two nervous boys at home and a steady stream of visitors, men and women who would tap on the door of an evening and be ushered into the dining room to describe the horrors they were facing. There were other places they could go, more official places, but they trusted him, and needed someone to vent their fears to. Wide-eyed children sometimes trailed behind, needing something to eat or a seat in front of the TV to keep them busy while the grown ups discussed things not for their ears. Hassan kept the children company, but wanted the calm of his normal life back. Samir had taken to hiding in his room.

"It's not good," she said. "Racist vandalism and low scale violence, all over the constituency. All over the city. My surgeries are full of frightened Muslim families, but it's Yusuf they want to talk to, not me."

"But he doesn't work in your office anymore. Right?"

"No. He moved to running the shelter when they changed the rules about MPs employing family members. It doesn't mean people don't come to him sometimes, though. He's built up a lot of trust."

"Ah." Michael exchanged a glance with John and leaned back in his chair. He rested his elbows on the armrests and clasped his hands in front of his chest. John sat up straighter, pulling his papers towards him.

"Anyway," Michael said, shuffling in his chair. "That's not what we're here to talk about."

She nodded. "Hayley Price. Bronzefield."

Michael's laugh rang out across the room.

"Bronzefield," he said, smiling at her. "You escaped by the skin of your teeth there."

She blinked, her face hot.

"Fortunate timing," he continued.

She stiffened. So far, there were twelve deaths from the Waterloo bomb. And five more were in a critical condition at St Thomas' Hospital. Only two had died in Birmingham, but that was two too many. How Michael could use the word *fortunate*...

He leaned in towards her.

"You need to put that behind you," he said. "We've got legislative plans. It'll have an impact on prisons. The prison population."

Jennifer looked at John, annoyed that he'd given her no warning of this. He scratched his cheek, the flesh loosening beneath his touch.

Michael sat back. "Let me explain."

7

NOVEMBER 2019. BIRMINGHAM

Jennifer slung her bag on the hall floor, glad to kick her shoes off at the end of a long and stressful week.

Her second visit to Bronzefield was haunting her. The panicked look in the governor's eyes. The jeers from the women as she passed through the prison. She'd been to plenty of prisons before of course, it came with the job. But this time was different. There was an extra layer to the usual hostility and gloom, a sharpness in the air she could almost taste. She may not have lost her job because of Hayley Price's death, but there were plenty who thought she should have.

She leaned against the wall and rubbed her eyes, not caring that her mascara would blur. In the kitchen she could hear voices. She went in, pasting on her best smile.

Yusuf was sitting at the table with both boys. This was unusual at this time of the evening. Normally Samir would be upstairs doing homework (or so she hoped) and Hassan would be getting ready for bed.

She coughed and they all looked up. Samir's face was

dark, his eyes flashing. Hassan looked gloomy and there was a guilty look on his face that he was trying to hide.

Yusuf gave her a smile that didn't extend to his eyes. "Evening."

She motioned towards the boys with her head. "What's up?"

Samir muttered something under his breath and Yusuf glared at him. Hassan started to cry.

She swept to the table, draping an arm around Hassan's shoulders. He leaned into her, sobbing.

"Shh, shh," she bent to whisper into his hair. "It's OK. We're here."

She looked up at Yusuf, flashing a question at him with her eyes.

Yusuf placed a hand on Samir's shoulder. Samir huffed and pushed his chair back, knocking it on the floor. He stomped out of the room and up the stairs, not looking at Jennifer. She heard the door to his room slam.

Jennifer watched in silence, feeling Hassan's tears soaking into her blouse.

"Tell me, Yusuf. What's happened? What's Samir done to Hassan?"

Yusuf's head shot up. "Don't jump to conclusions."

She shrank back. *What have I done wrong?*

Yusuf slumped in his chair and shrugged his shoulders. "Sorry," he muttered.

She looked down at Hassan. "What is it, sweetie? You can tell Mummy. Nobody's in trouble."

"I said don't make assumptions," repeated Yusuf.

"Well, tell me what's going on," she hissed. She could feel her palms growing clammy. "Did something happen at school?"

Hassan let out a loud sob and pulled out of her embrace. "It's James."

James was one of Hassan's school friends. "OK, " she replied. "What's up with James?"

"He's not my friend anymore."

Jennifer shot another question at Yusuf with her eyes. "I'm sure that's not true. James is one of your best friends."

"Not any more, he's not," muttered Yusuf.

"He's not Hassan's friend. He's a racist little shit."

Jennifer looked up to see Samir in the doorway, his cheeks blazing.

"Samir!" Jennifer lifted herself in her seat. "We'll have none of that kind of language."

Samir looked at Yusuf. "Sorry," he said. "But it's true."

Yusuf stood and crossed to Samir. "Come on, we don't know that for sure," he said, holding an arm out. Samir batted it away.

Jennifer was feeling increasingly irritated. "Will someone please tell me what's happened?"

Yusuf dragged a hand through his beard. Samir watched him speak, fidgeting. "Hassan was supposed to go to James's house after school today. I stayed at home, expecting James's mum to pick him up, then I got a phone call from the school at four o'clock. Asking if someone was going to fetch him."

Jennifer felt her heart pick up a beat. She looked at Hassan. "Were you OK, love?" He nodded.

"So I went to get him," Yusuf continued. "Turns out James's mum had left without him."

"OK," breathed Jennifer. Surely it was a misunderstanding. People forgot these sorts of things all the time.

"When I got him home there was a message from James's mum on my voicemail."

She nodded. An apology, she imagined. "I'll bet she felt

really stupid." She knew James's mum; had chatted to her in the playground on Fridays. She was a nurse who worked at the local hospital and seemed friendly enough.

"No," replied Yusuf. His face darkened.

"What?" she said. "Will you just tell me?"

Samir spoke. "She doesn't want her son playing with a Muslim."

Jennifer looked at him. "What?"

Samir scowled. "You heard. Racist bitch."

"Samir!" she shouted. "That's enough. Yusuf?"

Yusuf pulled his phone from his pocket. "Here's the text."

Hassan shuddered in her arms.

She took the phone and read. *James won't be playing with Hassan anymore. With everything that's happening, we want to protect him. I'm sure you understand.*

She let the phone slip from her hand onto the table. "What the—" she gasped. "What is she on about?"

Yusuf shook his head. "I can't be sure."

Samir clenched his fists. "Of course we can, Dad. She wants to protect her *precious little boy* from Muslims like us."

Jennifer looked at Yusuf. "It could be anything," she said. "It might not be—"

"I'm inclined to agree with Samir." Yusuf glanced at Hassan, who had buried his face in his arms on the table. "But let's not talk about it right now, hey?"

Samir grunted and threw himself upstairs. The door slammed again and the house fell silent apart from the rhythm of Hassan's sobs.

Yusuf was upstairs, trying to get Hassan to sleep. Jennifer had read him a story and brought Rufus to him. But even having his beloved cat purring on the pillow wasn't enough. Yusuf was on the bedroom floor now, lying quietly while he waited for Hassan to sleep. Something he hadn't done since the boys were toddlers.

Jennifer sipped at a glass of wine, trying to calm herself. The liquid dragged in her throat, sharp and heavy. The TV was on but she was oblivious: some drama she hadn't been following. She didn't have the energy to find the remote and turn it off.

She cradled her glass in her hands and slumped into the sofa, feeling the energy drain from her. Maybe James's mum would see sense in the morning. Maybe Yusuf had misunderstood. Maybe – probably – Samir was overreacting.

She turned words over in her head, intent on speaking to James's mum, on clearing things up. If it meant getting to the constituency office late, then so be it.

She had an early meeting with the police commissioner. She couldn't miss that. She put a fist to her temple, feeling a headache coming. When did it all get so hard?

The toilet flushed upstairs and Yusuf padded down. She put her glass on the coffee table, willing herself into alertness.

Instead of joining her on the sofa as normal, he took the armchair next to her. She watched him pick up the remote and flick through the channels.

"I've got a meeting I can't get out of in the morning," she said once he'd settled on a channel. "Can you speak to James's mum?"

He froze, remote in mid-air.

"This needs sorting out, quickly," she continued.

He winked the TV off. He didn't look at her.

"I'll be at the mosque," he said. "Besides, it's not as easy as that."

She said nothing. From upstairs she heard a noise. Hassan? They both listened for a moment, staring ahead. There was quiet.

Yusuf scratched his beard again and turned to her. "If this woman is what Samir says she is, d'you seriously think she's going to respond to me?"

Jennifer swallowed. "But we've known her for years."

"No," he said. "*You've* known her for years. If chatting to someone on the playground once a week counts as knowing them."

"That's not—"

"She doesn't talk to me. I've never thought much of it – a lot of the mums don't like talking to the dads. Maybe they think it'll look like they're poaching us. But now I think about it, I don't think she's ever actually talked to me. Not properly."

Jennifer felt herself grow cold. She couldn't believe that this woman who she'd happily exchanged pleasantries with for the last five years was a racist.

"Do you really think—"

Yusuf stood up. "I wish you could understand."

She rose with him, working to keep her body language as open as possible. He stared towards the window, his eyes dark.

"I'm not talking to her," he said. "I'll talk to the school, see if they can resolve any problems between Hassan and James. They're good at that sort of thing."

"OK. But I want to talk to his mum too."

He said nothing. She reached for his hand. It was stiff

but he didn't pull away. She ran through the next day in her head.

"OK," she whispered. "I can do the afternoon school run, speak to her then. Let's talk about something else. I've had an awful week."

He turned to her. "Awful week? You don't know the half of it. The boys are like china, work is manic. It's getting worse, you know. People like James's mum, who a week ago would never... Now it's OK. Don't you see? Do I need to spell it out for you? Being wary of Muslims has become acceptable."

She struggled to hide her frustration. Why was he making her feel as though this was all her fault? "I do know. D'you think it's not happening in London? I was walking to work on Tuesday and there was a gang of kids throwing insults at an old couple. Telling them to go home."

"What did you do?"

"I told them to get lost, of course. Yusuf, you don't think I'm going to stand by and watch that sort of thing happening?"

"No. Of course not." He was looking at the photo over the fireplace. An enlarged print of the four of them when Hassan was a baby, taken in a photography studio. They were all smiling. Samir was tickling Hassan who laughed hysterically, his pink mouth open in an excited O.

He turned to her, his shoulders sagging. "But Michael. I'm not sure what he'd do. And that's what counts."

"You know I can't—"

He shrugged and stood up. "I'm tired. I'm going to bed."

She opened her mouth to protest but he was gone, clattering onto the lower steps and then catching himself and slowing as he remembered the sleeping boys. She fell into the sofa and blinked at the TV, her stomach twisting.

8

NOVEMBER 2019. LONDON

"The Right Honourable Member patronises us all if he thinks we don't know what this Bill is really about."

Maggie O'Reilly, third term MP for Hull in the North East of England, was the third backbencher to respond to John's latest statement in the House of Commons, and the first to attack it. She was a large, impressive woman with a penchant for brightly coloured scarves and a habit of rebelling against the government.

Jennifer felt John tense beside her. Beyond him, Michael was stony faced. He muttered to himself through clenched teeth.

John had announced new measures to combat radicalisation in prisons; the measures Michael had wanted to talk to Jennifer about. Officially, any prisoner converting to any faith would be subject to increased vigilance. But Jennifer, like everyone else, could read between the lines.

Maggie continued. "The government wants to victimise prisoners who convert to Islam. I know they talk about *all religions* but let's be honest here, that's not what they're talking about."

The benches hummed with muttering and the shuffling of papers. Jennifer folded her arms and shook her head, knowing people would be watching her.

"So let me ask a question, seeing as that's what I'm supposed to do of course."

More muttering. The Speaker sat forward, ready for a rebuke. Maggie glanced at him.

"Apologies, Mr Speaker. I promise not to go too far."

The Speaker pursed his lips; he and Maggie had clashed plenty in the past.

She took a deep breath and puffed out her chest. "So, my question. Would this legislation have done anything to prevent the October attacks?"

There was a silence broken by a cough from somewhere behind Jennifer. Opposite her, the Tory home affairs spokesman looked uncomfortable. Attacking the Home Secretary should be his job.

Maggie wasn't finished. "It wouldn't, would it?" She looked at the Speaker again. "That was a question. And so is this. Can my Right Honourable friend the Home Secretary tell me if any of the perpetrators of last October's bomb attacks were recent converts to Islam *or any other religion*, can he tell me if they were British, and can he tell me if they'd recently – or ever – been in prison?"

She smiled and sat down. A hubbub rose behind Jennifer, a mix of agreement and dissent. Jennifer felt the seat back behind her shudder as people hit it with their palms. John smiled tersely and the Tory front bench looked uncomfortable; Trask knew he was missing out on an opportunity, and would loathe having a Labour backbencher, however notorious, steal it from him. Many of the Opposition MPs were on their feet, ignoring the Deputy Speaker's cries for order before shuffling back into place like a class of naughty toddlers.

John stood up, stirring the air. A bead of sweat was working its way down the back of his neck into his shirt collar. Trask and his home office spokesman smirked and relaxed into their seats.

John turned to face Maggie, smiling.

"Mr Speaker, I'd hate to deny certain members of this house the opportunity to make political capital from this tragedy that has taken the lives—"

But however far he raised his voice, John couldn't be heard above the shouting. A dozen or so Labour MPs rose to their feet and the Tories joined in, feigning indignation. There was a shout of 'hypocrite'. Around Jennifer the mood was sinking. Next to her two Cabinet members muttered together, looking sidelong at John.

Finally the noise subsided and the Speaker addressed himself to John.

"I would like to advise the Right Honourable Gentleman to take care in the precise form of words he uses to describe the actions of members of this House."

John nodded and swept a hand across his forehead. The back of his collar was damp and his grey-blonde hair was darkening at the tips. He cleared his throat, drew himself up and continued.

"As I was saying, the tragedy that hit us in October isn't something for politics. I'm pleased that the Prime Minister" – here he motioned towards Trask – "has put away political rivalry so we can demonstrate this House is united in its determination to stop terrorists. Don't forget what happened in October. An organised group of terrorists infiltrated our transport systems and created carnage. Dozens of people died and many more were injured. This can't happen again. I've already gone into detail on the recruitment taking place in prisons; I shouldn't have to repeat myself."

He paused and wiped his brow. "Ask yourselves: do you want to do everything you can to prevent another disaster, or not? If you do, then you have to support this Bill."

He sat down amid more shouting and thumping of feet. The bench beneath Jennifer shook. The same two Cabinet members who had been whispering were now falling over themselves to reach past her and pat John on the back. John turned to her and winked, taking her by surprise; she didn't manage a smile in return.

~

J ennifer rushed back to the Home Office building. She had a lot of paperwork to get through and a briefing on prison security at six pm. Then there was a networking event with business leaders from the constituency, something she wasn't looking forward to.

Her personal assistant Donna looked up as she passed. Jennifer smiled at her. "Sorry," she said. "John took longer than usual. Too many questions. I know you need me to get those papers signed."

Donna shook her head. "That's not the problem."

Jennifer ground to a halt. "Oh?"

Donna paled. "There's been... an incident... in your constituency."

Jennifer's shoulders dropped. "Oh." She didn't ask any more; as a civil servant, Donna's job was confined to government matters, not constituency ones.

"Thanks," she said, and hurried into her office. She

tapped at her keyboard and opened the BBC website. It was streaming live footage from Spaghetti Junction.

The phone on her desk buzzed.

"Sorry, Minister. You might want to turn on the news."

"I have already. What is it?"

There was a pause. Jennifer frowned and replaced the handset. She would have to see for herself.

She fell into her chair. In the background was the familiar sight of the diggers and cranes, with not much changed since she was last there. In the foreground, a crowd of people. Or rather two crowds, separated by the police.

Jennifer pinched her nose and stared at the screen. On one side was a group of a dozen or so white men, fists jabbing at the police in the centre and placards clutched in tattooed and scarred fists. *Immigrants go home. Stop terrorism. England for the English.* And worse.

On the right of the screen, facing them down, was a smaller but more mixed group; white, brown and black skin, young and old. There was one placard at the front: *Hope Not Hate.* And another behind it: *Socialist Workers.* Jennifer sighed. The Socialist Workers' Party always found their way to these things.

She turned up the volume. There was no commentary; just the sound of angry confrontation.

Then she spotted him. She frowned and leaned into the screen, her throat dry.

His face was indistinct, turned sideways from the camera. He was shouting something. A policeman approached him, putting a hand up between them. He shook his head and turned back into the crowd, becoming hidden from her.

She picked up her mobile. It rang out four times and then voicemail kicked in.

"This is Yusuf Hussain. Sorry I can't come to the phone right now. Please leave a message."

She tightened her lips and hung up, turning back to the screen.

The crowd was parting now, more police coming between the two groups. Someone threw a bottle and there was a moment of calm followed by a surge as both groups pushed towards each other.

She put a finger to the screen. There he was again.

Could she zoom in, on a live feed? She tried pinching her fingers on the trackpad but nothing happened. She bit her lip, impatient. *Yusuf, what are you doing?*

Words were tracking across the bottom of the screen. *Violent demonstration – right-wing groups – local community – Spaghetti Junction.* None of it made any sense. Had he been there before this had started, or had he gone after seeing it on the news, like she was now? They only lived a few streets away.

The camera zoomed in on the anti-racist protestors, finding its mark. The commentator paused for a moment, as if listening to someone. Then he spoke, haltingly.

"We believe that the husband of the Prisons Minister Jennifer Sinclair is in the crowd."

Yusuf, what have you done? Why didn't you talk to me first?

Then she remembered that he had. And she'd defended Michael.

He turned towards the camera, spotting it on him. He frowned and looked away, muttering to a woman standing behind him. Then he turned back again.

It was as if he could see her, watching him. Yusuf stared at the lens, at her. It was like a challenge.

9

DECEMBER 2019. BIRMINGHAM

Jennifer drove through the darkened streets, picking her way home from a meeting with the Assistant Chief Constable. She'd spoken at a press conference with him, trying to calm the situation. Mohamed Yazami, MP for the city centre constituency where the protests had spread from Spaghetti Junction, was there too, offering solidarity. But the violence had started to spread north, and she wasn't sure she'd ever get home.

Every now and then she would hit a road that had been cordoned off, turning what should have been a ten-minute drive into an ordeal. It was going to be at least an hour until she was home.

Her phone had been buzzing constantly, but she didn't dare pick it up; the streets were too unpredictable. Cars had been left at odd angles, abandoned by their owners, and people darted into the road with no warning. She gripped the steering wheel, peering ahead like a learner on her driving test. As her phone hummed for possibly the tenth time, two shapes appeared in her headlights and she slammed on the brakes. Two men, hoods up, turned to her.

She felt her heart accelerate and glanced down at her phone; would help come, if she were to call? Or were the emergency services too busy?

Almost as quickly as they'd appeared, the two shapes vanished into the darkness and her headlights fell on nothing but the road ahead. It was strewn with debris. An upturned shopping trolley lay in the gutter, and the tarmac was littered with broken glass, bricks and pieces of wood that got under her wheels. She took a deep breath, checked the door locks once again, and eased her foot onto the accelerator.

She'd been forced to take an unfamiliar street, one she'd only ever seen in daytime while out canvassing. It was quiet, but to her right she could hear the sounds of sirens accompanied by the hum of raised voices pierced by the occasional splintering sound. She shivered.

The press conference had gone smoothly enough, without too many questions about Yusuf. But the kids out on the streets tonight wouldn't be watching TV. Instead, their parents would have been watching, sitting in terrified silence and wondering when and if their kids were coming home. So far there'd been fifteen serious injuries and twelve arrests in Birmingham alone. More arrests would come later, in the cold light of morning.

She took a right turn, relieved to be back on familiar streets. The road was in semi-darkness, only half of the street lamps working. Up ahead was a crowd of people, spilling into the road. She swerved as a police van sped past. It stopped between her and the crowd, its occupants slamming doors and lifting riot shields in front of them. Sparks came from over the heads of the crowd and the noise intensified.

She stopped the car, unsure whether to push on and

take the turning between her and the rioters, which led home, or to reverse. Up ahead, the police advanced on the crowd, pushing it away from her. She decided to risk it.

She drove slowly, debating whether to turn off her headlights. As she approached, they illuminated the backs of the police, the handcuffs on their belts catching the light. Her phone buzzed again and she looked at it. It would be good to hear Yusuf's voice. Even if she was still angry with him for being at Spaghetti Junction when this all started.

She stopped the car and fumbled for her phone, hitting speed dial.

"Jen? Where are you? It's mayhem out there."

"I know. I'm in the middle of it."

"What? No, Jen. Come home."

"I'm trying. I'm nearly home, just need to get past a crowd. The road's full of people."

"What? OK, so turn back. Take the long way round."

"There isn't a long way round."

Jennifer, unlike so many other MPs, had chosen to live in the heart of her constituency. She hadn't taken the easy route with a house in the leafy suburb to the north, which was Tory anyway. As a junior minister and not a member of the Cabinet, her house had no police protection. It was right in the eye of the storm. Should she push on?

"Jen, listen to me. Go back into town. Stay in a hotel, if you need to."

"No. The boys need us both there. I'll be fine. I'm going to put you on hands-free."

She slid the phone into its holder and started to ease her way forward. The wall of police backs was moving away from her, but more slowly now. She could see the turning. Once she took that she would be two minutes from home.

"Jennifer? Can you hear me?"

"Yes. Where are the boys? Are they OK?"

"They're downstairs, watching TV."

"You're not with them?"

"No. I didn't want them hearing this. I don't like you doing this, love. Think about the—"

"I'm at the turn. I'll just be a couple of minutes. You go back to the boys. They shouldn't be on their own."

"Jennifer, please—"

"Love you."

She reached out to end the call, her eyes leaving the windscreen. When her gaze flicked back to the road ahead, there was a man standing in front of her car. He was skinny and pale, his skin almost translucent in the beams. He wore a torn T-shirt and jeans darkened by stains.

She waved for him to move aside. He stayed right where he was, blinking at her. She stared back, transfixed, her stomach churning. She considered reaching for her phone but didn't dare take her eyes off him. Had she locked the doors?

There was a yell from one side and the man turned. More forms appeared out of the darkness, from the right and then from the left. The man moved towards them, his shape blurring in front of her. The crowd closed in on the car, blocking the light from the street lamps.

She tried to edge forwards but she could feel bodies thudding against her car, hands scrabbling at the paintwork.

Behind her, a siren sounded. The crowd shifted, jostling her car. She squeezed her eyes shut, just for a moment, wishing she hadn't hung up the phone. Were those going to be her last words to Yusuf?

Then the car rocked and there was a scream. Her eyes flew open and she twisted round in her seat, her breath ragged. The crowd had pulled back. She heard shouts from behind and glanced in her rear view mirror to see police running towards them.

There was a scream.

Had she hit someone?

She looked at the door next to her, eyeing the handle. Going out there was madness, but she couldn't just drive away. She threw open the car door. A wall of sound hit her – screams and shouts and over the top of them, the ever-present sound of sirens.

She slid out. Surrounding the car was a ring of people. On the side furthest from her was a line of young Asian men, their eyes wide. And on the side nearest her was another group, larger, of white men and women, all young, all wearing hoodies. One man was gripped on either side by two women, holding him back as he lunged towards the Asian men.

There was a groan. Between her feet and the front wheel of the car, a man was crouched on the ground, holding another man in his arms. The injured man's face was turned away from her, cast in shadow.

She *had* hit someone. "Oh my god. I'm so sorry!"

"Not your fault." The crouching man frowned over at the huddle on the other side of the car. He got to his feet, his face white with rage, and pointed a trembling finger.

"You!" he shouted.

A man emerged from the crowd. He was short and plump with black hair that curled around his ears. His green bomber jacket was covered in blood.

There was another groan from the man on the ground. She went over to him.

Someone in the crowd shifted and the beam of the streetlight lit up the man's face, grey and lifeless. He was wearing a blood-soaked T-shirt. It was the man she'd caught in her headlights.

She suppressed a cry and swallowed hard. She crouched down and put her hand on his wrist. No pulse.

Then she spotted it. A blade, glinting. On the ground beside him was a knife.

Behind her, a woman screamed. She felt hands on her shoulders pulling her back and out of the way. Then they were surrounded by police, working their way through the crowd, roughly grabbing hold of people and dragging them back to their van.

10

JANUARY 2020. LONDON

"How are you?"

Jennifer was in John's office, sitting opposite him at his meeting table. Normally they used the chairs near his desk, something that hadn't been lost on her when he ushered her in.

She shrugged. "OK, thanks. Still shocked."

"Nasty business. Really nasty. I'm sorry you were caught up in it."

She looked down and twisted her hands in her lap. She'd been having problems sleeping, and was struggling to maintain the calm façade her family needed right now.

At least the riots were over. The weather had turned, a cold snap making going out on the streets at night less pleasant than it might have been. The night after Jennifer had seen that man get stabbed, the numbers had almost halved. The next night they were down to a trickle. And then Christmas had got in the way. But it was too late for the man, who had died the next day in hospital. He was only eighteen.

She'd run over those moments in her mind till her head

hurt. Had she seen even a glimpse of the stabbing? When exactly had it happened? She'd been so focused on getting out, she'd paid too little attention to what was happening outside. Was it her fault? If her car hadn't been there, would things have played out differently?

"I think we should get you police protection," John said, dragging her out of her thoughts. "I know it's not normal for ministers at your level, but this is different."

She shook her head. "No. Anyone could have been in that situation. I was just unlucky. It was nothing to do with my job."

"It was bloody stupid of you to drive through that area—"

"That area is my constituency. It's where I live. And if I get police protection, what does that say to the family of the boy who died? To the people who voted for me? It's a safe neighbourhood, John. I don't want people thinking otherwise."

"They're not ministers. Those voters."

"No, John. I appreciate it, but no thanks."

He shrugged. "OK. But tell me if you change your mind."

She nodded.

"Anyway," he continued. "I've been meaning to speak to you. There's some new legislation we're planning. It'll affect you."

"Oh?" She sank into the chair he had pulled out, as he took the one opposite. The table between them was glass-topped and cold to the touch. She had her back to the room and her view was of a wall of pristine books behind John's head. She wondered if any of those books had ever been read.

"Look, I'm going to be straight with you, but you can't

talk about this outside here. Not yet." He looked up and grunted as his secretary came in with a pot of coffee. He waited for her to finish pouring and leave, closing the door behind her. "We have to stop this kind of thing happening again."

She shrugged. "What kind of thing?"

"The riots. Look, sorry if this is delicate for you—"

"No. Don't be daft." She took a deep breath, forcing away the panic that kept pushing at her. Maybe this conversation would exorcise it. "Go on. What have you got planned?"

"OK. So we've put security around Spaghetti Junction, and Waterloo. Anywhere that could be a focus."

"It wasn't just because of what happened at Spaghetti Junction—"

"Everything's got its source. This time, it was that demo."

"It's not as simple as that," she said. "After the bombs, people started scapegoating. They looked for someone to blame. We need to counteract that. We've got to put the communities back together again."

Her own community was still reeling. Things were calm, for now, but there was a festering undercurrent that made her nervous. The waiting rooms at her surgeries had become segregated of their own accord, and the streets were deserted after dusk. Yusuf had started taking Samir to school instead of letting him walk alone, something that hadn't gone down well.

"That's just words, Jennifer. We need action." He licked his lips. "So we're going to be restricting demos like the one that started it all. The one Yusuf was at."

"Now hold on—" *Don't drag my husband into this.*

"Sorry." He held up his palms. "That was below the belt. Not his fault. But why the blazes did you let him go?"

She laughed. "He's a free man, John. Despite being married to a government minister."

"Hmpff. Well, I'd be grateful if you kept him in line."

She took a deep breath. Yusuf wasn't a pet dog. "Tell me about this legislation."

"Right. So we're introducing police powers to break up any large gathering not notified in advance."

"Large gathering? What does that mean?"

John shrugged. "Difficult to define. We're working on the language, but it'll be less about numbers, more about intent."

She cocked her head. "How many demos have you been on in your time?"

He blushed. "Too many to count."

"And now you're getting too old, you want to stop other people doing it."

"Ouch. Never too old. But yes. And it could be temporary. We can reverse it when things have calmed down."

"That's rubbish, and you know it," she said. "Legislation like that is never reversed."

"Maybe, maybe not." He eyed her. "When this goes public, what will Yusuf do?"

She stiffened. "I don't see what that's got to do with anything."

John leaned back, pushing a stray lock of hair into place. "Come on, Jennifer."

"I don't know. Maybe you should ask him yourself."

"OK, so it's like that. Well, I'm not all that surprised at what he did. Not really."

"Sorry?"

"Don't forget I knew Yusuf when he was young. We

were both gobby bastards, but we had our principles. His are coming to the fore now."

"And you want to abandon yours."

"That's not fair. We need to be practical. Sometimes when you're in government, you can't afford the luxury of principles. Not when people's lives are at stake." He sipped his coffee, looking pensive. "And we're going to be tracking the people who were there when this all kicked off. Including people at Spaghetti Junction."

"Including Yusuf?"

He closed his eyes. "Yes. Look, I admire him for taking a stand. But we can't give him special treatment. Maybe if he helps the police, gives them information—"

She snorted. "What sort of information?"

He continued, talking over her. "We need to stop this happening again. In a year or so things will have calmed down. You have to understand the imperative here. It's for people's safety."

"Imperative?" Now she understood. That wasn't his language; it was someone else's. "You've been talking to Michael."

"Of course I bloody have."

"Was this your idea, or his?"

A blush rose up his neck. "His."

Jennifer nodded. "Yusuf won't go along with it. And I'm not sure I want to." She shook out her shoulders, feeling tense. "Anyway, it's not my department."

John rose from his chair, looking out of the window at a rainy Whitehall. Street sounds floated up: taxis, delivery vans, messengers, chatter, the regularity of Westminster life. He dug his hands in his pockets and continued.

"This is going to be a difficult one to sell to a lot of people. A large chunk of the bleedin' heart party membership, for starters. But there could be backlash in Muslim communities. We need to make it understood that this isn't scapegoating. It's prevention."

He turned and came to her side of the table, leaning on the armrest of her chair. She could feel the warmth of his breath against her skin and when she looked up at him, she could see the network of broken veins in his cheeks.

"The stabbing you witnessed didn't help. Only one death during the riots, and it was a Muslim kid stabbing a white kid. Do you know how that plays out in white working class communities?"

"That's a bit of a gen—"

He thumped the table. "No, Jennifer. Wake up. These restrictions were the only thing we could think of that didn't directly target Muslims."

"*What?*"

"You should have seen the alternatives. Restrictions to mosques, amongst others. I talked Michael down from that one."

"Good." She unclenched her fist; she'd been squeezing her thumb so tightly it hurt.

He sat back behind the desk, fixing her in place with a stare. "Things have calmed down now. We've managed to put the fascists back in their box, and the community leaders want to demonstrate they're peaceful. But no one's happy. We need to show that we're doing something, that we won't let it happen again."

"So you remove the fundamental right to protest."

"No. Not if the protest is notified to the police a week in advance."

"It's the principle, John."

He pulled back. "I wouldn't even be considering it if we had any choice. Look, I don't need to explain myself to you."

"So what is it you're asking me to do?"

"You've got connections. You've got the respect of the Muslim community, and not just because of Yusuf; the work you've done in Birmingham hasn't gone unnoticed. And people in the party don't see you as a poodle. We need you to help sell it for us. And we need you to keep Yusuf in his box."

"And if I refuse?"

He smiled. "Well, I'd rather think about what will happen if you accept. Obviously helping us out would be good for your ministerial career."

He had her achilles heel. She was ambitious. But she knew what Yusuf would say.

"I'm going to have to think about this."

"I'd rather you agreed sooner rather than later, but if you have to discuss it with Yusuf, then that's fine with me."

She looked up at the mention of Yusuf. "It's not up to him."

He shrugged. "How did you feel about him being at that protest?"

"We've talked it through. It's fine."

"Hmm. Anyway, I'm giving you until Monday. After that, the ship sails, with or without you on board. There are plenty of other people who can be of use."

11

JANUARY 2020. BIRMINGHAM

ON THURSDAY NIGHT, SHE GOT HOME FROM A TWO-hour train journey to find the house in darkness.

She crept into the living room, turning on a table lamp and shivering against the cold of the sleeping building. Shrugging her coat off and dumping it on the sofa, she slumped down and rubbed her eyes. She'd been ready to face Yusuf, had rehearsed what she would say on the train. Now she felt untethered.

She gathered her coat up and took it into the hall, hanging it next to Hassan's bright yellow soft-shell. She glanced up the stairs. She'd been so eager to confront Yusuf when she got home. It hadn't occurred to her he'd be in bed by eleven pm.

She headed upstairs. Passing Samir's closed door, she rested her head against it, longing to disturb him, to find out how his week had been. She sighed and crossed to Hassan's room. The door was ajar and a dim light shone next to his bed. She knelt on the floor and bent over him, smiling.

There was a movement by his feet. She turned to ruffle

the fur between the cat's ears then gave Hassan a light kiss on the cheek and left.

She paused at the door to her and Yusuf's room. She burned to talk to him and felt guilty about her reticence on the phone the previous night, the way she'd shrugged off his queries about her day with a mumbled *it was fine*.

Yusuf was asleep, a book dangling from his hand. She felt her shoulders slump; all that adrenaline, wasted. She leaned over to shut off his bedside light. The book fell from his hand and she caught it before it hit the floor.

Pulling in a deep breath, she crept to her own side of the bed and quietly undressed, easing herself in next to him. She lay on her back, staring at the ceiling, the crack that snaked across its blank expanse.

She turned away from Yusuf, careful not to disturb the duvet. She gazed at the light around the curtains, listening to the plunk of the pipes, catching fragments of conversation as people passed in the street outside. The curtains were thin and the orange mist of a streetlamp suffused the room. Tree branches moved across it from time to time in the wind, casting shadows across the room.

Yusuf turned over, making the bed shudder. He made a small, distressed noise: a bad dream. Unable to lie still, she slid from the bed, taking care to leave the duvet over him, and made her way to the bathroom. Its soft carpet welcomed her cold feet and muffled their sound.

She sat on the toilet lid for at least half an hour, playing the anticipated scene with Yusuf over and over in her head. She heard a sound from Samir's room and froze, waiting for him to open the bathroom door. How would she explain sitting here in the middle of the night?

No-one appeared. After a few moments holding her breath, she headed back to her room.

Yusuf was sitting up and rubbing his eyes. He turned on his bedside lamp and yawned.

"Jen? What time is it?"

"Almost midnight. Sorry. Go back to sleep."

"I'm awake now," he grumbled, swinging his legs over the side of the bed and heading for the bathroom. After a couple of minutes the toilet flushed and he shuffled downstairs to the kitchen. Jennifer listened to the thrum of the pipes and considered what to do. She grabbed her dressing gown and followed him downstairs, casting a glance at the boys' doors as she passed.

He was standing at the sink, gripping a mug of water and scratching his chin. He flinched as she appeared, as if he'd forgotten she was home. He pulled his dressing gown tight around him and sat at the kitchen table, looking at her between sips.

"What's up?" he said. "You look like death."

She nodded. *Now or never.*

"I'm not sure you want to hear this, but I have to tell you about something that happened at work."

He looked at her, his expression flat. She took a seat opposite him.

She told him about her conversation with John – about how they wanted to restrict demos, giving the police powers to break up gatherings. How they wanted to stop a backlash. He listened in silence, and when she had finished, explaining that she had to give her decision in four days' time, he drained the last of his coffee and headed back to the sink. She watched him, trembling.

"Yusuf. Please talk to me."

"You've got a nerve, Jennifer."

"Uh?" She wasn't expecting this.

"Telling me this in the middle of the night, with the kids

asleep upstairs. You know damn well that I can't react, or I'll wake them. So what do you expect me to do?"

"I don't know. I don't expect you to do anything. I just have to decide what I'm going to do, and I wanted to discuss it with you first. Like we always do. I know you hate this; I hate it too. But it's going to happen anyway, and people are going to get pissed off about it. We could do something to try to stop that."

"Jennifer, I don't want to talk about this now. You seem to have made up your mind, and I can't see how what I think has anything to do with it. Let me go back to bed."

This was the only way to deal with him. Let him retreat into himself, sort out his own feelings, and then approach him when he was ready. As long as he was ready in the next couple of days.

"OK. I'm sorry, love. I didn't want all this to happen any more than you did. I love you."

She kissed him before he was able to move away, feeling his lips tight against hers. She squeezed his hand, receiving nothing in response, and watched him retreat towards the stairs.

For the next two hours they lay awake, each with their back to the other. From time to time the bed moved, and Jennifer heard him sighing. She fought the urge to turn and try to explain herself.

Jennifer was relieved when at long last the alarm buzzed. She dressed and left as soon as she had her make-up on, giving Hassan a gentle kiss while he slept and casting Yusuf what she hoped was a conciliatory look before leaving. She grabbed breakfast on the way to work, but was unable to eat it. After a late meeting with the local victim support programme manager, at seven pm she made it back to the house.

Which was empty.

She panicked. By this time they should all be at home, with Hassan being nagged into bed and Samir a zombie in front of YouTube. But the house was heavy with silence. Frantic, she jabbed at her phone to dial Yusuf.

Voicemail.

She threw her phone onto the hall table, cursing herself under her breath. *Where are they?* She rattled into the kitchen, tossing her bag onto the table and attempting to calm herself with a cup of tea, spilling hot water on her hand in the process.

As she turned away from the sink she spotted a folded up piece of notepaper on the floor with her name on. She grabbed it. *Taken the boys for pizza.*

She slumped against the fridge door, her heart slowing. This had happened before, when Samir was small. They'd argued about her campaign tactics and Yusuf had disappeared with Samir, taking him to a funfair. And then two years ago, when Samir was a protesting twelve year old and Hassan a puzzled eight, he'd taken them all the way to Derby, driving forty miles before reconsidering and turning back.

She stood up, clenching and unclenching her fists, and was about to grab her phone when it rang. It was Yusuf.

"Yusuf? Where the hell are you?"

"Calm down. We'll be home later."

"You could have told me. I was scared stiff." Her breathing was shallow. She put a hand to her chest and willed her heart to slow.

"Sorry. But you owe me an apology too. Telling me that in the middle of the night." He was whispering. She wondered if the boys were with him, or if he'd found a moment alone, sent them off to the toilet maybe.

"I didn't mean to. You gave me no choice," she replied.

"Whatever. I don't like it."

"I didn't expect you to."

"And I know I can't stop you from doing what you want."

"Come on Yusuf, you know it's not like that."

"I can't. I shouldn't. I'll keep quiet, I won't rock the boat. But I'm not getting involved. I'll see you later."

"OK. How are—"

But he had hung up.

12

JANUARY 2020. BIRMINGHAM

JENNIFER STARED INTO SPACE IN THE LIVING ROOM, jumping out of her seat every time a car drove past. She'd heated a curry in the microwave; it sat on the table in front of her, cooling. She'd been tempted to let the cat have it when he'd leaped up to try his luck, but thought better of it and shooed him away distractedly.

Finally a pair of headlights didn't pass but instead turned to beam into the room. She smoothed her clammy palms on her skirt, wishing she'd taken the time to change out of her work clothes. She felt tight and uncomfortable in them, aware of the grime of the day settling on her skin.

She walked towards the front door, wondering who would be through it first. A weight landed against it and she heard giggling. Hassan.

She smiled and threw the door open, catching him as he fell. She landed a kiss on his head and tousled his hair.

"Hello, sweetie. Nice pizza?"

"Yeah. Daddy let me have the all-you-can-eat ice-cream."

That would have stretched things out. "Lovely. Now it's late. Go upstairs and get your pyjamas on."

He groaned but did as he was told. Samir sidled past, giving her a curt teenage hello, and disappeared upstairs. Finally only Yusuf was left, emptying the car of the boys' coats and school bags.

She stood in the doorway, calming her breath. Watching him while trying not to look threatening. What mood would he be in?

He gave her a quick kiss then pushed past and started putting things away.

"You OK?" she asked.

He looked up the stairs and then motioned towards the living room. She followed him in there. He shut the door and she felt ice run down her spine.

"Hassan will be back down in a minute," she said, her voice shaky. What did he want to say, that demanded a closed door?

He took a deep breath, his chest rising and falling, his eyes on her.

"I know. I'll be quick."

She nodded.

"I've made a decision."

She put a hand to her chest, her skin tightening. "What?" Her voice was brittle.

He licked his lips. "I'm fed up of standing on the sidelines while you and John do whatever you want to do."

She frowned, puzzled. "I'm sorry."

"Let me continue." He looked up at the ceiling and then back down, his gaze landing on the curtains behind her. She heard a car pass outside and the sound of the boys' voices upstairs.

He scratched his beard. "I love what I do at the shelter."

He paused. She waited. "But it's not enough. I can only help people so much."

"I think what you do makes a huge difference," she said. "More than me, sometimes."

"Do you really think that? Really? Or are you just patronising me?"

The accusation was like a barb in her chest. "I'd never patronise you, Yusuf." She blinked.

"Whatever," he said, sounding more like Samir than himself. "I sometimes think you're more interested in keeping John happy than you are me."

"That's not true."

"Really? Where are your priorities, Jen?"

His eyes were on her, his face hard. She met his gaze, trying not to tremble.

"Here. You and the boys. You're my priorities."

"It doesn't feel that way."

"Yusuf, that's not fair. We talked about what it would mean when I became an MP. We knew there'd be compromises. That's why I'm so grateful that you—"

"Grateful? Is that what it is?"

She could feel her thumbnail in her palm; the nervous tic. "I don't know what it is you need me to say. They're going to do this without me. You know that. Maybe I can improve it, temper it a bit."

"You've already said that."

"I know. There isn't much else to say."

He turned away from her, looking at the family photo over the fireplace. "Anyway, I know I can't stop you doing what you want to at Westminster, but I can do more myself."

"OK." She had no idea what he meant. Was he going to

speak to John? To try to sway him somehow? She wasn't aware they were still in touch.

"So I'm going to stand for the city council. I can do that while still keeping up my work at the—"

She all but collapsed in relief. "I think that's great."

He frowned. "Do you?"

"Of course. You'd make a great councillor."

He stared at her for a few moments. "Thanks," he said, not sounding as if he meant it.

The door clattered open and Hassan was in the room. "I'm hungry!" he cried.

Jennifer turned to him. "You've just had pizza. How can you possibly be—"

"I'm hungry," he repeated, folding his arms and slumping onto the sofa. Jennifer looked at Yusuf, giving him a hopeful smile. He didn't return it.

13

JULY 2020. LONDON

IT WAS A STIFLING MORNING IN JULY. THE temperature had been nudging the thirties for at least a week and the *Evening Standard* was reporting record temperatures on the tube. Jennifer was on the phone to Yusuf when John came breezing into her office, throwing open the door and sending a welcome draft of air her way. She'd just recovered from a bout of food poisoning and was struggling against the heat. She had moved to one of the armchairs in her office, desperate for comfort. She'd spent the morning roaming her room like a cat in heat, searching out a cool spot. Truth be told, she probably shouldn't be there at all.

"Morning, John. How's things?"

"Oh, not brilliant. I can't really talk to you about it – sorry."

She nodded, still focused on what Yusuf had been telling her about Samir's school report. All they talked about now was the boys. Weekends were spent in tense silences broken only when one of them went out to work, which was often. He hadn't even discussed his council campaign with her, and her only involvement had been professional – knocking on doors, standing behind him at the count when his victory was declared.

By contrast, in the past six months she'd established an easy rapport with John, a sense of comrades-in-arms struggling against a common enemy. The restrictions on demonstrations had worked so far, with the protests grinding to a halt. But with the heat came the threat of renewed unrest. Scattered pockets of violence had broken out over the last few nights; Manchester, Leeds, East London. Not Birmingham yet; the stabbing Jennifer had witnessed still cast a shadow. This gave John a wild, haunted look whenever he spoke of it. He was under pressure from Michael: Jennifer sensed that he feared for his job. She went along with this new friendship, knowing it might help John and that it could only benefit her career. And she secretly liked the fact that with John, there were no arguments.

"Was that Yusuf?" he asked, throwing his jacket onto a chair and slumping on top of it. Jennifer winced.

"Yes. Samir just had his school report."

"School report? But he's only twelve, isn't he?"

She smiled. "Fifteen now. GCSEs next year." She pictured Samir in his school uniform, scowling at his dad as he drifted off to school in it every morning.

"Oh." John smiled to himself. "I remember my first school report. Eleven and just started at grammar school."

He gave her a suspicious look. "You didn't think I'd have gone to grammar school, did you?"

She shrugged. "Now what would make you think that, John?"

"Anyway, I had some old battleaxe for a teacher. Miss Humphreys her name was. Seventy if she was a day, and obviously no one had seen fit to marry her in all that time.

She said I was a bad influence on the other kids. Me! Can you believe it?"

She smiled. "Maybe."

"It was them who were the bad influence on me. Was it my fault the other boys encouraged me to steal the caretaker's bike and ride it round the playground? Was it my fault when they cheered me on as I melted stationery equipment in the Bunsen burners?"

Jennifer laughed, relieved to see John so relaxed. Her stomach gurgled and she put a hand to it. Not again.

A shudder jolted through her. She placed a steadying hand on her desk and looked at John.

"You OK?" he asked, colour draining from his face.

She gave a tight nod, lips clamped together.

"You're not going to throw up, are you?"

She shook her head. "No."

She was contradicted by a wave of nausea.

"John," she whispered as it subsided. "I need to be alone."

He headed for the door. "No problem."

Another jolt went through her. John turned, holding the doorframe.

"Was that you?" he asked.

"What? I don't think so." The room was swimming, but she was sure she hadn't moved.

"I felt something." He looked unsettled. He approached her, putting his hand on the cracked leather of her chair.

There was a loud noise from behind her, a bang followed by a deep, slow rumble. She turned to see grey smoke obscure the window, filling the courtyard outside. John pushed past her. He leaned over as far as he could against the sealed casement, trying to get a better vantage point. She pushed herself up to hover behind him. All she could hear was shouts and the peal of a distant alarm. As John pressed his face closer to the glass it shattered, propelling him onto the floor.

There was a thick, eerie silence. Jennifer stood over John, mesmerised by the glittering shroud of glass covering his prone body. A sharp, acrid smell burned her nostrils, making her gag. Blood started to seep from a cut above John's right eye.

Frozen, she clutched at her stomach, trying to calm her nerves. She pulled her hand away and saw blood on it. She moved it across her abdomen; when she reached her hip, she felt something sharp against her fingertips. She pulled at it and lifted it to her face; a shard of glass, no more than an inch long, tipped with blood.

Almost immediately, there was a security guard in the room. She stared at Jennifer, her eyes flashing. "Get downstairs, in the basement, now! There's been a bomb."

Jennifer looked down at John, still unconscious on the floor. "But...?"

"Don't worry about him. I need you downstairs quick."

Jennifer moved towards the door, swallowing hard.

The guard stared at her. "You OK?"

There was a shout from further down the corridor and the guard rushed away before Jennifer could tell her about the blood. She put her hand on her hip again, her eyes widening. She took a deep breath and followed, heading for the lift as fast as she could. Barring her way was another security guard.

"You'll need to use the stairs. It's for your own safety."

"But I've—"

He turned away, shepherding more people towards the staircase.

Jennifer joined the growing crowd jostling its way to the

broad staircase that snaked down the centre of the building. Worried about losing her balance, she clung to the railing as she fumbled her way down. She held out an arm in front of herself in an effort to avoid being elbowed by the people pushing past.

Finally, they arrived in the gloom of the basement. She was ushered to an office by yet another guard. This one couldn't take his eyes off her bloodied hands.

"Have you been injured?"

She looked down. "I think so." The room was blurred and she felt like she might lose her footing.

"Here. Sit down. I'll get an ambulance. Have you got anything you can hold against it?"

She shook her head, feeling the room sway.

The office was spartan, furnished with an empty desk and a couple of low chairs. Two of her ministerial colleagues were already there, standing below the high window. The view up to the street above their heads was obscured by a cloud of smoke and dust. She blinked at them, unable to remember their names.

Jennifer let the guard usher her into a chair. By now she was having to focus hard on keeping conscious. She slumped into the chair, sweat beading on her face.

"Jennifer! Are you OK? My God, you look terrible." One of the ministers, a woman with dark curly hair, sank to Jennifer's eye level, her eyes wide with panic.

"I've been injured."

Moments later, a wheelchair appeared and the same security guard who had ushered Jennifer down to the basement was wheeling her along unfamiliar grey corridors. She was too busy battling the nausea and faintness to ask where they were going. She couldn't feel any pain; there was just a chill in her hip, as if she'd stabbed herself with an icicle. A paramedic met them and took the chair, then shoehorned it out of a narrow door leading to the courtyard below Jennifer's office.

"We'll be at the ambulance in a moment," he said. "But I need you to hold this to your wound."

Jennifer blinked and saw a white object in front of her. She fumbled for it and let him guide her hand to her hip, pressing on it as best she could. The iciness subsided and the faintness eased. But now there was pain. Hard, sharp pain. She gulped down air, not sure whether to fight it or let it consume her.

As they started to move again, she put up her other hand to block the sun from her eyes. Clouds of dust swirled and settled, making it difficult to see. To one side, two paramedics were crouched over a whimpering woman. Blood covered the woman's face. Jennifer recoiled, panting now, pushing her breath in and out. A man Jennifer recognised but couldn't place limped past, nodding when he spotted her. Something she preferred not to identify was sticking out of his leg and another paramedic was hurrying behind him, begging him to slow down. In a corner, hoses arced into the open windows of downstairs offices. The windows glowed orange through the dust and spray.

The air was full of shouting – injured people crying out, emergency workers calling to each other – punctuated by the rising wail of approaching sirens. She turned in the wheelchair, craning her neck to find people she knew, but a stab of pain flung her back. Finally she was pushed through an archway and cried with relief as the paramedic wheeled her into one of the waiting ambulances.

14

JULY-SEPTEMBER 2020. LONDON

"It's my turn!"

"You've already had five minutes. Dad said—"

"Boys. Shush. Mum's awake."

Jennifer opened her eyes. Yusuf was next to her, his eyes wide. Samir and Hassan were on the other side of the bed, squabbling over Samir's phone.

She was groggy but managed to piece together the events of the previous day.

"Yusuf!" she whispered. "You shouldn't have brought them down here – after what happened—"

"Don't worry. I had no choice; they wouldn't let me come without them. They wanted to know you were OK."

She raised her head to look down at her hip, but it was covered by a sheet. She lifted it to reveal a lump under her hospital gown: bandages.

"Am I?"

He smiled. "You got a surface wound. The fact that you were already ill made you feel like you'd lost more blood." He hesitated. "Why didn't you tell me you had food poisoning?"

"It didn't seem important."

He grabbed her hand. "It's OK. I'm just glad you weren't hurt. I mean, seriously hurt." He looked uneasy, wary of her reaction.

She twisted her hand to hold his. "Thanks. How long have you been here?"

"Since this morning. We were brought from the station in a ministerial car, with a security guard. The boys loved it." He smiled at her, his face soft. "I'll take them home tomorrow."

She sighed, too exhausted to argue. Still, at least Yusuf seemed to have dropped everything to come to her. She wouldn't have laid a bet on that, the way things had been.

Yusuf patted Samir's arm.

"Stop arguing, you two. Here's some change. Samir, take Hassan to the vending machine."

Jennifer watched them leave, her chest tightening. Yusuf hadn't willingly been alone with her for weeks.

"How do you feel?" he asked. "Does it hurt?"

She sent her mind into her hip, poking about for sensation. "No. It's numb."

"They gave you a painkiller. An injection."

She nodded, shifting in the bed. The movement brought a dull pain to the wound.

"How's John?" she asked.

"He's fine. They brought him here too. He had cuts from the broken glass, mostly his face. I saw him leaving this morning – apparently they're superficial."

"But what was it? The blast?"

"It was a car bomb. An extremist group has claimed it, a new one. A man drove it into the front of the building, killed himself. " He tightened his grip on her hand. "And two civil servants. And there are twelve missing. The building's a mess. One side's collapsed. People are still trapped."

Jennifer closed her eyes and slumped into the pillows. She pictured the grand Queen Anne façade with a hole ripped through it, rubble strewn across the street and smoke and dust obscuring the windows. She thought of the scene in the courtyard the day before. Bile rose in her throat.

"Are they still looking for people?"

"Of course." Yusuf nodded. "They'll find them. I'm sure. I saw them pull someone out on the news before I left this morning."

She was shaken by the thought of this happening in the full glare of the twenty-four hour media. People she worked with – had shared arguments, and jokes, and battles with – were in there, struggling to survive. Maybe counting the minutes until the air ran out. And the media were out front, getting it all on film, making sure they didn't miss a thing.

She knew that the casualties were fewer this time than the last time, but this felt so much worse.

"How are you?" she asked him.

He shrugged. "Relieved. Now I know what you went through with the Waterloo bomb, not knowing where we were. But I feel oddly delirious. I hate myself for it."

"Don't. Panic does that to you."

Yusuf clutched Jennifer's hand tighter, his eyes searching her face. "I'm sorry, love."

"What?"

"You know. John – the protests. All that. Let's not let politics come between us again."

She felt her shoulders relax. He bent to hug her and she let him take her weight. "No," she whispered. "Let's not."

The boys were soon back, brandishing their loot. Jennifer widened her smile and held out her free arm, welcoming them onto the bed. Hassan climbed up and hugged her neck. He brushed against the wound and she grimaced but didn't tell him off. Samir only perched on the bed but put a hand on her arm.

Jennifer gathered them to her as Yusuf pulled his phone out to grab a selfie.

~

Two weeks later, she was back in Westminster. Her team had been allocated temporary offices in the Treasury. As she introduced herself to the receptionist at the imposing front desk, she felt an urge to turn and flee. She pushed it down and waited in silence while Donna came to fetch her.

Donna was relieved to have her boss back. She chattered as she led the way down winding corridors and up staircases which took Jennifer back to the day of the bombing. She felt the stairs above pressing down as they ascended, and had to stop and pause for breath. Her hip was still sore and she struggled to keep up.

Finally they were at the corridor outside her office. The admin team sat at desks in the hallway and civil servants were dotted along the corridor in pokey offices. Jennifer smiled at each of them in turn as she made her way to her own office at the end. These people had worked with her for months or years yet they felt unfamiliar here, as if she'd just met them.

"This is you," Donna said, pushing open a featureless door.

Her new office was small and dark, with little natural light. The one high window looked out over air conditioning units. She swallowed and stepped inside, lowering herself to her new chair. It squeaked under her weight.

"Sorry," Donna muttered. "It's not brilliant, is it?"

Jennifer's shoulders dropped and she forced out a smile. "We'll cope, I'm sure."

"Yes," Donna replied and backed out, closing the door.

Jennifer sat in the stillness of this new space. Her files were still in boxes beside the desk: not unpacked yet in case of another move. She lowered herself to them, searching for something to personalise the space.

Beneath a wad of papers was a photo of Samir and Hassan. She bit her lip and pulled it out, placing it on the empty desk. She'd need to get a new one.

Donna opened the door. She saw Jennifer on the floor and gasped. "Oh! I'm so sorry! You don't need to do that."

Jennifer looked up. "It's OK. I'd rather."

Donna blushed.

"Ease me in gently," Jennifer continued. "You get on with your work. I'll call you if I need anything."

Donna picked up the phone on the desk, listened to it and then replaced the handset. "Dial 1," she said. "If you need me."

"I will."

She waved Donna away and returned to her task, dreading the day when she would have to do this again in the Home Office.

15

OCTOBER 2020. LONDON

"Come in!"

Jennifer's office door opened and she pulled back from her desk, unaccustomed to visitors.

"John? What are you doing up here?"

He pushed the door further open – it was blocked by the armchair – and ignored the question, slumping into the chair. His face had taken on a pinched look. He'd lost weight and seemed to have aged a decade too.

She smiled. "How are you?"

"I'm well, how are you? Recovered?"

"Yes. The odd twinge when I bang my hip on something but much better, thanks. Your scars are healing well."

He lifted a hand to his face, tracing the shadow of a scar beneath his eye. "Thanks. I wish it was all that simple."

Jennifer raised an eyebrow. John sighed.

"I can't stop thinking about the staff."

She nodded.

"Five of them died," he muttered. "Five people who worked for me. Two straight away, in the blast, and three more who we didn't reach in time." He paused, looking towards the window. A shiver ran through him and he turned back to her, his eyes drilling into her face. "They suffocated under the rubble," he muttered.

"John, you couldn't possibly have..."

"I know Jennifer, I know. But I feel responsible, you know? Maybe it was me who should've died."

His face was lined with worry. Dark shadows under his eyes threatened to suck Jennifer in. Where had the joker gone, the man who'd been sharing stories of his school days?

"John, have you spoken to anyone about this?"

He glowered. "Of course not. I don't want Michael thinking I'm not up to the job. The recruitment's getting worse now. We're going to need tougher legislation. He's relying on me."

"I don't mean that. A counsellor. Someone who can help you work things out."

He grunted. "Ha! Oh no. No. Definitely not."

"But John..."

He stood up.

"You can't tell anyone what I've just told you. Keep it to yourself, yes?" he hissed.

But before Jennifer could say anything he'd left, his heavy footsteps hurrying towards the lift.

~

"We can't do that. It's a racist policy."

John had summoned Jennifer to his office early – so early, in fact, that she'd wondered if he'd had someone watching for her arrival. He'd sat her straight down and launched into telling her the government's latest plans, with no preamble.

"It's a practical policy," he replied. "Designed to protect people."

She took a deep breath, forcing herself to stay patient. "Do you *really* believe that?"

"This is the next step in our battle with the terrorists. I need you to sort it out."

Jennifer stared at him. She was horrified at what he was proposing.

"Why do you think that this will cut immigration? Why do you even think that immigration has security implications?"

"There's no escaping the facts, Jennifer."

"What facts? You're saying you want to impose restrictions on immigration from countries you suspect of harbouring terrorist organisations."

"Yes. We want to keep them out."

"But that won't stop the terrorists, if they're determined. They just get false passports."

"We have to do something. This sends a message. Tightens security."

"I don't believe you really think this."

He said nothing.

"So which countries are you talking about?"

He swallowed. "Pakistan, Afghanistan, Saudi Arabia. A few more."

"Muslim countries."

"Countries harbouring terrorist organisations."

She shook her head.

"Like I say," he said. "If you help with this, it means a promotion. Immigration Minister. We – I – need you to push it through."

She looked at him. The Home Office bomb had got to him, yes, but not like this, surely?

"I'm sorry," she said, her breath shallow. "I can't support this. We're still the Labour Party."

John sighed. "We're in government, Jennifer. We have to do what it takes to keep this country safe."

Jennifer looked at him, thinking of all the speeches she'd watched him make over the years, before and after becoming an MP herself. All that passion, all that anger; was this what it had come to? Then she thought of Michael, smooth-tongued in his expensive, perfectly tailored suits that matched his private education.

"Tell me you had nothing to do with this idea," she said.

"That's irrelevant, and you know it. We're government ministers, and we act together. Or there's chaos."

She sighed. "I can't believe he'd go this far." She paused, judging the wisdom of what she was about to say. "Does it ever occur to you he's in the wrong party?"

"Who's in the wrong party?"

She span round to see Michael Stuart at the door. Don't blush, she told herself. Don't show him how rattled you are.

John spoke for her. "No one. We were just gossiping."

Michael narrowed his eyes. "That's not like you, John." He turned to Jennifer. "I assume he's told you?"

"He has," said Jennifer. "I don't understand why you're here."

Michael shrugged. "It's handy having you in the Treasury. I can come straight through from Number 10. Maybe I should move all the Cabinet here. What do you think?"

"I think they should stay with their staff."

"Not about that. About what John's told you. Your chance to be in the Cabinet."

"If I go along with these immigration proposals."

"Yes."

She shook her head. "It's not right, Michael. We all know that you can't stop terrorism by keeping innocent people from moving around. And think about what the backbenches will—"

He waved a hand. "That's not your concern. And as for it being right, since when was protecting the people of this country not right?"

"This won't protect anyone. It'll just erode human rights and make us look even more right wing than Trask."

A shrug. "Again, not your concern. My priority is security and protection. No one else will die at the hands of extremists – not on my watch."

Jennifer looked from him to John; why was John saying nothing?

"This will happen," Michael continued. "I'd prefer you to be involved. John believes your experience and reputation will help. But if you refuse, it won't change anything."

He turned and left, his footsteps muffled by the corridor's carpet. Jennifer resisted the urge to follow, to check he hadn't stopped to listen in.

She turned to John. "Tell me that wasn't planned."

"It wasn't. He pops in here every now and then."

"Did he know you were seeing me?"

"Yes." A pause. "So? What's your answer?"

She felt her palms turn sticky. Her mind was reeling and she needed to sit down. John watched, raising an eyebrow. His scars had healed now and were all but invisible. He looked healthier than she'd ever seen him.

"What Michael said. He will make this happen without you," he said, his voice low and firm. The voice Jennifer adopted when she was trying to make the boys behave. "There are others who would be more than happy to take your place, and spearhead this."

She closed her eyes. She knew there were other junior ministers snapping at her heels.

"Are you threatening me?" Her eyes snapped back open. "Are you *sacking* me?"

"No. No, Jennifer." John stood up and their eyes locked across the desk. He glanced down at Jennifer's knuckles, turned white as she braced herself against the desk. Then his face softened. "Please – calm down. But you have to know we will make this happen whatever. Michael has his heart set on it."

"Don't tell me to calm down." She straightened up, backing away from him. Was this who she'd been working for, all along?

" I won't be any part of this," she said, her voice trembling.

John shook his head. "Now, look, don't be—"

Her chest filled with heat. She cut off the rest of his words, heat running through her.

"I resign."

PART II

OCTOBER 2020 - FEBRUARY
2021. LONDON AND
BIRMINGHAM

16

OCTOBER 2020. LONDON AND
BIRMINGHAM

IT WAS RARE FOR JENNIFER TO BE OUTDOORS AT THIS time of day.

Eight am and she was sitting on a bench in Green Park, aware that the damp wood was staining her skirt but too angry to care.

Struggling to remember how she had found her way here, she looked around, numbed by the normality of the surroundings. A tree overhung the bench, the last leaves clinging to it. An expanse of grass glistened in the thin sunlight, and beyond that a layer of mist cloaked a silver-grey pond. Jennifer shivered, realising she'd forgotten her coat. How cosseted she'd been, hidden away in a ministerial car or first class rail carriage.

Around her, people were enjoying the bright chill of the autumn day. A pair of disheveled women sat on the next bench along. Their grey-rimmed eyes followed a trio of toddlers running around on the grass in front of them, bulky in their fluffy pink coats. A teenage couple giggled between syrupy kisses, sitting on a leather jacket spread on the grass.

People were exercising dogs, jogging, power-walking, or just taking a diversion on their way to work.

Jennifer picked her phone out of her bag and brought up Yusuf in her contacts. She stared at the phone for a moment, thinking. Slowly she tapped his name and then held the phone to her ear.

She waited while the phone rang out twice then shifted to voicemail. She slumped and snapped the phone off, putting it back in her bag.

She shivered again, and not just from the cold. *What have I done?*

She didn't regret her decision. What John had proposed was a step too far. Jennifer couldn't live with herself if she played the leading role he was asking of her. Let alone live with Yusuf.

But embarrassment at her response was already gnawing at her. Storming out like that made her look petty and emotional. And, what was worse, she would have to go back. She had exploded from John's office, momentum pushing her out onto the street, avoiding the gaze of the puzzled front desk staff asking if they should call a car. She hadn't taken a detour via her own office or picked up any of her things. She hadn't even formally resigned. John would be assuming this was a fit of pique, that she would sidle back later, tail between her legs, agreeing to do the PM's dirty work.

That wasn't going to happen. But she owed John the courtesy of making her resignation official. And she didn't want to lose what few of her own belongings were among the packing cases.

She stood and turned towards the street, hailing a taxi.

$\sim$

Back at the Treasury building, she slipped in via a side entrance and managed to make it to her desk without speaking to anyone. She turned on the PC she'd barely used to type a resignation letter: one copy for John and the other, more formal version, addressed to the Prime Minister. She found a plastic bag in a bottom drawer and swept her personal belongings into it: a photo of Yusuf, more of the kids, a couple of paperweights; her Law certificates, framed. Not much to show for a glittering career.

She left the office, easing the door closed behind her. She stopped to place the sealed envelopes on Donna's desk. Donna looked up from her screen. But Jennifer didn't have the words – or the nerve – to tell her.

She swallowed. "Make sure those are sent to John and Michael Stuart immediately, please."

"Certainly, Minister."

"Thanks."

Donna looked at the envelopes and then back up at Jennifer. There was a question in her eyes, but she said nothing. Jennifer berated herself for being such a coward; for not being able to tell her staff, who had been so hard-working and loyal, for not giving them the satisfaction of a proper farewell.

She forced a smile and tugged on her coat as she left the little suite of offices for the last time.

As Jennifer walked through the door of her empty London flat, her mobile buzzed: Yusuf.

"Hello love, what's going on? You're on the TV. Is it true?"

"Is what true?" She wedged the phone under her ear and turned on the news. Sure enough, archive footage of her was being shown: speaking at party conference, visiting a school, campaigning in the constituency. The film cut back to the studio.

"We've heard that Ms Sinclair has resigned to spend more time with her family, but we haven't had official confirmation from the Home Office, nor have we heard anything from the former minister herself." The presenter turned to a pundit sitting next to him. "Vanessa, do you think we should be reading between the lines here?"

"Well, Tom. Many a politician has resigned to 'spend more time with their family'. And it normally means something else. But in this case, Jennifer Sinclair's family situation, with her Muslim husband and sons, could be making things more complicated."

The phone dangled from Jennifer's hand. She heard the tinny sound of Yusuf's voice and lifted it back to her ear.

"What's going on? Is it true? Have you resigned? Why didn't you talk to me about it?"

"Yes, it is true. But not because of what they're saying. Believe me, you'll be glad when I tell you."

She recounted her morning to him: the summons to John's office, the hasty resignation, the trip back to pick up her things.

"*Shit.* You did the right thing. But what can we do to try and stop them?"

"Nothing, at the moment. Nothing I can think of. They haven't made their intentions public yet. Now I've resigned, I don't have access to that sort of information any more."

She paused, her head thick with a threatening headache. "Yusuf, did I do the wrong thing? Should I have stayed and tried to stop it from the inside?"

"No, love. There's a line you don't cross. You know John wouldn't let you undermine him like that. At least you had the satisfaction of walking out before they sacked you, which it sounds like he was threatening to do."

"You're right, I know you are. But first I want to clear up all this family rubbish. I won't lie down and let them say that your faith means I can't be a government minister."

"Just be careful. You don't want to say anything that'll be misquoted. They'll be frantically briefing against you."

"I'll be careful – I promise. I'm going to make a couple of calls and then I'll be on the first train."

She hung up and called John.

"Ms Sinclair." It was Amanda, his PA, who normally addressed her as 'Minister'. It felt like she'd been erased.

"Hello, Amanda. Can I speak to John please?"

Amanda didn't miss a beat. "I'm sorry, but he's unavailable at the moment."

"Well, can I leave a message?"

"I'll tell him you called."

"Thanks."

Amanda's tone made it clear that the call wouldn't be returned. Jennifer still didn't know where the news story had come from; had the Home Office told them she'd resigned to be with her family, or had they jumped to their own conclusions?

She dialled Lucy Snape, a political correspondent on the Guardian. Someone she'd been able to trust in the past.

"Lucy, I need to ask you something off the record. Do you know why they're saying I resigned because of my family? Is that what they've had from the Home Office, or are they making it up?"

"Don't you know? I thought the Home Office would be working from a statement you prepared."

"No, they're not."

"I just got a press release. Says you've decided you need to spend more time with your family, and that you're taking a break for a while."

"*What?*"

"Jennifer, is there something going on here? Why did you resign, exactly? I take it you did resign?"

"Yes, I did resign." She thought fast, sifting through options, deciding not to act. *Not yet.* "But I can't tell you why."

"You sure? I'd have thought you'd want to tell your side of the story."

"Yes. No. Sorry. Look, we've worked together before. If I tell anyone it'll be you. But I'm not ready. Not now."

"OK." Lucy sounded wary, but excited. "You know where I am, yes?"

"Yes, I do. Thanks."

So, thought Jennifer. John had chosen to hide his own plans by releasing lies about her.

She was angry and not in a fit state to make clear decisions. Yusuf's rational head was what she needed, so she packed a bag and phoned for a taxi.

Outside, the press pack had started to gather. She could hear their voices through the door before she even opened it. She steeled herself to push through them, then opened the door. The noise exploded.

She made her way down the steps, feeling the press of their bodies as they threw questions at her, making her chest tighten. She avoided eye contact and elbowed her way through.

"I'll speak to you when I'm ready!" She dove into the welcome depths of the cab. "Euston," she snapped at the driver, turning her face away from the cameras.

Three hours later, she arrived home in Birmingham, in another taxi. They were waiting there, too. Two men bounced out of separate cars, falling over each other in their haste to get at her. She flew to the front door, grateful that Yusuf was ready.

"Let me in," she panted, slamming the door behind her and turning the lock.

In silence, they walked through to the kitchen. It was gone six o'clock, and as Yusuf turned on the lights the windows blackened. Jennifer felt a stab of anxiety that someone might be out there, watching from the dark of the garden. She shook her head, reminding herself that they had lights with motion sensors. She wished they'd thought to install blinds. She slumped down at the table.

Yusuf sat next to her, his hand enveloping hers. He'd pulled a chair round to face her.

"Yusuf, what have I done?"

She collapsed into him, trembling. They sat like this, until her breathing slowed.

At last she let go.

"I bet you haven't eaten, have you?" he asked, standing. As she watched him move around the kitchen, she realised she hadn't seen the boys yet.

"The boys are at my mum's," he said, as though reading her thoughts.

She left Yusuf stirring pasta sauce and slipped upstairs. She needed to change her clothes.

"Hi there." Yusuf had appeared in the doorway. "Food's ready."

She walked to him, her arms out, and gave him a hug. He smelt of garlic mixed with aftershave. It was true, she hadn't eaten since a snatched breakfast at six.

They ate in silence. As Jennifer cleared the plates away,

Yusuf broached the subject of John's proposals. She didn't feel ready to think about it, but they needed to start planning.

She sat down and put a notepad between them, chewing a pen she'd pulled out of a drawer.

"What's he planning to do next?" Yusuf asked. "We need to anticipate and respond."

Jennifer sighed. Her mind felt thick and heavy. "I've no idea."

Yusuf gave her a concerned look. "But you can work it out, can't you? How did he seem? Worried? Pressurised?"

She thought of John's body language over the last few months, the way he had changed before her eyes. She had no idea if he was the same man Yusuf had been at university with, the same man they'd sat round tables with late into the night, drinking whisky and putting the world to rights.

"He's frazzled," she said. "Michael's putting him under pressure."

"OK," said Yusuf. "So they're probably going to start the ball rolling sooner rather than later."

Jennifer sighed. She wanted a break, some time to rest and get her energy back. She nodded. "You're right."

"So, what will you do?"

"Talk to the press. Clear up this family nonsense first." She took a long sip at her mug of tea, throwing ideas around in her head. "If there's nothing in the Guardian tomorrow, nothing about my conversation with Lucy Snape, I'll give it to her."

Yusuf frowned. Jennifer looked at him. "I rang her. I needed to know who'd told them about my resignation."

"Was that wise?"

She felt herself stiffen. "I had to. It's fine. It'll be fine."

Yusuf pulled back. He was nodding but didn't look convinced.

"Look, if she hasn't leaked it tomorrow then I'll talk to her," she said. "What I tell her can go public anyway, so it won't matter."

"And what will you say?"

She leaned back. "My god. I've got no idea." She pushed out a long breath. "I can't do this on my own."

He leaned in again and stroked her hand. "You've got me, love."

"That's not what I mean." He frowned and started to pull away and she quickly grabbed his hand, holding it between hers. "Sorry. It's just – I'll need other people with me. To help me beat Michael." She paused, examining Yusuf's face. "And John."

Yusuf nodded.

"Are you OK with this?" she asked. "He's your friend."

"This is more important," he muttered.

"OK. I'm tired. Let's go to bed. I'll ring Penny, get her over here. We'll need to get the constituency on board."

Penny was Jennifer's agent, a brusque, efficient woman who didn't always appreciate Yusuf's involvement in her campaigns. He pursed his lips. "You're right."

Jennifer squeezed Yusuf's hand. "Thanks."

OCTOBER 2020. BIRMINGHAM

"Jennifer, hi! Glad you decided to call back. So are you going to tell me the real reason for your resignation?"

"Lucy, I want you to know how much I hate doing this. You know how committed I've been to this government, and John Hunter goes back a long way with my family. I don't want you to publish the fact that it was me who talked to you. Say 'unattributable sources in the Home Office', or something like that."

"Anything you want, if it means I get the story. Have you talked to anyone else?"

"No other press, if that's what you mean. I hoped you might handle this a bit more sympathetically than some of the others."

"Thanks. So—?"

She really wants this story, thought Jennifer. She took a deep breath and nibbled at a wayward fingernail. She was standing next to the bed in her room, one of the few places she could be alone.

"OK. Well, to start with, I did not resign because of my family. I want to make that very clear."

There was silence while Lucy waited for her to continue.

"Lucy, you know I don't like doing this. I know leaking something like this isn't a very – well, honourable – thing to do, and I hate doing it. But I really believe that by making this public, it will help to prevent what I think is a very unwise move."

"Which is?"

"I resigned because I was asked to introduce some new legislation. Banning immigration from a number of Muslim states. The idea is that it will stem what is believed to be a tide of actual or potential terrorist recruits entering the country."

"Jennifer, am I hearing you right? A blanket ban from Muslim states? Which ones, exactly?"

"I think you need to ask the Home Office that." Put John on the back foot, she thought. Make him confirm or deny her accusations.

"So because of a small number of extremists, they want to ban all Muslims from entering this country?"

"Well, not all."

Jennifer's heart was pounding now, and her fingertip was bleeding. She pictured John's solid face, the way he had looked at her when she told him she would have no part of this. She plunged on.

"But yes, that's the general idea. Regardless of how many of the people committing these crimes are actually immigrants, or even visitors."

"Right. But hell, Jennifer, that's huge."

Jennifer sat down on the bed, her skin turning cold.

What were the implications of her disloyalty? It was too late now.

"Thanks for this, Jennifer. Look, I've got to go. Catch the press and all that." The call clattered to an end.

Time to implement Yusuf's damage limitation plan.

Jennifer ran downstairs. In the kitchen Yusuf had his back to the door, along with Penny, who had arrived while she was on the phone. The two of them were caught up in a stilted conversation about the garden, standing on opposite sides of the kitchen. At Jennifer's arrival they turned, surprised.

Penny approached Jennifer, giving her a sympathetic look that made her feel like an invalid. She hugged her and Jennifer stood stiffly in her agent's arms, unaccustomed to the contact. At last Penny let go and held her at arm's length, looking into her face.

"I'm proud of you, Jennifer. You've done a great thing."

Jennifer shrugged and looked down at Penny's necklace of purple beads. It lent a grey pallor to her skin.

"Thanks. Didn't have much choice really," Jennifer replied, shaking her off. Penny sat down opposite Yusuf and Jennifer took a place at the head of the table.

"They're outside," Penny said. "Hacks."

Jennifer smiled inwardly: Penny had never liked the press. They got in the way of the voters, as far as she was concerned.

"Well," Jennifer said. "I've just been on the phone to one."

Penny's face darkened. "Yusuf told me."

"Right." Jennifer's voice became businesslike. "So, Lucy Snape has the story now. It won't be long before everyone else does. Let's get working on that statement."

'M inister Quits Over Immigration Ban' ran the Guardian's headline the next morning.

By the time Jennifer had ploughed through the new morning routine of getting the kids dressed behind closed curtains, the radio and TV channels were running the story too. She sat at the kitchen table, Yusuf opposite her. He watched her reactions as she read the story on her iPad. The crowd outside the front door had grown in the early hours, and getting the boys off to school had been a trial.

The other papers were still reporting that she'd resigned for the sake of her family, although that had by now been relegated deep inside, on the political or comment pages. Jennifer knew that her resignation was nothing to the uproar this legislation would cause; that she had become only a small part of the story. Despite the disappointment at being made aware of her own inconsequence, she was relieved.

"I think we should go and stay somewhere else for a while." Yusuf pushed the iPad out of the way, forcing her to look at him. "You can't think straight while you're under siege."

"No. I've made my bed and I'll lie in it. If it's too much, we can let the boys stay at your mum's for a few days. A treat for them. But I don't want to hide."

"But what will you tell them?"

"Nothing. At least nothing they don't already know. Not till I've had a chance to talk to some backbenchers. Or, rather, some of the other backbenchers." She smiled. She'd have to get used to that title. Having resigned from her ministerial job, she was back to being a backbench MP.

Yusuf looked worried.

"Thanks for being with me on this, love," Jennifer said, taking his hand. It was soft and warm. She looked at him properly, maybe for the first time in weeks. He was wearing a blue silk shirt, one she'd bought him for his birthday. It brightened his skin and made him look alive. "I know it's not easy for you. But think of the support you'll get on the council."

"I know. Not all of them. But most, yes." His eyes were steady on her face.

Jennifer smiled at him and put down her cup of tea, which had grown cold. "So. What's next? I'll stay here for a few days, see some more of the kids. Battle my way through some advice surgeries. Then on Monday I'll head back to London, start stage two."

Yusuf returned the smile. Jennifer was surprised to feel his grip tightening on her hand, transferring its heat. He rose from the table, pulling her up. The shirt shifted, light catching on it. He'd tucked it into his black jeans. Suddenly she was taken back to their first date, to the sight of his slender hips in smart black trousers, the shirt he'd worn. The years had been kinder to him than to her, she thought.

She followed as he pulled her out of the room, through the hallway and to the stairs.

"Let's take our minds off it for a bit," he said.

Her breath caught in her throat. Surprised, she followed him upstairs.

18

OCTOBER 2020. LONDON

It was a Wednesday night and Jennifer was deep into a meeting of the campaign team she'd pulled together in the fortnight following her resignation. Maggie Reilly, the rebellious and larger-than-life MP Jennifer had watched in action so many months ago, was dominating the meeting with a description of her techniques for dealing with the Labour Whips.

"You just have to switch off, Jen" she said.

"Jennifer, please. Only Yusuf calls me Jen."

Maggie shook her head. "Then I'll call you Jenny."

Jennifer opened her mouth to protest but Maggie had regained her flow.

"It's like being in a room with a toddler throwing a tantrum, or trying not to bait a snake. I just go into a zone." She closed her eyes, raising her arms as if in a trance. "One where I know I'm right and I shouldn't be swayed by these jumped up bastards. They wouldn't know a genuine opinion if it smacked them in the face with a wet kipper."

She opened her eyes and cracked a grin, settling back down on the sofa in the tiny living room of Jennifer's

London flat. Jennifer had raced through an emergency tidy-up before the meeting, stuffing papers into bins and shoving some in her bedroom. The others laughed as Maggie glowed like a leading lady in the warmth of the spotlight.

Colin Hayes was perched opposite, on a hard-backed chair dragged in from the bedroom.

"That's all very well, Maggie. But what we must come back to is how all this plays out in the press. The Whips have friends in the media, and we need to cultivate them too."

Colin was a new MP in a rock-solid South London seat which he'd won in a by-election as the 'local guy'. He hadn't made much impression on Jennifer or anyone else but he was a former journalist and his media contacts might prove helpful.

The final member of the group was Javed Iqbal, the son of Pakistani immigrants whose loathing of this bill trumped his untrammelled record of loyalty. Javed had a puffy, lived-in face and stark white streaks snaking through his thick black hair. Maggie was dismissive of his former loyalty and Colin struggled to understand why he couldn't be a back-slapping socialite like him, but Jennifer valued his insight.

Tonight they were planning a strategy for influencing ministers. Media attention had swelled and ministers were proving unwilling to make statements; the BBC had taken to keeping seats empty in the studio when a government spokesperson couldn't be found.

"Look, both of you," Jennifer interrupted. "We're not talking about the press or the Whips tonight. We need to divvy up these ministers and decide what order we'll try to meet them in."

Maggie nodded. "I say you take the meetings, Jenny."

Jennifer squirmed. "You know full well they won't listen to me."

Jennifer sighed. "I don't have good relations with all of them. Certainly no one in the Home Office..."

"It's not worth talking to the Home Office," Javed said. "Concentrate on the others."

He was right. "OK," Jennifer said. "Let's write out a list, identify the ones worth talking to, and who we're friendly with. Then we can work out who talks to each one. OK?"

She grabbed a piece of paper.

The next morning Jennifer was woken by the buzz of her mobile rattling on the bedside table. She fumbled for it and looked at the display: *number withheld*. Hoping it wasn't a journalist, she answered it, stifling a yawn as she settled the phone on the pillow beside her ear.

"Jennifer? It's John. John Hunter."

"John? It's not even six in the morning." She didn't bother to hide the drowsiness in her voice.

"Yes, I know. Look, we need to talk. Can I see you in an hour? Come to my office. I'll have someone waiting for you so there'll be no problem getting in."

He hung up. Jennifer sank below the duvet, letting herself drift back into sleep, until ten minutes later the alarm clock went off. She climbed out of bed and dived into the shower. As the hot water brought her to life she wondered what John might be up to. She sure as hell wouldn't be responding to any requests to back down.

Fifty minutes later she was at the main entrance to the Home Office, now repaired and open for business. Sure enough, a man she'd never seen before was there already – the 'somebody waiting'. She followed him inside, taking the familiar route.

There were small changes. The hallways had been redecorated and the place smelt of fresh paint mixed with dust. And there were subtle shifts she couldn't place; maybe the pictures had been moved, or the carpet colour changed. She felt like an exile returning to the country of her birth; at once familiar and unwelcoming.

Outside John's office, the man left with another curt nod. There was no one else around. Jennifer gave a sharp knock on the door. "Come in!" came the response.

John was behind a monstrous new desk, angled for the best view of the door and window. In front of it were two sofas and a low table, with a cafetiere of coffee and some pastries. The smell of coffee mingled with the paint tang and the fuzzy, hay-feverish scent of new carpet. Every surface gleamed.

"Jennifer," he said, smiling and gesturing towards a sofa. "Please take a seat."

She sat on the sofa. He rounded his desk and cleared a spot on the other, which was strewn with newspapers. He leaned forwards and poured two coffees, placing a pastry on a plate and handing it to Jennifer. He didn't take one for himself.

She took a sip from the coffee and turned towards him. Behind him, through the large window, the sun was rising over the buildings opposite. She frowned and shifted in her seat to bring it behind his head, not to be blinded. She wondered if this was deliberate.

"Let's get straight to it, shall we?"

Jennifer nodded, ignoring her pastry.

"I s'pose you're expecting me to try and talk you out of

your little campaign, to offer you your job back, or something like that. Right?"

"Ah! Damn." Jennifer had spilled her coffee – on her trousers, not on the beautiful new cream sofa. She fumbled in her bag for a tissue and mopped herself up. John watched in silence, a patronising smile dancing on his lips. When she had recomposed herself he was still giving her a level stare. It seemed Jennifer was expected to speak.

She put her damp rag on the table.

"To be honest John, I really didn't know what to expect. You surprised me."

"OK, I accept that. But seeing you again yesterday, it made me realise how bloody rude I've been."

She waited.

"Yes, I know you've been trying to contact me," he said. "And that poor old Mandy has been fobbing you off. Not her fault, of course." Jennifer nodded; of course it wasn't. "So I thought I should do the decent thing and get in touch. Have a chat. Let you know how things stand."

She smiled, intrigued. "I'm glad. You and I go back a long way, and I'd hate for us to become – well, enemies."

"But you know we can't be friends again, just because of that," he replied. "I trusted you. I talked the PM into promoting you way beyond your experience, because I knew how committed you were, how determined. I thought to myself, *That's the sort of girl I need. Someone who'll stick with it, battle through the flack and stay with us through thick and thin.*"

Jennifer stiffened and decided to let the *girl* go. She hadn't been expecting a lecture.

"But I was wrong, wasn't I? I stuck my neck out for you – gave Michael the impression you were the type who'd never do what you did. Who'd never resign like that, and most of all, would never leak things to the bloody press in such an underhand way."

His face had turned red. Clearly, he wasn't as calm and in control as he was trying to make out. was red and a lock of hair bounced over his left eye as he spoke. Jennifer dug her fingernails into her palms, suppressing the anger that threatened to mirror his.

"There is no evidence that I leaked anything," she said, pushing down the tremor in her voice.

He gave a sharp shake of his head. "Come on, Jennifer. Don't play the innocent with me. I know how friendly you are with Lucy Snape. When I saw her by-line on that story, I knew straight away. A bit of rooting around, and I had it confirmed by the end of the day."

He pushed his hair back and raised his cup for a long, noisy sip. Jennifer didn't know what to say. At length, he put down his cup and looked at her. The fire in his cheeks was fading but his eyes still had a sharp gleam.

"Nothing to say for yourself? No, I thought not. What I wanted you to know, Jennifer, is that I wouldn't offer you your job back if you were the last bloody candidate on earth. The PM gave me hell after you resigned. He couldn't kick you so he kicked me. And all this shenanigans has made him stubborn about this bill. If it doesn't go through, I'll have to resign. So you've just made him more determined."

Jennifer leaned forward. "I know what he can be like. But I also know that there's a large part of him that is pragmatic, conciliatory. If it looks like the government could lose a vote, I think he'll negotiate. And we're willing to find compromises, you know."

John gave an exasperated laugh.

"You really think that, don't you? I know you don't mean to hurt the party, I know you're too loyal for that." His eyes narrowed. "Or you were. But you *are* hurting the party by carrying on like this. Michael won't back down. And come to that, neither will I. We'll take this to a vote, and we'll win. The Tories may be condemning us now, but when it comes to it, this sort of stuff is right up their alley. They know if they opposed us, their voters would be up in arms. So we'll get it through comfortably, don't you worry about that."

"That remains to be seen, I think."

"You believe what you want. I just want you to know that there will be no negotiating from this office, or from Number Ten. Message clear?"

"Loud and clear."

He sighed, his stare fixing her in place like a startled bird. Jennifer slammed down her cup, not caring about spillages now, and stood to look down on him.

"We're not going to give up, John. This is a shitty piece of legislation, and you know it. I'm just sorry it had to be like this."

Then she left before saying something she might regret.

19

NOVEMBER 2020. LONDON

"WILL THE PRIME MINISTER CONFIRM THE VERACITY of today's reports that he is seeking to extend the terms of his new proposals to include other minority groups as well as Muslims?"

The Leader of the Opposition sat down and a deafening roar erupted, making Jennifer's ears smart. All around her, Labour MPs were yelling: *Bollocks! Shut up! Sit down!* On the benches opposite, the Tories were cheering: *Got him! Disgrace!*

It was five minutes into Prime Minister's Questions. Michael Stuart approached the dispatch box calmly, eyeing Trask and the rest of his tormentors. His face was calm but his usually sleek, dark hair curled around his earlobes; he needed a haircut. Behind him, John sat in the front row, a look of scorn on his face as he eyed Trask.

"The Right Honourable Gentleman should not believe everything he hears outside this chamber. He knows as well as I do that our proposals do not take into account an individual's religion or race. I wonder if he has forgotten what he himself said in this house a few short months ago?" He paused to look around the chamber, ignoring the muttering that buzzed along the benches. "Mr Speaker, if I may quote."

There was quiet while Michael looked at his papers, broken only by a muffled laugh from opposite. Jennifer knew he didn't need them; he'd have his words memorised. But Michael was always the master of the dramatic pause.

"'The risk of the ranks of terrorist organisations being swelled by immigrants is great, and that risk is highest in the case of those immigrants coming from Islamic states.'" He looked up, waving a hand to take in his colleagues, to invite them into a conversation. Then he leaned forward, looking at Trask. "Did he, or did he not, say that?"

More jeers from both sides, so intense now that Jennifer couldn't tell what was coming from the government benches and what from opposite. The effect was like being plunged into a trough of water in the middle of a football terrace. The Prime Minister paused, his brown eyes surveying the Tory front bench. He raised an eyebrow and took a deep breath. "Will he not agree with me that since the first terrorist attack so near to this House, he, like me, has been actively seeking to reduce the number of potential terrorist recruits entering this country? And that he, like me, believes that the best way to do that is by restricting immigration from high-risk states? I ask him, did he say that on March the seventeenth this year, or did he not?"

He sat down again to a riot of shouting. Jennifer glanced at Maggie, sitting next to her.

"Order, order!" The Speaker was standing now, trying to bang his gavel hard enough to be heard. The rumbling subsided as Leonard Trask rose. Someone placed a hand on Jennifer's shoulder from behind, making her flinch. She turned: there was an approving smile too. Plenty of them.

"The Right Honourable Gentleman knows full well that he takes what I said out of context. I will concede that I did indeed state those views. However, if he read his *Hansard* correctly, he would know that I suggested negotiations with high-risk states over eligibility for immigration. Not a ban!"

Eventually the noise abated, the jousting ceased and it was time for the lowly backbenchers; their weekly opportunity to seek the PM's attention. Some did it to get their face seen, others to raise an issue in their constituency. Many did it to boost their standing with the PM. But Jennifer was none of these. She actually needed an answer to a question.

Each time a question was answered, she sprang up like a grey-suited jack-in-the-box. Others were just as quick, and after five questions she still hadn't been called. She tapped her fingers on the file in her hand, impatient.

At last the Speaker called her name. A hollow feeling sucked at her chest and she grabbed one hand with the other. She took a deep breath and turned towards the front bench.

"Will the Prime Minister confirm reports I have received from officials that he is considering widening his restrictions on immigration to include all Arab states, including those with secular governments, and is consulting on the possibility of forcibly repatriating male immigrants who have entered this country from those states since the summer's terrorist attacks?"

The room erupted. Papers were waved and the rumble of the benches shuddered through Jennifer as she sat down. She smiled at Maggie, who grabbed her hand and squeezed it. Her palm was as damp as Jennifer's was dry.

Michael rose to his feet, shuffling papers. The hair at the back of his neck was damp. He turned briefly towards her, not making eye contact, and then turned back to face the dispatch box.

"May I thank my honourable friend for the question. Such reports are based on wild rumour and speculation only and I do not wish to lower myself to respond to them. However, given her penchant for scandal, I would be interested to hear what the papers have to say about this tomorrow."

Behind Jennifer, one MP let out a spluttering laugh. Jennifer shook her head, miming disbelief. On the front row, across the aisle from the ministers, Javed Iqbal was waving his papers in the air and laughing. His eyes gleamed with something, as if he could taste victory. Maggie's face had the look of an animal about to catch its longed-for prey.

Jennifer bit her lip. Tomorrow's papers would be reporting Michael's failure to deny her accusation, hot on the heels of Trask's which was so keenly rebutted. But they hadn't won yet. As John turned to look at her, his eyes full of steel, Jennifer worried she had begun a fight to the death.

∿

The next morning's press was full of it. Splashed across the front pages of the left-leaning papers were accusations of hypocrisy, of isolationism. The more upbeat right-wing papers, in contrast, chose to credit Trask with a kind of victory over Michael.

Jennifer hid in her flat, her phone switched off. A small press pack was gathering in the street below, their babble reaching her second floor window.

At eleven she had to leave for a meeting. She toyed with using the fire escape to make a sneaky exit, but this would mean climbing down two flights of stairs which were little more than ladders. Besides, she could handle the press – when she was ready.

She opened the front door to the street. It was narrow, with Victorian buildings looming on either side, opening right onto the pavement. The press pack was causing quite an obstruction.

"Good morning," she said breezily.

They lunged at her. "Ms Sinclair! Can you tell us where the information you revealed at PMQs yesterday came from?" one of them asked. Polite; broadsheet. Jennifer pushed through, saying nothing.

She started walking. Not too leisurely: she didn't want to give the appearance of grandstanding. And not too fast: she couldn't have them thinking she was afraid. The cold morning air stung her cheeks.

They followed closely, the pack shuffling along the pavement behind her. "Jennifer! Why d'you want to bring the government down?"

The words were like a dart fired into her back. She froze. Thinking fast, she took a deep breath, turning to face them. She squinted and they became a grey amorphous mass: no faces, no individuals.

"I don't want to bring the government down. Britain has gained massively from having a Labour government and it's the last thing I want for that to be lost. I just want to stop a law that's unjust and counter-productive."

They started pushing again. They could trap her here if she wasn't careful, goad her into saying something she regretted.

"Now if you don't mind, I need to be at work. Excuse me, please."

She retreated, the click of her heels echoing off the red brick walls. She looked back to see them breaking up,

118

knowing she wouldn't return for some hours. She quickened her step towards the everyday rush of Waterloo, where she hailed a cab and made her escape, feeling like a character in a film noir.

At the Houses of Parliament she hurried to her office, a tiny third floor room much like the one from her first term. In the eaves and with no windows, it was dark and stuffy and smelt of the accumulated sweat of generations of occupants. She spent as little time here as possible, but today it was a refuge. She slumped into the solitary armchair, squeezed in between a desk and two small bookcases.

There was a knock on the door. She stared at it. *Go away.*

"Jennifer? It's Maggie. I have news."

Jennifer let her in, going round to the chair behind her desk so Maggie could take the armchair. The room was at full capacity.

"You were great yesterday," Maggie grinned. "Everybody's talking about you."

"Thanks. But I don't want everyone talking about me. I want them talking about the bill."

She laughed. "Oh, come on, Jennifer. You don't have to be all high and mighty with me. Number Ten are in a spin, briefing and counter-briefing all over the place. I'm not even sure if Michael Stuart knows what's going on. This is *great.*"

Maggie's green eyes shone. She loved this: the game, the fight.

Jennifer hated it. All she wanted was the best outcome with the fewest possible casualties. *Minimum collateral damage.* But she couldn't get this morning's accusation out of her head.

"Maggie, I was doorstepped today."

"That's excellent! They're really taking notice."

"It's not excellent, not at all. One of them asked me why I wanted to bring the government down." She leaned back, looking at the low eaves. *What have I done?* "I don't want to bring the government down. But they think I've got some sort of vendetta and that's why I resigned."

"Don't worry, love. It doesn't matter what they think. What matters is that they're paying attention, they're listening."

Jennifer looked back at Maggie. "Can I ask you a question?"

"Course you can."

"If it came to it, if this bill *was* going to bring down the government... would you keep going, would you take it that far?"

"You know I'm not one to shirk my responsibilities. If something's wrong, then I'll vote against it. And if Michael Stuart insists on introducing racist laws, then yes, I'll vote against him, whatever that means." She clasped her hands together and smiled. "But it won't come to that, you know. They're going to cave in. And even if we win, why should it bring down the government?"

Jennifer shivered. "Oh, I don't know. Something about the way John spoke to me the other day. They've got a lot riding on this. The tabloids support it, the Americans have done much the same thing already. Michael Stuart won't want to look indecisive."

"OK." Maggie came to perch on the desk. "So what about you?"

"Hmm?"

"Jennifer, would you carry on with this whatever?"

She hesitated. "I really don't know. I can't imagine it happening, can't picture it in my head. We're different, you and me."

20

JANUARY 2021. LONDON

It was a Tuesday morning and Jennifer didn't have to be in Parliament until nine o'clock. She ran a hot shower in the hope that it would wash away some of her tension. As the steaming water plastered her short hair to her skull, she closed her eyes and tried to clear her head. Finally, relaxed but not purged, she stepped out, wriggling her toes on the bathmat and reaching for a towel.

She froze. There was a familiar voice coming from the bedroom, on the other side of the door.

Yusuf? She frowned and crept to the bathroom door but couldn't make out what was being said. It definitely wasn't her husband, though. She shrank back, her hand on the door handle.

She knew that voice.

It was John.

What the hell was he doing in her flat – in her bedroom? Had he come to give her a dressing down?

How had he got in?

She reached for the pull-cord and turned off the light, silencing the extractor fan. The drain made its habitual gurgling sound and a pipe gave a single bang deep in the wall.

Now there was another voice.

Jennifer scanned the bathroom, looking for her phone or at least some clothes. But she hadn't brought anything in with her, not even a dressing gown.

She pulled the towel tighter and pushed the door open, peering through the crack.

The bedroom outside was empty.

She hesitated, clutching the towel.

Be bold, she told herself. She pulled her shoulders back and pushed the door open with feigned confidence, painfully aware of the towel wrapped around her.

She fell into the room and collapsed onto the bed, weak with relief and embarrassment. *It's just the radio!* It had come on while she was in the shower. She stared up at the ceiling for a moment, heart still thumping.

John was still speaking.

"...which is why it's crucial that the police and other law enforcement bodies have all the support and resources they need do their job..."

"Mr Hunter," interrupted the interviewer, "you haven't answered my question. Is it true that you're going to extend this bill – that you're going to restrict immigration from all the Arab and southern Asian states?"

Jennifer sat up. This was the first time John had spoken publicly since PMQs, and the first time her question had been put to any Cabinet member on air.

"Look. The terrorist attacks were a tragedy, and something we have to make sure doesn't happen again. That's my priority – and I'm doing everything I can."

"Yes, Home Secretary." The interviewer's words were respectful, his tone less so. "But that wasn't what I asked..."

"Look, let me continue. The Home Office attack showed the terrorists are as desperate to stop us catching them as we are to stop them getting to us. Terrorist groups are recruiting right here in the UK. And they're recruiting young men in the Middle East, especially Pakistan, who they get to come here to recruit more, and with some of them, to commit acts of terrorism."

"So why haven't there been more attacks?"

"The police and other authorities are working hard to find terrorist cells. We've been working closely with the Americans. They've got this problem in the States, but recruitment isn't so high, 'cause they don't have such a big Muslim population. So..."

"Hang on a minute. I must stop you there. Are you meaning to say that a sizeable Muslim population inevitably leads to more terrorist activity? That's a very bold statement."

"That's not what I said." John's voice was hoarse now and he had picked up pace. Jennifer could picture him on the phone to the studio from his office, leaning over his desk. Sweating.

"You don't need me to tell you," he continued, "that the majority of Muslims in this country are peaceful and want no part of this. But there are young men being taken advantage of because they're disillusioned with the West."

"So – to return to my first question – you say that terrorist cells are sending people to this country specifically to undertake terrorist activity. So why don't you make sure those individuals are prevented from entering the country, rather than imposing a blanket ban?"

"We don't know who they all are. Most of them have got no traceable connections to terrorism when they leave their home country."

"So how do you know they are terrorists?"

"We find out later on. I can't tell you how, but we've got good evidence. Very good."

"Which means that we have to believe you based on evidence which you are unable, or unwilling, to provide? I'm sure many people will be very worried by that."

"Look..."

"But to the second part of Ms Sinclair's accusation."

Jennifer's heart jumped at the mention of her name.

"Will you be forcing people to return to where they came from, even if they entered this country legally? What does this make of the Department for Employment's policy of encouraging migrant workers in order to address skills shortages?"

"Ah, now Jennifer – Ms Sinclair – wasn't right on that one. We *will* be repatriating people, but only those we believe are involved in terrorist activity. We won't be deporting everyone, not at all."

"But the evidence you've been able to gather against people so far is pretty flimsy. What court of law will decide whether these people are guilty of the crimes that you're accusing them of?"

"Look. We don't have the luxury of time. We're creating a review system run by the police and the immigration service, with a judge presiding. It'll be able to make speedy decisions."

The interviewer spluttered. "So people will be deported, despite entering the country legally, for allegedly committing a crime which no court has found them guilty of."

John inhaled. His voice became shrill. "It's not like that. The alternative is more terrorist attacks – something I'm sure your listeners want us to stop."

Jennifer blinked up at the ceiling. If this was a Conference speech, John would have been jabbing the air with his fingers. His face would have been red. It probably was. But would the hall have been applauding?

"Minister, thank you very much for your time."

John coughed. "OK. No. Yes. Thank you. Thank you very much."

Jennifer realised that she'd been holding her breath. She was cold and the bed was growing damp. She stood up and started to get dressed.

As she pulled on her shirt, she was interrupted by the phone. A journalist, wanting her response to John's interview. She rebuffed him, preferring to check her facts before responding to accusations of lying, and turned her phone off yet again.

~

Over the next week, Jennifer felt like she'd released the brakes on a runaway train. High-profile rebel MPs were appearing on TV calling for Michael Stuart's resignation. The number of backbenchers publicly supporting her campaign grew and even a few ministers started to wobble. Michael called a special Cabinet meeting at Chequers; they were all pestered by the press for information on what was said. And John, wind in his sails, was appearing whenever and wherever he was given the opportunity to defend himself and the government. It wasn't long before those calling for Michael's resignation were demanding his too.

At home, Jennifer was attracting even more attention than ever. Yusuf was being approached on the street and congratulated for his wife's stand, and the latest party meeting had been packed out. But the attention wasn't all positive. Walking to the House one morning, she was spat at by a man leaning out of a car window. He yelled after her, his words lost as he sped away. And a series of accusatory letters started arriving at the constituency office, ranting about how she was making the country unsafe and that if only immigrants would go home, they'd all be better off.

The following Wednesday evening, Jennifer was walking through the division lobby for a routine vote on gas meters. Other people crowded around her, jostling. She hated the predictable chat and enforced jocularity of the division lobby, and retreated into herself.

An elbow jabbed into her as someone pushed past.

"Hello, John," she said to the retreating figure. "How are you?"

He froze.

"It's OK. I won't bite."

He turned, casting his eyes about to check who was watching.

"Oh, Jennifer, it's you," he said, failing to sound surprised. "I'm well, thanks." He smiled but his eyes were hard. "How about you? Fighting the good fight and all that?"

"You know it's not like that. If things could have been different—"

"No, but they weren't different, were they?" He stepped closer, his breath hot on Jennifer's face. Dark circles ringed his eyes. "You turned your back on us, and now you want to be friendly? Don't bother."

Next to them, two MPs paused in their conversation to listen in. Jennifer scowled at them and lowered her voice. "Please don't make it personal. You know it's not—"

"If I lose my job, it bloody well will be," he hissed.

Jennifer stared at him. "He won't sack you, surely?"

"Hmm?" He raised a spidery eyebrow. "Don't be so sure. Michael is a man on a mission. Have you been reading the papers?"

She rolled her eyes. The tabloids were supportive of Michael, applauding his tough stance. Photos of the carnage from the Waterloo and Spaghetti Junction bombs had been plastered across the front pages, as a reminder of what the government was trying to prevent. The broadsheets were more mixed; the Telegraph sceptical but reluctantly supportive, the Times combative and the Guardian full of indignation. The online news sites were a soup of anger, accusations and threatened violence, internet forums being closed down on an almost hourly basis. The trolls weren't Jennifer's concern; it was the 'I'm not a racist but...' types, increasingly supportive of Michael, that she had to worry about.

"Of course," she said.

"Then you'll know public opinion's behind us. People are scared, Jennifer. They want strong government."

She searched his face for signs of ambivalence, for the truth behind his words. But his eyes were steady on hers.

"I'm sorry," she said. "I didn't want to hurt you, Jo—"

"Don't. I'm not that fragile."

Maybe not, she thought. But she felt uneasy about betraying John, who she'd known for so many years, and respected. "I'm sorry. But I couldn't let you – him – do it. Not without a fight."

"Well, you got your fight all right."

He started to push through the people ahead of him, trying to escape. After a few unsuccessful attempts, he turned back. "And Jennifer?"

"Yes?"

"Don't leak this conversation, will you?"

With that he pushed even harder and was soon on the other side of two solid men, giving Jennifer no chance to defend herself.

She looked around, wondering who might have heard, and spotted Colin Hayes. She waved him over.

"Colin! Over here!" she hissed. It was difficult not to attract attention while attempting to be heard over the droning buzz of conversation.

He blinked at her as if coming to a decision. Then he said something to his neighbour, who looked up at Jennifer and smiled. Colin squeezed through the crowd, muttering apologies. "Jennifer, hi. How's things?"

"Not brilliant. John Hunter just gave me a tongue-lashing."

"Oh, don't worry about him. I happen to know that he's out of favour these days."

She frowned. "Do you? Who told you that?"

He looked down at his thin, almost translucent hands, his pale face turning an unattractive blotchy pink. "Oh, no one. No one you know."

She sighed. "Fair enough. So, see you tomorrow night, then? We need to go over the plan for the last few days before the vote."

"Err... Maybe – I mean yes, of course. I'll see you then."

Once again a man was fighting through the crowd to escape her. Was it something about her, or were they all up to something?

21

JANUARY-FEBRUARY 2021. LONDON

Jennifer was woken the next morning by her mobile ringing in the next room. Rubbing her eyes, she groped her way out of bed, stumbling over her slippers and catching a toe on the door frame. She clutched at it, falling into a chair as she grabbed the phone.

"Yes?" she muttered, studying her crimson toe.

"Ms Sinclair, what do you have to say about Colin Hayes's announcement today?" It was a male voice, one she didn't recognise.

"Sorry, what announcement?"

"Hasn't he told you? He's switched sides. Voting with the government."

"What!" Jennifer leapt to her feet, the pain in her toe suddenly forgotten.

"Any comment to make, Jennifer?"

"No. Absolutely not."

She ended the call. The phone immediately rang again.

"You sure you don't have anything to say?" The same voice.

"Who are you? Leave me alone."

She hung up and headed to the bathroom. As she closed the door she heard it ringing again. She went back to answer it, setting herself next to the window. Outside was damp and grey, with none of the birdsong that she'd chosen this flat for. She felt a drop of rain hit her cheek and shut the window.

"Maggie! I'm glad it's you."

"Have you heard?"

"About Colin? Yes, I've heard. What the hell is he doing?"

Maggie's voice was brittle. "The little bastard has turned on us, that's what he's doing. Gone to the papers accusing us of having our own agenda. I suppose Michael's offered him a nice job of some sort at the next reshuffle."

"Do you really think so? God, they are desperate. Colin wouldn't have got a government job in a month of Sundays."

"Well, I'm prepared to lay money that one miraculously turns up for him. Just you wait."

"So what has he said?"

"Plenty. Read your papers. And we need to meet, this morning."

"Right. See you at nine, here. Can you ring Javed?"

"No problem. See you then."

Jennifer found her iPad and shuffled to the kitchen, flicking up news sites as she went. It was as bad as Maggie had said. Colin had sent out a press release late the previous night, too late for them to get wind of it before their meeting. He was claiming that the long-term future of the country was at stake and he didn't want to jeopardise that by putting a Labour government at risk.

As if.

She turned on the radio to hear Christian Smith, her replacement as prisons minister, welcoming Colin back into the fold. "Colin Hayes has seen the sensible course of action, and I am confident that others will follow in his wake," he said, adding that it was important for the government not to be complacent and that the outcome of next Tuesday's vote was still touch and go.

Maggie arrived half an hour later, with Jennifer still drying her hair.

"Don't worry, I can wait." Maggie sat on the sofa and yanked a cigarette out of her bag. She caught Jennifer's frown.

"I'll lean out the window," she snapped.

Jennifer nodded and headed back into her bedroom.

"Bloody Colin Hayes," Maggie snorted from her vantage point by the window. "Never liked him from the moment I clapped eyes on the weedy little bugger. Opportunist. Sell his own granny, he would."

Jennifer emerged from the bedroom, her hair still damp. She looked at her watch; where was Javed?

Maggie yanked at the window then leaned out, taking a long drag. She ignored the rain. Jennifer sat in silence, thinking over their next move.

When Javed appeared, Maggie had finished her cigarette. She flicked it out of the window and twisted her mouth at Javed. He sat on the sofa while Jennifer made coffee. She could hear Maggie starting on a plan to get on the phone and make contact with their supporters.

The government was already doing the same thing. Over recent days Jennifer had noticed waverers having lunch or dinner with ministers; meetings for which they would normally have waited months.

Javed was quiet, listening to Maggie in between jabs at his phone. Eventually, Maggie turned on him.

"Cat got your tongue, Javed?"

He blushed and shrank back. He looked as if he'd slept in his clothes. Jennifer was sure they were the same ones he'd been wearing the previous night.

"Leave me alone, Maggie. This is getting to me. Maybe Colin did the right thing."

"Right thing? Bloody hell, Javed! You want them stopping immigrants from Pakistan? What would that have meant to your parents, eh?"

Jennifer stared at Maggie.

Javed pulled himself up, eyes blazing. His face was almost grey. "That's out of order, Maggie. This isn't about my family. It's about a principle. And don't worry, I'm not going to switch sides. I'm just under a lot of pressure from the Whips, that's all."

"But surely you're under just as much pressure from your constituents?" Jennifer asked.

"Yes, and not just them. Can't you see, this is tougher on me! A whole community is expecting me to deliver for them on this. It's alright for you two, with your high-mindedness and your political correctness. This is about reality for me!"

"Now hang on a minute, Javed," Jennifer said. "I'm pretty close to it too."

"You and your bloody husband. You haven't got a clue. Parading your relationship around like a political badge of honour. It makes me sick!"

"Javed!" stormed Maggie. "Get out! Now!"

"Happy to."

He slammed the door behind him as Jennifer and Maggie stood incredulous in his wake.

"Where the fuck did that come from?" Maggie gasped.

~

Despite Javed's empty threats, Colin Hayes's defection proved to be little more than that: one man changing sides. There were no throngs of rebels following in his wake; in fact, no one went with him. This strengthened the rebels' position and calmed Maggie, even made her a little smug.

"Always knew he was Billy-no-mates," she beamed, sitting in Jennifer's flat two days after his defection – and Javed's outburst. Javed was keeping his distance but hadn't switched sides. And he hadn't spoken to the press, a fact which made Jennifer relieved if not Maggie, who was still unforgiving.

On the Thursday night five days before the vote, Jennifer sat down at her desk, jotting names and numbers on a pad. She calculated that over thirty Labour MPs were planning to rebel. With the Opposition, that gave them a projected majority of eighteen. Even if some decided to abstain in the final days and hours, there was a real chance of winning.

She sighed and went to her bedroom to pack for the weekend. What she needed was time with her family.

She stood at the door to her flat and looked at her dishevelled living room, scene of so many planning meetings and arguments. On the windowsill was a loose pile of mail, unanswered while she'd been so distracted. She sighed, wondering what the return to normality would be like on Wednesday morning, once it was all over. How the result would affect her mood. Not to mention her standing in the party and the constituency.

Too late to change anything now. She picked up her case and turned out the light. A weekend at home would recharge her batteries. But things would be just as hectic there, her mobile would be pestering her all weekend. She was due in the BBC Midlands studio tomorrow morning, to record an interview that would go out on Sunday. She hoped that whatever she said would still apply by then.

She closed the door and clattered down the stairs, pushing away numbing fatigue and a rising sense of dread.

22
FEBRUARY 2021. BIRMINGHAM

AT HOME, THE HOUSE WAS QUIET. HASSAN WAS already in bed and Samir was out with friends.

"Which friends?" she asked Yusuf.

He shrugged. "Not sure."

She frowned. "Shouldn't we know where he is?"

"You didn't even know he was out till you got back. He texted me, went to a friend's after school for homework." He sighed. "I'm sorry. He'll be fine."

Jennifer bit her lip. This wasn't her territory to encroach on. "OK. If you say so." She leaned towards him and squeezed his arm. He looked up from the onions he'd been chopping and smiled. Emboldened, she gave him a kiss.

"Stop it, I'm making a curry!" he laughed.

She tickled him under the ribs, thinking of Hassan, who loved and hated being tickled in equal measure. "Sorry," she breathed into his ear.

Samir slid home while they were eating, bowls perched on their laps in front of the TV. Jennifer paused, fork in mid-air, and listened to the sound of their son trying to be stealthy.

Yusuf stood up, pushing his bowl roughly onto the arm of his chair. He walked to the door and yanked it open. Jennifer tensed, feeling cold.

"Samir?" came Yusuf's voice from the hall. "You're late."

There was a muttered reply.

"Pardon?"

"I said I'm sorry!" Samir shouted, thundering up the stairs.

Jennifer followed Yusuf. He was standing at the bottom of the stairs, his face dark with anger.

She put a hand on his back. "Let me speak to him," she said, and slid past him onto the stairs.

"I'm not sure—" he said, but she waved his doubts away and padded upstairs.

She paused at the door to Samir's room, then walked on the spot for a moment so he would hear her footsteps. She knocked.

"Only me, love," she said. Not waiting for a response, she pushed the door open.

Samir was on his bed, reading a book. She was surprised; she hadn't seen him doing that for a while.

"Good book?" she asked.

A grunt. *OK*, she thought. *This is how it's going to be.* She approached the bed, painting a smile on her face. She could hear her own shaky breathing. *Why am I so nervous?*

"Go away," he muttered. "I'm fine."

She perched on the end of the bed. "I know you're fine," she said. "But your dad isn't. He doesn't like it when you shout."

He looked up. His eyes were blotchy and she had a sudden urge to hug him. "How would you know?" he asked.

She felt her shoulders sag. "What's that s'posed to mean?"

"Nothing."

"Samir."

He shrugged. "Just, you're never here. And when you are here you don't talk to us. Or to Dad. All you want to talk about is John Hunter and Michael Stuart."

He was looking at his book, but his eyes weren't moving across the page. There was tension in his face. Had he gone too far, he was probably wondering. *Well, has he?*

"That's not true." She thought of her weekends at home, the hours she wasn't rushing around on constituency business or sitting in surgeries. There weren't many of them. She blinked and scratched her nose.

He looked up. "You know you're lying, don't you?" He stared at her, trembling ever so slightly. He looked down. "Typical politician."

She leaned in. "*What?*"

"You heard." His focus was back on his book now, and his face was pale. She heard a noise downstairs: Yusuf, clearing away their dinner.

"I've never heard you talk like this before," she said. "You know me, love. I'm not like—"

He ran a hand down the back of his neck. "Like who?" he said. "Like that ridiculous Maggie you've been hanging out with, a walking joke? Like John Hunter, willing to do his master's bidding like a good dog? Like Michael Stuart, purveyor of racist laws?"

She frowned. These weren't the words of a fifteen-year-old.

"Who've you been talking to?" she asked.

He shot up from the bed, letting his book fall to the floor. *Accusations Against the Imperialist State.* Her lip curled in an involuntary grimace. How long had he been reading this stuff? She felt her shoulders slump; she hadn't been paying enough attention to him.

He was standing over her now, imposing despite his leanness. "There you go again," he shouted. "You're laughing at me! You're all the same."

He walked to the door and pulled it open. "Go away!" he shouted. "Leave me alone!"

She stayed on the bed, smoothing her hands on the duvet. "No. We need to talk," she said.

"Mummy?"

Samir's head shot round as Hassan shuffled into the room, rubbing his eyes. Jennifer stood up. "Yes, sweetie?"

Samir put a hand on his brother's shoulder. "Go away." The hand twisted.

"Ouch. You're hurting me," said Hassan. He started to cry.

"Samir!" Jennifer crossed to Hassan and pulled him away from Samir, folding him in a hug. "Shush now, just a bad dream. Let's get you back to bed."

She steered her youngest son out as her eldest slammed the door behind them.

∼

On Sunday Jennifer woke early. She'd slept fitfully the past two nights, torn between worry about Samir and dread of the vote. She'd dreamed of the Houses of Parliament collapsing into the Thames and Samir standing in the wreckage, pointing at her. He'd stayed out till late on Saturday, and refused to speak to her or Yusuf when he got back. This morning they were going to tell him he was grounded.

Yusuf was still asleep. His eyes flickered under their lids and he grunted, flinging an arm out and batting her hip. She watched him, wondering what he was dreaming about. All of their talk recently had been of the bill and the campaign; but would it invade his sleep the way it did hers?

She eased herself out of bed and tiptoed downstairs. She picked up her iPad in the living room, anxious to check the news. When she got to the Sunday Times front page, her breathing stopped.

PM DECLARES CONFIDENCE VOTE.

She dropped onto the sofa, scanning the accompanying story. According to 'anonymous sources', Michael Stuart was going to attach the immigration vote to a vote of confidence in the government. She shook her head and pulled back control of her breathing. She reached for the TV remote, hand trembling.

A reporter was stationed outside the door of 10 Downing Street, talking to the presenter in the studio.

"No, we have no official confirmation of this yet – nor do we have a denial. We've been told the Prime Minister will emerge shortly to give a statement. However—"

The door behind him opened and he scurried out of the way. Michael was emerging. He was alone, followed a few paces behind by two advisors. His face was pale, his eyes swollen, and he'd acquired some grey hairs. He forced a tight, fixed smile and shuffled to a solitary microphone. The camera panned out to show the famous black door and Michael's wife Jane standing to one side. She had the wide-eyed look of someone who hadn't slept.

He coughed and reached in his inside pocket for a sheet of paper.

"Good morning," he said. He cleared his throat again then looked ahead. "As you will be aware, there have been reports this morning claiming that I have changed the terms of the vote on our anti-terrorism bill."

He paused to survey the waiting journalists and cameras. There was a silence broken only by the echo of a bird singing nearby.

"Everyone in this country is concerned for their safety and wellbeing, and that of their children. The threat of terrorism means people feel less safe in their homes and as they go about their daily business. I feel that concern too. I have a family of my own, and don't want my children to grow up afraid."

Jane Stuart looked down at her feet, playing with her wedding ring. Then she disappeared as the camera zoomed in on her husband.

"This is why I am determined to rid this country of terrorists and their supporters. I'm sure every man, woman and child watching or listening today would support me in that." Another pause. "As you know, there are those who would prevent me from doing this." He licked his lips, leaving a faint sheen, and stared into the camera. "I say to these people, do not let our children suffer fear and terror. Do not let our country be violated by those who would seek to destroy what we value most. This is your chance to show that you, like me, want to make Britain a safer place."

He swept his gaze across his silent audience, steadier this time.

"Because I feel so strongly about this issue, I have decided that the future of my government must rest on it. Without these measures, I and my colleagues will be unable to protect this country's citizens, and we will have failed in our duty. So I have decided to attach the vote on this issue to a vote of confidence. I say this to the dissenters."

He paused, his eyes narrow. He leaned forwards and clasped hold of the podium.

"Now it is time to decide which way your loyalties lie."

He smiled, his eyes gaining a hint of their usual sparkle, and nodded at the press. With a brief *thank you* he was gone, swallowed up by the familiar black door.

Jennifer sat frozen, her iPad on the floor. She rubbed her temples.

There was movement behind her: Yusuf.

"What are you going to do?" he said.

"God only knows," she replied.

23

FEBRUARY 2021. LONDON

BACK IN LONDON, SHE WOKE EARLY AGAIN ON TUESDAY, the day of the vote.

Leaving her flat for the chilly darkness of the street outside, she strolled to work. The sky was lightening, a denim tinge rising over the river, and the city was starting its day. Postmen were making their rounds, a pub was receiving a delivery of beer, and one or two commuters shuffled towards Waterloo. She wondered if these people's lives, so different to her own, were easier. But as she approached Westminster Bridge and saw the Houses of Parliament looming ahead of her, she smiled. Soaring from the banks of the Thames, the building had a grandeur today. The faint haze on the river lent it a sense of majesty and mystique. The place still had the capacity to make her pulse race.

Once over the river, she decided to keep walking past the front entrance, enjoying the early morning calm. Only a few jet-lagged tourists huddled outside for selfies. The solitary protester's tent on Parliament Square was quiet.

She turned into the southernmost entrance, on the Lords end, and made her way through inner courtyards, passing yet more postal deliveries and vans unloading catering supplies for the kitchens. The clatter of pans and hubbub of voices rang out, and she was accosted by the smell of frying bacon. She sauntered, unwilling to rush to her poky eaves office. Eventually she turned into the back half of the building. But instead of squeezing herself into the rattling lift to the third floor, she headed for the tea room in search of breakfast.

The tea room was all but deserted. A still calm hung over the space, intensified by pockets of light dotting the tables. It was as if the room itself was taking a deep breath in preparation for the rigours of the day. Few MPs were in the habit of getting in this early and only a couple of tables were taken, each with a single occupant. One of those occupants was in a large armchair in a corner, almost obscured by a copy of the Guardian. John Hunter.

Jennifer hesitated then decided it would be worse to ignore him. Swallowing hard, she approached his chair. He looked up.

"Hello, John."

"Jennifer! What are you doing here?" He'd paled.

"Sorry. I can..." She motioned towards the door.

"No, no. Stay here. I imagine you're feeling much the same as me, eh?"

She nodded, taken aback by his friendliness. Last time they spoke, he had hissed at her not to leak their conversation. And he'd been scared of losing his job. Was that still the case?

She fetched herself a pot of tea and sat back down. John folded up his newspaper, dropped it on the unoccupied chair, and turned to her. Behind her, two MPs passed them, talking loudly; she wondered who they were but didn't turn. John nodded at them then sipped his coffee. Jennifer shifted in her seat and John pulled at his collar.

Finally they were alone.

"Funny how things turn out, isn't it?" said John.

Jennifer looked up from her tea tray, raising an eyebrow.

He smiled. "I mean, you and me. We were just starting to get along so well. We've been through a lot together."

"We certainly have." She sipped her tea, nervous of what this might be leading to.

"I'm sorry we ended up on opposite sides. You had bags of potential, but I can't imagine Michael having a need for that now." He chuckled to himself.

"Are you OK? You seem different."

"Oh, me I'm fine," he replied. "It's him you need to worry about. A man possessed, he is." He leaned back and scratched his ear. Hairs were sprouting from it; that was new. "Thought I'd come and escape for half an hour or so. Funny for you to do the same thing. You don't normally come in here this early."

"No. First time. I didn't realise how peaceful it could be."

"Yes. Not like it gets later."

"Are things OK with you? You and Michael?"

His face hardened. "Of course. Why shouldn't they be?"

"It was just when we—"

"Forget that conversation, Jennifer. I've done what Michael required of me, and today it'll all be over."

She opened her mouth to contradict him but realised he was right. Whichever way today's vote went, this phase of the lives, of their careers, would be over. What was she going to do with herself?

He downed his coffee and picked up his paper, recomposing himself. "Anyway, I should be getting on. I'll see you later, no doubt."

"Yes, see you later... John?"

"Yes?"

Jennifer stopped herself, resisting an urge to wish him good luck. "Nothing."

He frowned and left the room, his footsteps reverberating in the quiet.

The time came to file into the chamber. It was as packed as during Prime Minister's Questions, or Budget day. Jennifer fought her way along a bench near the back; Maggie was already in place. As she passed through the crowds finding their seats, chatting and trying to get comfortable in the tight space, she felt people's eyes on her.

She smiled back at them, trying her best to seem calm and optimistic. She reserved her broadest smiles for fellow rebels, but didn't get the response she'd expected. One or two looked swiftly away.

She frowned, confused. Were they all about to turn back to Michael?

Most of the people she passed were not rebels, and would only have disdain for what she was doing. Their eyes bored into her. By the time she sat down, she was sweating.

She took a few deep breaths and wiped her face with her sleeve, glad she'd worn a dark jacket. Maggie was on one side and another Birmingham MP on the other. Other dissenters were scattered around the government benches. They had decided not to sit together, so that when speeches were made, it would look as if they were coming from a larger number, more widely scattered throughout the party.

The debate started with John, who began without flourish; words prepared for him by the civil servants. Formalities over, he launched into full flow, repeating the arguments Michael had made on TV two days before. It was a good performance – he knew his career was on the line.

Dawn Goodwin, the Tory Home Affairs spokesperson, responded less convincingly. The only punches she managed to land were those mocking the Prime Minister for blackmailing his backbenchers so that he could keep his job.

Her comments were greeted with laughter by the Tory benches. Around Jennifer, Labour MPs called out criticisms. She sat in silence, waiting for her turn.

John and Dawn traded a few more blows, until it was time for contributions from the backbenches. Jennifer jumped up and waved her papers, disappointed when someone in front of her was called. He made an ingratiating speech, praising the government's tough approach to terrorism and asserting that tighter immigration controls were a price worth paying for greater security. More were called; Labour MPs defending the government, Tory MPs attacking it. One MP, who had told Jennifer just half an hour before that she was still rebelling, delivered a short speech saying she had returned to the fold.

Jennifer was beginning to lose hope when at last she was called. She rose to her feet, ignoring the whispers around her. She heard someone mutter 'turncoat'. She felt Maggie shift her weight next to her. She, like the others, was relying on Jennifer.

It was time.

24

FEBRUARY 2021. LONDON

"I STAND BEFORE YOU TODAY WITH A HEAVY HEART AND a troubled conscience," she began, to the sound of muted jeers from the Opposition.

"The Prime Minister has given us a choice: to support this bill or to stand against him. As you will know, I am not someone who finds it easy to vote against my government. Until recently, I was its loyal servant."

The jeers came again, louder this time. Some were from the Labour benches. Jennifer pinched her fingers together, willing herself to stay calm.

"But if we support this bill, what will we be allowing to happen?

"There are families in my constituency who are watching this house with fear today. Women and children afraid that their husband or father will be banned from joining them in this country. Elderly people desperate to have their sons here so they can be supported in old age. Brothers and sisters separated with little hope of reunion. People who feel that this country is rejecting them, at a time when life is at its hardest.

"This country has a long tradition of offering a welcome to those who would make a new life here. Throughout our history, we have been an immigrant nation, comprised of people who have come here to do the best they could for themselves and make a contribution to their new home.

"The many thousands of people in this country who came here from Muslim states, or whose parents did, have an undeniable stake in our country's future and are an integral part of it. Yet how must they feel when they are told that they should not have been allowed here in the first place?"

The House was quiet. She glanced around and pushed on.

"I remind you that the government wants to ban immigration of men between the ages of eighteen and fifty from Muslim states. The men themselves do not have to be Muslim, or even resident in those states for all of their lives.

"The government seems to think that all men who have lived in a country where Islam is the main faith are potential terrorists. This group would include my own husband, and his father. It would include two members of this House. It would include over three hundred men in my constituency. People who came to this country to forge a better life for their families, some to escape political tyranny in their home country for a better way of life here."

She paused, thinking of Yusuf. He'd be at work, watching this on the TV. Surrounded by colleagues. Or would he have hidden away in his office? She hoped she'd do him proud.

"Does the Prime Minister think he can protect our freedom and democracy simply by denying them to others?"

The House erupted on both sides.

"Order!" cried the Speaker.

Jennifer smiled. She glanced down again at her notes, reminding herself of the next few lines so she could deliver them whilst maintaining eye contact with her audience.

At last there was quiet. She looked ahead and continued.

"Colleagues, before you support this bill, consider this – of the thousands of men who legally came to this country from Muslim states in the last five years, how many were terrorists?"

She paused. Behind her, she heard Maggie whisper to someone.

"The answer is just one. The majority of those who have committed terrorist acts in this country came here illegally or under false papers. This bill would do nothing to stop them. And those who did not come here illegally, who were British citizens, were born here. This bill would be powerless against them.

"There is just one man who came here legally and went on to become a terrorist – the man who drove a van laden with explosives into the Home Office."

There were a few intakes of breath. Jennifer knew she was taking a risk but pressed on regardless. She looked at John, who was staring ahead.

"For the sake of this one man, the government wants to close this country off to people who have a legitimate reason for coming here. In revenge for what one man did to us – I was there too, remember – it wants to punish thousands.

"I know what is at stake here. And as I have already acknowledged, this is not an easy decision for me, or for anyone in our party who has spoken against this bill today."

She looked around the Government benches. The chamber was quiet. She could just make out the sound of the protesters outside on Westminster Square, at least half of whom were on her side. They were listening to her, she was sure. She could turn this round.

"But in government or not, we are the Labour Party, built on principles of fairness and inclusion. I know that what I am asking you to do is difficult. But what do we sacrifice for the sake of power? Our ideals? The right of frightened, hungry people to cross borders in search of a better life? Or simply our own pride?

"I urge you, look deep into your hearts and ask yourself if you really want to make that sacrifice."

She sat down to silence, and a familiar squeeze on the shoulder from Maggie. After what seemed like an age, voices rose around her. MPs were on their feet, eager to be the first to respond, to slam her down or lift her up. She felt cocooned in this wall of noise, an invisible curtain shielding her and Maggie, who smiled and kept hold of her arm.

"Fantastic, Jenny," Maggie mouthed. "Bloody brilliant!"

~

Jennifer was pushed towards the 'no' lobby by a wave of jubilant Tory MPs. She shrank away from them, wishing she didn't have to physically join them to vote. She was shivering.

"Come on, Jennifer, stick the knife in!" one of them shouted.

She felt sick. She understood how, by attaching this to a confidence vote, Michael had separated the government's survival from the immigration bill. Even MPs who hated what he was doing wouldn't help her destroy the government.

But after making that speech, after leading the campaign

for so long, and after throwing in her ministerial career for it, she couldn't back out now. She shuffled through the crowds of opposition MPs, trying not to show her dejection.

On her way through the voting lobby, Jennifer was accosted by Leonard Trask.

"I wish the Labour Party had more of your sort, Ms Sinclair," he said. "Heaven knows you've got enough fools and cowards, but traitors – no, you don't come across those every day."

He moved closer, and she was forced to look into his small blue eyes, bright against the fake tan. A thin smile spread across his face.

"Still," he continued, "once we're in government, maybe you can help us out some more!"

Jennifer held his gaze, determined not to look away. He laughed and strode off, becoming lost in a crowd of his own MPs.

After passing the hard-faced Whips with just five other Labour MPs, she sidled back to her seat. Maggie joined her. She'd seen the encounter with Trask.

"Ugh," she said. "I hate that man even more than I hate Michael Stuart."

Jennifer felt her stomach hollow out at the words. This wasn't about hating anyone.

There was a low hum, mutters making their way round the chamber; speculation, calculations. John and Michael took their places at the front, stony-faced.

Finally, the Whips entered and the door was closed behind them. In a row four abreast, they moved towards the speaker. Jennifer watched them shuffle into place, knowing that the order in which they stood would give away the result.

As they settled into position, she felt her chest tighten. The House quietened and the Whip on the far right spoke.

"Ayes to the right, three hundred and one. Noes to the left, three hundred and two."

We've won, thought Jennifer, her heart pounding.

A thunderous roar of voices and hands pounding on seat backs rose around her. Her skin tightened. What had she done?

Just six Labour MPs had voted against the government. Had one of them switched sides, or even abstained, the vote would have gone the other way.

A man in front of her turned and glared. "Hope you're happy now."

PART III

OCTOBER 2020

25

APRIL 2021. LONDON

"My government will introduce legislation enabling people to save for their own retirement, and be less dependent on the state..."

Six weeks and one forced election later, and it was the one time that MPs were allowed to enter the chamber of the House of Lords. In front of Jennifer were rows upon rows of peers, their finery gleaming under the lights. The MPs looked drab by comparison, packed in together like cattle. If they thought the Commons was crowded, this was worse.

It was the first Queen's Speech of Leonard Trask's new government. At the front of the crowd of MPs were Trask and Michael Stuart, forced for once to be friendly, to walk together through the corridor dividing the two houses and stand side by side while the Queen made a seemingly endless speech detailing Trask's plans.

Jennifer was surrounded by Labour MPs, a meagre bunch now. Most of the Cabinet – Shadow Cabinet, she reminded herself – were gone, and Michael was clinging onto the leadership despite mutterings that he should go. The party was haemorrhaging members, disgusted by his willingness to sell short their ideals, and things were looking bleak.

Three rows ahead, right behind Michael, was John. His face was calm but he was staring at the back of Michael's head. Jennifer had a good idea what he was thinking.

That morning, reluctant to face her office, she had taken a walk up Whitehall, glancing towards Downing Street as she passed on the opposite side. In there would be Trask, plotting for the day with his ministers and assorted underlings. She tried to push the thought of her enemies around the Cabinet table from her mind.

She arrived at Trafalgar Square. Ready to rest and throw some caffeine into her system, she spotted a line of commuters outside a corner coffee shop and joined the fast moving queue. Latte in hand, she cast around for somewhere quiet to sit. The coffee shop was dark and cavernous and it was difficult to make out which tables were occupied. Voices rose up, bubbling towards the ceiling with its frescoes and fake ageing. The tourists liked it, she imagined.

"Jennifer!" A man's voice came from the depths of the shop. He had his back to Jennifer but was watching her in a greyed out mirror that loomed over his table.

She approached him, her gaze flitting between the back of his head and his reflected face in the mirror. She forced a smile. "John."

He stood and turned, grabbing her hand for slightly too long. His grip was warm and solid and he was smiling, his eyes crinkling.

"Good to see you. Please," he gestured at the table with a broad sweep of his arm. "Join me."

She lowered her tray to the table and lifted her cup, taking care not to spill anything this time. She propped her tray against the table leg, waiting for a lecture.

"How are you? How's Yusuf? The kids?"

The election campaign had brought them together; Yusuf had taken time off to help with canvassing and even Samir had managed to knock on a few doors for her. She'd been relieved to hold her seat, despite Labour losing power. Yusuf's work on the council would become more important now, as Labour still held the city.

"Fine, thanks. You?"

"Well, I've surprised myself, but I feel great. Less stressed than I have for years."

He was right. The bags under his eyes had receded and his skin had lost its unearthly pallor. His voice was clearer too.

"Er, OK. I thought you'd hate being in Opposition."

He laughed under his breath. "That's the thing. So did I. Dreaded it, after that vote, when you—" Jennifer's cheeks grew hot. "Well, let's not talk about that, eh? Anyway, turns out it's been a tonic." He slurped his drink. "Sheila says it's the first time in years she hasn't had to worry about me dropping dead of a heart attack." He paused and licked his lips. "I've even found the energy to stand up to Michael." He cocked his head, still looking at her.

"You?" Jennifer replied. "Surely you've never had problems standing up to anyone?"

His smile broadened into a smirk. "Aha, you don't know me as well as you thought you did. Let's just say Michael could have done with a few more people standing up to him. People like you even."

Her eyes widened.

"Hang on, John," she said, not knowing whether to laugh or cry, "you hated me for what I did. Told me I'd ruined your career."

He waved a hand in dismissal. "That! That was the strain talking. Not your fault. Michael's."

She paused to take this in. John was still working with Michael – he'd stayed on as Shadow Home Secretary after the election – and there were rumours he might take over as Party Leader.

"So you weren't as supportive of Michael as you said you were?"

He looked at her in the way Samir would when she said something stupid.

"No, Jennifer. Publicly, yes, of course. But privately. Well, I had a fair bit of respect for the stand you took."

"But I brought down the government!" she hissed, aware that the next table was only a few metres away.

"Michael did that, by announcing that bloody stupid confidence vote. I tried to talk him out of it."

This was news to Jennifer.

"Really?"

He nodded.

Hindsight was a wonderful thing, she considered. "So where does that leave you now?"

He smiled. "Oh, I'll carry on. For now." He tapped his nose. "But as for the future, well who knows, eh?"

Jennifer allowed herself a smile. Party leader, maybe? He'd certainly be an improvement. She wondered how he planned to do it, whether there was to be a night of the long knives or if Michael was already planning his resignation.

She shook her head. This time, she wasn't getting involved.

"What about the Queen's Speech?" she said, changing the subject. "Know anything about what's going to be in it?"

～

"...**M**y government will introduce measures to increase security and combat radicalisation..."

And now they were listening to that speech, to what Leonard Trask was planning. Including a harsher version of the immigration bill Jennifer had fought so hard to defeat. She watched John and wondered what he was plotting as his eyes bore into his leader's back.

26

APRIL 2021. LONDON AND BIRMINGHAM

"Is THIS SEAT TAKEN?"

Jennifer looked up from her newspaper. A tall neat woman with dark hair scraped back into a ponytail was smiling at her, gesturing at the seat opposite. Surprised, she looked around the train carriage. Every other table had at least two occupants.

She smiled. "No. Help yourself."

"Thank you." The woman stowed a black leather holdall on the shelf above and dropped into the seat. Jennifer watched through her eyelashes. She knew this woman; they were currently working together on a bill committee, scrutinising an education bill before its third reading. They'd spent long hours cooped up in committee rooms together and had even visited a school. They were on friendly terms and Jennifer found herself warming to this woman, despite being from different parties.

Catherine Moore was the Tory candidate who'd defeated Jack Scholes, MP for the semi-rural seat next door but one to Jennifer's. A Labour seat for twenty years but now – since her betrayal – Tory.

Jennifer smiled. "I didn't know you took this train."

"Well, I don't normally make it, but today everything fell into place. I didn't leave my bag in the cloakroom like I often do, is the main reason."

The Members' Cloakroom was an archaic space, with members' hooks arranged alphabetically by constituency and a pink ribbon on each hook that was designed to hold a sword. No one was allowed in it except the members themselves, not even staff.

"I'm a bit of an admirer of yours, you know."

Jennifer let the paper drop. Why a Tory first termer should be an admirer, she had no idea.

"That's kind of you. Unwarranted, but thank you."

"Oh I know you probably think I'm a bit odd, admiring someone across the floor, as it were. And it's not because of..." she hesitated, "...it's not because of how they say you helped us get into power."

Jennifer frowned.

"Sorry, that came out wrong." She was blushing, rubbing her palms on her skirt. "What I meant to say was that I admire your strength, your courage. I've been watching you on the committee; you're tenacious, but reasonable. I'd like to be a politician like you. Someone who doesn't abandon what she thinks is right." Another hesitation, her cheeks reddening further. "Does that make sense? I mean it as a compliment. Really."

Jennifer half-smiled, thinking of similar conversations with party activists. But this was the first time with someone who'd benefited from her treachery.

"Thank you. I'm really not sure I deserve any admiration. But if you don't mind..." She glanced down at her paper, hoping to make it clear that she had work to do.

Catherine's blush spread to her neck. "Of course. Me too. I'm sorry."

≈

An hour later an announcement came over the tannoy. A train was stuck between Rugby and Coventry and they were being diverted. *Apologies for the disruption to your journey*, etcetera.

Jennifer gazed through the smeared window at the dark fields creeping by, the dim shapes of Rugby's new solar array. She placed the papers she'd been reading on the table, careful to cover them with her newspaper, and pinched her nose, breathing deeply. A headache was forming behind her temples.

The guard bustled past, pausing to answer questions from disgruntled passengers. What snippets she managed to catch didn't tell her anything new. She slipped her phone out of her bag and sent Yusuf a quick message, then rooted around inside the bag for painkillers. Nothing.

She looked across at her companion, who was reading a novel. Jennifer couldn't remember when she'd last had the time or mental energy for that. Jennifer coughed and Catherine looked up.

"Excuse me, but you don't have any painkillers with you by any chance?"

A smile spread across Catherine's face. "Of course. Let me find something for you."

She heaved her handbag onto the table between them and delved into it, placing items on the table as she discarded them: a green leather purse, a charging brick, a scuffed mobile phone. She pulled out a clear plastic makeup bag that bulged with foundation, blusher, mascara, more than one bottle of nail varnish and plenty of medicine packets. Jennifer watched in silence.

Catherine placed two packets on the table.

"Paracetamol or Ibuprofen?" she asked.

"Paracetamol, please."

She slid the packet across the table. "Keep it. Just in case. Let me get you some water."

The trolley was approaching. Catherine flagged it down for a bottle of water and Jennifer thanked her, keeping quiet about the bottle she had in her own bag.

"Thanks," she repeated, feeling awkward.

"Not a problem. I can tell you when we're at New Street, if you want to sleep."

Jennifer thanked her again and closed her eyes.

~

Jennifer was woken by the gentle tug of Catherine's hand on her arm. Blinking, she looked out of the window. The familiar lights of Spaghetti Junction, now rebuilt and improved, were passing in the darkness. She stretched and yawned, hoping her sleep hadn't been too undignified.

"We're nearly at New Street," Catherine said. "Only fifteen minutes late after all. I hope your head's feeling better."

"Yes. Thanks." Jennifer closed her eyes and took a few calming breaths before gathering her belongings. Soon they were shuffling towards the carriage doors, Catherine in front.

On the platform she turned and held out her hand. "It's been good to meet you, Ms Sinclair."

"Jennifer – call me Jennifer, please."

"Jennifer. And I'm Catherine. Have a good weekend."

She walked away, scanning the departures board. Jennifer dragged her bags towards the taxi rank, smiling despite herself.

27

MAY 2021. LONDON

Jennifer began to travel home with Catherine: not every week, but maybe twice a month. Sometimes they would sit in silence across the table, both reading, staring at their phones or grabbing some time to relax. But they also found opportunities to talk, to find out about each other; their families, backgrounds and careers.

They skirted around political topics and resisted the temptation even to discuss the effect of government policy on their constituencies. Catherine's constituency was an affluent one, with two towns between which she split her time, anxious not to show favouritism. She wasn't local but had grown up in rural Suffolk, the daughter of a head-teacher and a high ranking civil servant. Politics had been part of her life from an early age just as it had been for Jennifer; but, instead of Greenham Common and CND marches, her education had been via the Women's Institute and the Young Farmers. The stories she told of the parties thrown by the latter made Jennifer laugh out loud; Catherine had been a lot less demure in her youth.

Jennifer found herself looking forward to these journeys, idle chat backed by the hum of the train speeding its way northwards. There was something freeing about spending time with someone who hadn't been there to witness her betrayal.

Few people on the train spoke to anyone; most were alone, heading home after a long day at work. They would occasionally bump into other Midlands MPs, who struggled to disguise their surprise at catching the two of them together and were eager to hurry away after brief pleasantries.

Eight weeks after the election, Michael gave up his tenuous grip on power and announced a leadership contest. John was the only viable candidate to replace him, and looked like he was going to win easily. A few days before the results were to be announced, Jennifer spotted him in the back corridor of the House of Commons as she was rushing to a committee meeting. He was flanked by advisors and muttering into his phone.

She slowed as she reached him.

"John," she said. "How's it going?"

He raised an eyebrow and looked up from his phone. "Jennifer, Jennifer," he laughed. "I wondered how long it would be."

Jennifer frowned. "I'm not after a job, if that's what you mean."

He raised his hands in mock surprise. "No?"

"Nope. Happy being a backbencher."

"Hmm." He didn't look convinced.

He whispered something into the ear of an advisor, then turned back to her.

"We need to have a chat," he said.

She sighed. "I've just told you I don't want a job."

"Not that. Something else."

She thought of their confrontations in the past, the way his head would tremble when he was angry. She'd had enough of all that.

"Come and talk to me," he said. "Tomorrow afternoon."

John's door was open. He was standing at his desk, leafing through some documents. His office was strewn with paperwork, opened newspapers and half full cups of coffee.

The battleground, Jennifer thought to herself.

He looked up without smiling.

"Hello there. Take a seat, please."

She perched on one of the chairs that faced his desk, placing a pile of papers on the other chair.

He sat down and shuffled some piles around, avoiding her eye.

Jennifer watched him. Having people avoid her eye was something she was getting used to, with many of her parliamentary colleagues behaving as if she had a communicable disease.

"So what's all the cloak and dagger then?" she asked.

"Catherine Moore," he said, staring at the desk between them.

She sighed. "Catherine Moore." He hadn't asked a question so she wasn't about to answer one.

"I have to admit I'm puzzled." He leaned back.

Jennifer waited.

"I know it's not uncommon for MPs to form cross-bench friendships," he continued. "Especially in their local area. But I never thought that would be your style." He cocked his head. "What's she like?"

"Catherine?" She was surprised to feel a pang of disloyalty. "She's – she's bright. A bit green right now, I suppose, but there's something there, I think. She's a decent woman, a decent politician."

John raised an eyebrow. She laughed.

"Yes, a decent Tory, John. I know you think they're some sort of mythological creature, but she is one. At least, she seems to be."

"Have you wondered why she's befriended you?"

Jennifer felt winded. "What are you implying?"

He gave her a look. "Oh, come on. Don't you think she might have been put up to it, that they're using you to find out what the Opposition are doing, or to plant ideas in your head?"

She spluttered. "Ideas! Come on, John. Do you seriously think the Tory party is going to successfully plant ideas in this head?" She rapped the side of her head with a knuckle.

"OK, maybe not ideas. But she could be sending information back to Trask. Have you thought about that, even a bit?" He steepled his fingers. "What do the two of you talk about?"

"You really don't have to worry. We don't talk about politics at all. I know all about her parents, her sick aunt, her most annoying constituents. I don't know anything about her views on Tory policy, or her feelings towards the Opposition. We just catch the train some weekends. We make small talk, we wind down at the end of a tough week. I'm not telling Catherine anything you wouldn't want me to. And she hasn't told me anything you'd want to hear." She paused. "Surely you trust me. I know we've had our differences in the past, but you know me better than this."

Jennifer waited, her breath shallow.

Eventually, he leaned back. "OK, I believe you." A pause. "Of course I bloody well believe you."

"Are you sure? It didn't feel like it there."

He leaned his head back and rubbed his neck. "I'm sorry, Jennifer. This was stupid."

She nodded. "So who told you?"

His hand stilled. "None of your business. But I know you well enough to know you wouldn't do anything stupid."

He seemed drawn. His expression reminded Jennifer of the way he'd looked at the height of their animosity, when he'd accosted her in the division lobby.

"Are you OK? You look stressed."

"I'm fine. I just don't like falling out with a friend." Jennifer raised an eyebrow and John grinned. "Well, not a second time, anyway."

She returned the grin. "Is there anything else? I need to get to the canteen. I'm starving."

"No. Not today." He sighed and stood up, still grinning. "Now, piss off and get something to eat before you fade away or something."

28

MAY 2021. BIRMINGHAM

The house was dark when Jennifer arrived home on Thursday. She'd spent an uncomfortable hour on the train trying to avoid questions from Catherine. Suddenly, an innocent request about her weekend plans felt loaded. She was tired, ready to kick off her shoes and slump into the sofa, and in need of someone to talk to.

But once again, the house was thick with emptiness. She moved from room to room, wondering where everyone was. The rooms were unnaturally tidy, even Hassan's. Normally she would walk in to a sea of mess and noise, Hassan refusing to go to bed, Yusuf trying to make calls around feeding the boys and Samir sulking about his homework.

She padded back downstairs, rubbing her eyes and realising that these memories were from months ago. The house was like this more often than not when she got home now. What had changed? She felt a pang at the thought of them living their lives without her.

She brewed a coffee, reluctant to have them arrive home to find her alone with a bottle of wine, and sat at the kitchen table. She brought out her phone and started scrolling through her emails. Twenty had arrived since she'd got off the train. She rubbed her eyes and sighed.

She looked up at the sound of the door. *At last.*

She leaned back to see into the hallway. The door opened slowly: not Hassan, then.

She stood and walked into the hall, cradling her coffee. A smile on her face.

"Oh. Mum." Samir looked startled. "You're early."

She looked at her watch. "No, I'm not. But you're late."

He shrugged. "Where's Dad?"

He said nothing.

"Where's Hassan?" she asked. Another shrug.

He squeezed past her towards the stairs.

"Can I get you anything?" she asked. "Have you eaten?"

"Mum, I'm fine. Already eaten."

"You been at a friend's house?"

He nodded. "Homework."

This wasn't enough of an answer. She stared at him, tongue-tied. *Since when couldn't I talk to my son?*

"Night then," he said.

"Already?"

Another nod. "School tomorrow."

"OK. Night."

She turned back to the hallway as he disappeared, his bedroom door closing with barely a sound. The front door opened again, more roughly this time. Hassan bounded through.

"Mummy!"

She opened her arms, letting him crash into them. Yusuf was behind him, struggling with bags. "Samir here?"

She nodded. "Just got back. Where have you been?"

His smile dropped. "D'you have to know our every movement?"

It felt like a slap. "No," she said. "That wasn't what I—"

"A council meeting dragged on and then I had to pick Hassan up from a party. Alright?"

"OK," she breathed, holding up her hands.

"Anyway, it's late, and Hassan needs to get to bed." He looked at her. "Will you take him?"

She felt cold. "Of course."

~

She went downstairs, leaving Hassan asleep. It had only taken half a page of his book; the party had worn him out.

Yusuf was in the living room, flicking between channels.

"You alright?" she asked.

He waved a hand. "Fine."

"You didn't sound it, when you got in."

He grunted. "Yeah, well."

"Yeah well what?" Her heart was pounding. "What's up, love?"

He threw the remote onto the table. It skidded and fell on the floor. Neither of them moved to pick it up.

"What's up?" she repeated.

He shook his head. "The usual."

She sat down next to him and put her hand on the sofa between them. He kept his own hand on his knee.

"What usual?" she asked. "The kids?"

He turned to her. His eyes were rimmed with deep brown shadows and his lips were swollen and pink, as if he'd been chewing them. "Not that."

"What? Talk to me Yusuf, please."

He sighed, scratching his chin. His beard was growing out and looked unkempt. "Casework, Jen. Leonard Trask and his bloody government. They're not exactly making it easy for people."

She slumped back. *Tell me about it*, she thought. She reached for his hand.

"I know," she said. "I'm sorry."

"Don't be. Not your fault."

She breathed a sigh of relief. At least someone wasn't blaming her.

"The council's divided. Even the Labour group."

"What d'you mean? Divided on what?"

"On what to do about Trask and his anti-terror measures. Whether the council has a duty of care to help the people affected."

The new Tory government had put forward a bill which included all of what Michael had failed to achieve, and added its own embellishments. The ban would no longer be limited to men under fifty, but would extend to older men, women and children too. And it included forced repatriation of immigrants who'd come to Britain in the last two years.

The irony of this wasn't lost on Jennifer; by defeating the bill when Michael introduced it, she'd only made it happen via Trask and his new government. She'd have hated herself for it, if her colleagues weren't already doing that for her.

"In what way?" she asked.

He turned to her, his eyes red. "There are families facing destitution because the main earner can't join them here. Even worse are the ones looking at deportation. And you know what's hardest about it?"

She shook her head.

"Nobody cares," he continued. "They're all obsessed with security, with blame. No one can see what Trask's really doing."

She nodded, still finding it hard to believe that such a divisive bill hadn't sparked outrage, rioting even. But the country seemed to be dulled, more concerned with security than with recognising the bigotry being paraded as anti-terrorism. The election campaign had been marked by right-wing rhetoric that tapped into a mood of fear and recrimination, rhetoric that the divided and beleaguered Labour Party had done nothing to counteract.

He turned to her. "D'you know what's happening out there?"

"Of course I do. We're fighting it, love. The party's united against it, and we're doing everything we can to sway wet Tories."

He shook his head. "You seriously think that will make a difference? You know what their majority's like. Some-times it feels as if you're hidden away down there in your Westminster cocoon – all of you – and you have no idea how this is playing on the ground."

"I know. I do surgeries, don't I?"

He waved a hand dismissively. "You and I both know they're all coming to me now."

She let out a long breath. "OK. Are you annoyed with me?"

"Yes. No. Oh, I don't know."

She squeezed his hand. He didn't squeeze back.

"I feel so powerless," he said.

She nodded. He wasn't alone.

29

MAY 2021. LONDON

"Catherine, you can't possibly support this! It's appalling."

For once, Jennifer had been unable to hold her tongue about policy. In the taxi to Euston, she'd confronted Catherine about the government's latest proposals.

"Of course I support it. The Islamists radicalise people by attacking the way they think. We want to get there first."

On Monday, two days after John's election as Labour leader, the government had announced a new policy for combatting radicalisation: the British Values programme. There was an oath, to be recited in schools and public sector workplaces. A vow of allegiance to the state. It made Jennifer shudder.

"But Catherine, this policy just won't work. This country is a nation of immigrants because people want to be here, to make a life here. You can't *force* them to love the state."

"So what about the kids who are travelling to the Middle East? The men who set off those bombs? You think they want to be here? You think they want to be loyal?"

Jennifer sighed. "Oh for god's sake, Catherine. Making them recite an oath of loyalty isn't going to change the way they think. Treating them with some respect might, but I guess Trask would never think of that."

"Jennifer! That's out of order."

She said nothing: to retract would be lying. The interior of the taxi dimmed as they dipped into the drop off zone under the station.

When it stopped, Catherine grabbed her door handle. Her knuckles were white. "I think we should travel separately tonight," she said, looking out of the window.

"Catherine, please."

"Catherine, nothing," she said. "I think you're being incredibly naive, trusting these people."

"These people? Who are these people?"

She shrugged.

"My husband, Catherine? My Muslim husband? My children? Are they under suspicion? Are they unwelcome?"

Catherine said nothing, slamming the door behind her. Jennifer sat in stunned silence as the clip of her heels echoed away in the dark space.

～

By the time Jennifer arrived home, she was bubbling with suppressed indignation. Yusuf barely had time to kiss her hello before she exploded.

"You won't believe what Catherine said tonight! I'm shocked. Speechless."

Yusuf peeled her jacket off – in her distraction she was getting her arms tangled in its sleeves – and hung it up. He steered her through to the kitchen, where the remains of the kids' dinner were still on the table.

"Yusuf! You haven't even tidied up yet!"

He raised his hands. "What? Hassan's only just gone to bed. You're pissed off with Catherine. Don't take it out on me."

She sighed and started clattering mugs around, spilling water as she tried to fill the kettle. Poor Yusuf, always at the receiving end of her anger at the world. "You're right. Sorry."

She felt his hand on her shoulder. "Let me do that. You'll break something. What's up? What happened with Catherine?"

She spun round. "You know Trask's British Values Bill?" He nodded. "She's only all for it. Thinks brainwashing is OK."

She stared at him. Normally she'd know how he'd react, but lately he was distant. It unnerved her; Yusuf was the biggest constant in her life and she in his. They'd always pulled together, through everything life had thrown at them. Failed campaigns, professional headaches, parenthood, even financial struggles. They'd faced it all together. But with her drive to stop Michael, and now her frustration at being unable to stop Trask, had she driven him away?

She looked at him as he put a wary hand on her shoulder, his brow creased. What could she say, to bring him back?

"Remember, love," he sighed. "She's a Tory. I know she's your friend. But she's one of Trask's MPs and even if she doesn't really think what you say she said, well – she'll support him, won't she?"

Jennifer pulled back, feeling her shoulders sag.

"Maybe John was right," Yusuf continued.

"*What?*"

"With what Trask's doing, with what she's voting for, how can you stay friends with her?"

"You don't understand," she snapped. "It's common for—"

He raised his eyes to the ceiling. "Yeah, yeah. I know. Cross-bench friendships and all that."

She nodded.

"But it's different, now," he said. "*They're* different."

Jennifer reached for him but he pulled away. "I think that – maybe – you're being naive, love," he said.

"That's not fair. Catherine's not like Trask, you know."

"No? How does she vote? Does she follow the whip?"

She shrank back. "She's just a backbencher right now. It's not the only way to—"

"They're not all like you."

She tensed, heat filling her chest. "What's that supposed to mean?"

He shook his head. "Don't you get it? Most MPs will support the party line no matter how bad it is. She's a first term MP, Jen. In a traditional seat. Are you honestly that surprised that she's supporting this bill?"

She shrugged. "I suppose not." She needed to listen to him. But whenever she got off that train, stepped into the House of Commons, the frustration overwhelmed her. Not to mention the self-recrimination. She still believed that if she could turn Catherine, make her see the faults in her leader, then maybe she'd atone somehow. It was the only course of action she could see through the haze.

"Well, then." Yusuf pulled her in and wrapped his arms around her. His body was hard and tense; he'd lost weight.

"I have no idea what I'm doing anymore," she whispered.

John's new office was furnished in a style that felt more fitting for Michael: pale green wallpaper and cream curtains with two emerald green armchairs and a compact sofa at the centre. The pale wood desk was small and covered in paperwork. Jennifer remembered John's ship of a desk in the Home Office and wondered how long it would be before this room was refurbished.

John was standing behind the desk, gazing out of the window. He turned as she entered.

"Ah, Jennifer. Sit down, please."

She sat on the floral sofa, jealous of the space he had here on the second floor of the Commons and of his view of the river. It wouldn't be long before there was a mahogany monstrosity in front of that window.

He lowered himself into one of the armchairs. It was small and hard, not suited to a man of John's proportions.

Jennifer leaned back – the sofa was too soft and made her back twinge – and then edged forwards again. She had an idea what this meeting was about, and wasn't looking forward to it.

He didn't hesitate. "I want to offer you a job."

She hesitated. "I already told you I'm happy on the—"

He waved a hand. "Yeah, yeah. Don't seek to serve, and all that. I know you better than that."

She had to admit the offer did make her heart race, maybe for the first time in weeks. But she needed to stay out of the limelight, for the time being.

It didn't do any harm to listen, though.

He laughed. "Not disagreeing with me then?"

She shrugged.

"Anyway," he said. "I want you to take the Home Office brief."

"Home Office? Your old job?" She hadn't been expecting that.

"Well, not exactly. It'll have the word 'Shadow' in front of it. Although you can't exactly complain about that."

"That's not fair."

"Isn't it? Anyway, I think if you're part of my shadow cabinet, your connection to Catherine Moore could help us."

She stiffened; this again. "How so?"

"One of my team suggested you might pass back information on what Trask's up to. Via your new friend."

Jennifer narrowed her eyes. He clearly didn't know that she wasn't on speaking terms with Catherine right now. But she didn't like the thought of him discussing her with his team.

He raised his palms. "But don't worry, I won't ask. Not after what you told me about her. The job offer is still there, though." He paused. "I liked working with you in government. I think we'd get on well in opposition too."

"Thanks," she said, surprised by the compliment. "Likewise. But Catherine and I aren't bosom buddies, you know."

She paused to consider. Did he want her for her experience, or her connection to Catherine? And did she want the job anyway? Was Catherine really her friend, or just another Tory clone, like John insisted? Knowing where her loyalties lay was one thing, but betraying her friend was another.

"But I do have some respect for her," she continued. "It wouldn't feel right, using her to spy on Trask."

"You're right. I respect you for it, honest I do. If there's one thing we can rely on you for Jennifer, it's integrity, eh?"

She shrugged.

"So, how about it? The job?"

She sighed. She really would prefer to keep to the back-benches right now, to steer clear of any more attention.

"I'm flattered. Of course I am."

"But?"

"But I think I'd be a liability for you."

He waved his hand again. "Ah, don't worry about that. Take it head-on, that's what I say. You go off and brood on the back benches, you'll just delay your rehabilitation."

Rehabilitation; so that's what it was. "What about the others? I'm not exactly popular around here."

"The rest of the shadow cabinet, you mean? Well, I haven't filled all the posts yet, and well, they'll just have to put up with it."

She allowed herself a smile. Sometimes, John made her heart warm.

"I'm still not sure," she said. She needed to think. To talk to Yusuf.

"Really?" He stood up, heading for the door. He pulled it open. She felt her chest sink; this was the biggest promotion she'd ever been offered, and she'd let it go.

She stood to leave. As she passed him he put a hand on her arm. "I'll give you five days," he said. "I can delay things over the weekend, just about."

"Oh." This was unexpected. He really did want her. "OK."

"If you want it, tell me on Monday morning. First thing. That's your deadline."

"Right. Thanks."

"Good. Monday morning. No later."

❧

She went up to her office, throwing herself into the armchair. It was green and threadbare in places, and a spring jutted into her thigh. She scratched at her skin through her skirt, working through what John had just said.

Had she been wrong to say no? Was she overthinking her unpopularity within the party? And was it time to forget about Catherine, and put herself first?

She stared at the wall, the notices and memos she had pinned to it a blur. She was still a pariah, someone people stared at when she passed along the corridors. Even if she took John up on his offer, this was going to be a struggle.

She ran through the encounters she'd had in the last few days, the colleagues she'd talked to. Not many had been friendly. Even Maggie was avoiding her; when it came to it, Jennifer wasn't enough of a rebel. She'd already been causing trouble for John, challenging him in the newspapers and pulling together a group of MPs to put pressure on him, claiming he wasn't providing a robust opposition to Trask.

But for Jennifer, their little rebellion – their stupid little rebellion – had been a one-off. Something she already regretted every time she watched Trask and his cronies crowing over their new-found power.

Could she redeem herself in the Shadow Cabinet?

The phone rang. Sighing, she picked it up.

"Jen?"

Yusuf. She smiled, glad of a friendly voice.

"Hi, love." It wasn't like him to ring at this time of day.

"You OK? You sound odd."

Jennifer looked up at the eaves. "Not really, love. John's just—"

"Sorry. But we don't have time to talk about John right now."

She hesitated.

"Jennifer?"

"I'm here. What is it?"

"It's Samir."

Jennifer closed her eyes. Another strop, she thought. Couldn't this wait?

"What's happened?"

"He got into a fight at school."

"A fight?" She frowned. That wasn't like Samir. "An argument, you mean?"

"No. A fight. He attacked someone. They sent him home early."

She sat up. "When was this?"

"This morning. Normally I wouldn't bother you at work but—"

"Of course. It's fine." But it stung Jennifer that she wasn't around when Samir was in trouble. She tried to picture him fighting but all she could imagine was him sitting apart from the other children, sulking. He'd never even been in trouble with his teachers. "Who with? Why?"

There was muttering on the other end of the line.

"Is he there with you?"

"No. He's upstairs. That was Penny."

"Penny? What's she doing there?"

"She's just dropping off some leaflets."

"Oh."

Jennifer tried to imagine her house at that moment: Samir upstairs like a thundercloud, and Yusuf and Penny in the kitchen dealing with constituency business. It felt like a different continent.

"How is he? Have you talked to him?"

More muttering, then the sound of the front door closing. "He's upset."

"Did he tell you what happened?"

"It was a couple of boys in one of the other classes. No
one we know. But it was about race, about the bomb
attacks."

Jennifer's grip on the armchair tightened. "Bomb
attacks? What do you mean?"

"He says the boys were saying something about the
Spaghetti Junction bombers, calling them racist names. He
snapped."

She exhaled, her voice quiet now. "Were they calling
him racist names?"

"No. He doesn't say so. Just the bombers."

"OK. So how did the fight start? What did he do?"

"He punched one of them and kneed the other one.
They weren't in a good way, according to the school. The
deputy head rang me."

Jennifer knew the head and deputy; good people. She'd
been a governor at the school, before her election.

"What about Samir? Is he hurt?" She wasn't sure which
was worse: the thought of Samir starting a fight or of him
being hit back.

Yusuf sighed. "He's fine. A teacher came along in time
to stop it before they retaliated."

"Did anyone see it? Were any of his friends there?"

There was a pause. "A teacher was there. She saw the
whole thing."

She tried to picture Samir being violent but still
couldn't see it. "Are you sure? They definitely didn't hit
him first."

"Jennifer, he doesn't deny it. I think he'd do it again.
The school has spoken to the boys about the language they

used. And to their parents. But their parents are more concerned about Samir attacking them, according to the deputy head. Not surprisingly, really."

Jennifer slumped in her chair, thinking of all the times she and Yusuf had talked to the boys about racist language and how to deal with it, how not to respond. The conversations they'd had about the bomb attacks and the racism afterwards, drumming into them the importance of not retaliating, not hitting out, no matter how horrible people were.

Samir, it seemed, had snapped.

30

MAY 2021. BIRMINGHAM

JENNIFER RUSHED HOME THE NEXT EVENING, ANXIOUS to see Yusuf. And Samir. John's comments – and his offer – were still nagging her, making her tongue-tied each time she encountered a colleague.

She needed to talk it over with Yusuf, to get his take. But he'd be more worried about Samir. She was too, but couldn't help wonder if the whole thing had been exaggerated. Maybe it was a scuffle, a misunderstanding.

One thought kept entering her head: *It's not like Samir*. In the chamber as she listened to a debate on emergency services; in the canteen as she went through next week's plan with her researcher; on the train as she tried to get through paperwork. Her son could be moody, and petulant. Bitter and sarcastic sometimes. But he had never been violent. Even when Hassan was a lively toddler and went through a stage of biting his brother, he hadn't once retaliated. When Samir was annoyed, he retreated into himself. He hid. He didn't lash out.

She was relieved to find everyone home, TVs blaring in more rooms than there were people, and music coming from behind Samir's door. Angry rap music. She resisted the urge to tell him to turn it down.

Yusuf was in the living room, tidying up a pile of Hassan's clothes. He gave her a peck on the cheek then beckoned for her to follow him. She paused to speak to Hassan, giving him a hug and listening to a tale about his teacher's pet dog before promising him a bedtime story very soon. Then she joined Yusuf in the kitchen.

Yusuf was clattering around, picking up crockery, as if trying to mask their voices.

She cast her eyes upwards. "How is he?"

Yusuf shrugged. "Fine. He had to stay home today. Tomorrow too. Two day exclusion."

"Seriously?"

He raised a hand. "It's the school rules. Get caught fighting, and you're out for two days."

She let out a long breath. "Have you spoken to them?"

He shook his head. "Tried to phone today. Couldn't get hold of anyone."

"Who did you call?"

"His year group head."

"We need to go higher than that. If there's racist abuse—"

Yusuf turned and put his hands on his hips. "Jennifer," he said. He sounded exasperated. She ignored it.

"Jennifer, nothing," she replied. "We've had no chance to defend him, and they've already kicked him out—"

"Not kicked him out, love. Two day exclusion."

"I still think they should investigate what prompted it. They know what he's like. It would have to take something big to provoke him like this."

"I know. I've tried to talk to him, but he won't tell me anything. All I've got to go on is what the school told me."

She felt her shoulders slump. Surely he didn't think Samir had just done this, for no reason?

"Is there something you're not telling me?" The room felt blurred. She took a deep breath and the feeling subsided.

"Of course not. I told you everything I knew, on the phone."

Yusuf approached her, reaching out a hand. She stiffened but let him place it on her arm.

"But it wasn't what they said," he said. "It was more the way they said it."

"How d'you mean?"

"You don't get it, do you? He's Muslim. The other kids were white. The school sympathises with them."

"Of course they don't. The school's got policies for this kind of—"

He gripped her wrist. "We don't live in that world anymore, love," he muttered. "Policies mean nothing. Not with the government doing what it's—"

A dry heat rose in her chest. "Oh, so this is my fault too, is it?"

"No. No, that's not what I'm saying. But schools used to be under pressure to stamp out racism. Back when you were in government."

"Of course. They still are."

He tightened his grip. "They're not."

She tugged her arm away and pushed past him, throwing herself into a chair.

"That's rubbish, Yusuf. You're being paranoid."

"I'm not. I'm closer to this than you are. Education is a local government responsibility. I see what goes on."

"What do you mean?"

"Things are changing, love. The mood. This is becoming a different country."

"Don't say that. We'll stop it. All of us. We'll stop Trask."

He shook his head.

"John offered me the Shadow Home Office brief," she muttered.

His head shot up. "What?"

She nodded.

"What did you say?" he asked.

"Nothing. I need to talk it over with you first."

He smiled; at least she was still consulting him on some things.

"But let's get this mess sorted out with Samir first, shall we?" she said. "I'll go and see Tina, in the morning." Tina was the headteacher. Jennifer had worked with her as a school governor, before her election.

"I don't think we need to—"

"Not we, me. I've known Tina for years. It'll just be an informal chat. I want to know more about what happened. I'm not denying that what he did is wrong, Yusuf. But he had to have been provoked."

He shrugged; they both knew what Samir was like.

"I'll ask her if she can investigate further."

"Maybe we just leave it, love. Maybe we should be talking to Samir instead."

"I won't go in all guns blazing," she said. "I just want to know more. Trust me."

~

"I'm very sorry, Ms Sinclair."

"Call me Jennifer, please."

The headteacher gave her a look. "I'm sorry, but I have to apply the rules evenly. Samir attacked the other students, and I can't be more lenient because of— because of your history with the school."

This wasn't going how Jennifer had expected. Tina had been terse when she welcomed her to her office, not the gregarious, welcoming woman she remembered from her time as a school governor.

"You know I'm not asking you to treat Samir differently. I'd never ask you to do that."

Tina sat back in her chair, checking her watch. Jennifer shifted in her place.

"So why are you here?" the headteacher asked. "I gather Mr Rush was already dealing with this."

Jennifer swallowed. Mr Rush was a new deputy head, and not someone she'd dealt with before. "I'm not trying to get round the system or anything like that. But I think it's important to investigate what it was that provoked Samir. You know him; he's not like that, not violent."

Tina raised an eyebrow. "He has got a good record up to this point, yes. How much did your husband tell you?"

Jennifer clenched her fists. *Don't try to play us off against each other*, she thought. Then she paused. *Was* there something Yusuf hadn't told her?

"He told me that Samir was accused of assault in response to racist taunts."

Tina leaned across the table. "Now hang on there. That's quite strong language to be using."

Jennifer frowned. "Yusuf told me that the other student had been using racist language."

"Directed towards Samir?"

She felt her toes curl inside her shoes. "Well, yes."

"So they called Samir racist names, is what you're saying? Because that's not what your son told us."

Jennifer wished she'd been able to talk to Samir. But when she'd gone up to his room he'd been unresponsive. This morning she'd tried again, but he'd told her to leave it alone. He didn't know she was here. "That's not what I'm saying."

Tina leaned back again, and gave her a smile that was a mix of patronising and wary. "Alright, then. I've spoken to Mr Rush and he's told me what happened. Another student said something that upset Samir and Samir retaliated. No one is alleging that any racist abuse was involved."

Semantics, thought Jennifer. "No," she said, her voice dragging. "But they were using racist language."

"As far as I've been informed, they were talking about the Spaghetti Junction bombers. Terrorists. Surely your son wouldn't believe they should be defended."

Jennifer pursed her lips. Outside in the corridor she heard shouting.

"It's not the fact that they were terrorists that was pertinent to this conversation," she breathed. "It was the fact that they were Muslim."

Tina leaned back further. "There's the rub."

"The rub?"

"Ms Sinclair, I know this is an uncomfortable question, but do you think Samir would have been defending the terrorists if they hadn't been Muslim?"

Jennifer reddened. "He wasn't defending them. What are you talking about?"

Tina let out a long sigh then looked at her watch again.

"We're going to have to draw this conversation to a close I'm afraid, I've got an assembly to take."

"We're not finished."

"I think we are. Your husband Mr Hussain told you that a staff member witnessed the whole thing?"

"Yes."

"And that Samir isn't denying what he did?"

She hesitated. "No."

"So I'm afraid the only option I had at my disposal was a two day suspension. I did speak to the Chair of Governors."

Jennifer tried to remember what she'd picked up of disciplinary procedure when she'd been a governor.

"I'll be taking it to appeal," she said finally. "All I want is a more thorough investigation. I'm sure you agree with me that there's no place for racist language in the school."

Tina stood up, pulling on a deep red jacket. It swamped the woman's slight frame. "That's your prerogative. I'll need something in writing." She ignored Jennifer's second comment.

Jennifer nodded. "You'll be getting it."

She stood as the headteacher rounded her desk and approached with her hand extended. Jennifer shook it.

"I shall keep an eye out for it. But you might want to consider moving Samir."

"I beg your pardon?"

"Well, I think a boy of Samir's – shall we say sensitivities – might be better off in a different kind of environment."

Jennifer frowned; where was this coming from? "What kind of environment are you talking about?"

Tina looked at her steadily. "You'll know about the new Muslim school that's opened in Perry Barr."

"Of course I do." Jennifer could hear her voice hardening.

Tina ushered her towards the door. "Well, he might feel more – more at home there."

Jennifer opened her mouth to speak but the other woman's hand was on her back, easing her into the corridor. A flood of teenagers rushed past, en route from one lesson to the next. She thought of Samir at home, missing this. She stood watching them, overcome by their chatter and energy. Is this what Samir was like when he was at school? She could barely imagine it.

She turned to the Head, ready to respond, to question this woman who just three years earlier had boasted of the school's ethnic diversity. But Tina was talking to another teacher, already onto the next thing.

She turned back to Jennifer. "Thank you for coming in, Ms Sinclair." She disappeared between the tousled heads that swarmed around her.

Jennifer could only stand and watch, her chest filling with hot anger.

~

"Yusuf!" she called, throwing the front door closed. "Are you here?"

She flung her coat onto a hook, ignoring it as it fell to the floor. She dropped her bag and kicked it at the wall.

Yusuf appeared, his face pale. "What's going on?"

"That goddamn woman. You're not going to believe what she said about Samir!"

Yusuf glanced up the stairs. "Please, calm down," he hissed.

She let out a long shaking breath. She was trembling. She had no idea how she'd got home and no memory of the route she'd taken. It was a miracle she hadn't crashed the car.

She stared at Yusuf, lost for words. "She told me he should be in a Muslim school."

His face fell. "Oh."

"Oh? *Oh?* Is that the best you can do?"

He scratched his chin. "Well, are you that surprised?"

She stared at him, suddenly feeling as if a wall had dropped around them, as if the two of them were trapped inside it. "Of course I'm surprised. That school prides itself on its diversity."

He pulled his hand through his hair. "It's part of a system that doesn't."

"That's not the point."

He put a hand on her shoulder. "Come into the living room," he said, looking upstairs again. She followed his gaze. Maybe it would be better for Samir to know about this. Or maybe not.

She slumped onto the sofa. "I can't believe this is what we've come to."

Yusuf came to sit next to her after easing the door shut. "It's not new." He was staring off into the distance, eyes unfocussed.

She turned to him. "How d'you mean?"

"That new Muslim school. The council are putting Muslim families under pressure to apply for it. Not to go to Samir's school."

She squinted at him. "First I've heard of it."

He shrugged. "I haven't seen anything official, but you read between the lines of the admissions letters they send out to parents and it's there, alright. They want to segregate us."

He looked at her. His face was hard and his eyes were hooded.

"Who's it coming from?" she asked. "Who's telling them to do that?"

"Who do you think? The Department for Education."

She shook her head. "Don't be daft. I'd know about it."

"I'm not being daft," he snapped. "It's true. MPs don't know everything, you know."

She stood up, ignoring this barb.

"Don't," he said.

"Don't what?"

He nodded at the door. "You're going to go up there, tell Samir what she said to you."

She looked at the door and clenched her fists. "No."

He raised an eyebrow.

"No, I'm not," she said. "I'm going to do something better."

31

MAY 2021. LONDON

"Have you heard about what the Department of Education are doing?"

Jennifer was in John's office; it had taken all her willpower to wait until Monday.

He rose from behind his desk and frowned. "What? Surely you're here to—"

"Have you? Do you know they're trying to bring in segregation?"

His brow furrowed. "Segregation?"

"Muslims. Muslim kids. They don't want them in the mainstream schools."

He stood up, pulling back as she leaned towards him. "Hang on. Let's just calm down a little—"

She sighed. "Jesus Christ, John. Are you aware of it, or aren't you?"

He looked her up and down, calculating. "Tell me what you've heard," he said.

She gave him an abbreviated version of what Samir's headteacher had told her, and a less abbreviated one of what Yusuf had said.

John rubbed the stubble on his chin. "OK," he said.

"OK?"

He put up a hand. "Don't get your knickers in a twist."

She glared at him.

He nodded. "We did already know something about this."

"Why haven't you said anything?" She knew Education wasn't her brief, never had been. In fact, nothing was her brief right now. But still, as one of only a few MPs with a Muslim family, she was shocked he hadn't warned her. Or maybe Yusuf. They still kept in touch via email and the occasional letter, something she found pleasingly quaint.

"Calm down, Jennifer. For God's sake just calm down. We will provide opposition on this, and a robust one too. But I'm waiting for the best time to attack."

He sat down and gestured for her to do the same. She slumped into a chair. The energy had left her and she felt drained. John had seen her raw side plenty of times, and she'd seen his. But now, given what he'd asked her on Thursday, maybe wasn't the time.

"Look, I'm not s'posed to be telling you this." He raised an eyebrow. "Not as things stand. But Deborah's got a team working on it. Gathering evidence. Then we'll hit him with it. In the next week or two."

Deborah was the new Shadow Education Secretary, or at least she would be today, when he announced his appointments.

"Do you think it'll make much difference?" Jennifer asked.

"Who knows? But that's why we've got to be careful. Plan for it. We can't just do a knee-jerk attack on anything we get wind of."

She swallowed. "Of course not. That's not what I was suggesting."

"No," he said. "Tell me everything you know, alright? And get Yusuf to keep his eyes open too."

"Of course. And John?"

"Yes?"

"Two things."

"Yes?"

"First, your request for me to spy on the Tories via Catherine Moore?"

"*Jennifer*," he hissed, glancing towards the door. "It wasn't—"

"Call it what you will. But let me think about it."

He raised his eyebrows. "So you're accepting my job offer then?"

She smiled. "Yes. Of course I am."

~

"Jennifer."

Jennifer paused and turned to face the person whose hand was on her arm. "Catherine. Hello."

Catherine cocked her head. "Are you OK?"

She flushed. Catherine had caught her running down the corridor to the lift, desperate to reach her office. To retreat. To think. And this was the first time they'd spoken since their argument in the taxi. Catherine was hardly around, now that she was a junior minister in the Foreign Office. Jennifer had watched her perform in the chamber, avoiding eye contact as if she could hide from her old friend. She'd even considered catching a different train.

She pulled in her breath, thinking fast. How was she

going to do this, without being a total bitch? "I'm fine. Thank you."

"It's good to see you," Catherine said. Her eyes were bright and she held herself taller. Jennifer glanced at the floor but Catherine's heels were lower if anything. The posture that came with a promotion.

"You too," she said, starting to move away. An advisor stood quietly next to Catherine. She could sense his tension; his body was still and he bristled, as if itching to tell Jennifer what he thought of her. She laughed inwardly.

Catherine's expression was warm. "What have you been up to?"

Jennifer shrugged. "I'm fine. It's good to see you. Anyway—"

"How's Samir?"

"He's OK." Why was Catherine asking after Samir?

Catherine smiled. "Good."

Jennifer nodded. She looked at the advisor, wishing he would whisk Catherine away.

"Morning, ladies."

She shifted her gaze to see Leonard Trask behind Catherine, smirking. She shuddered.

He pressed his hand on Catherine's shoulder, close to her neck. Catherine's eyes widened.

"Prime Minister," Catherine said, her voice betraying a slight tremor. "How are you?"

"Oh, Catherine. Call me Leonard. Please." He looked at Jennifer, his eyes dancing. "And who's your friend? Jennifer Sinclair, none other. I knew you liked to stick the knife in, but I didn't know you were planning on crossing the floor."

Jennifer willed herself not to retaliate. He wasn't worth it.

"Hello, Prime Minister. No plans to join you, I'm afraid. So sorry to disappoint."

She met his gaze. He looked her up and down then turned his attention to Catherine.

"So," he said. "How are we enjoying the new job?"

Catherine gave a tight smile. "Very well, thank you."

"Good. Do us proud." He let her go.

"I'll bid you ladies good day then." He breezed off, not waiting for a response.

Catherine was massaging the spot on her neck where Trask's hand had been.

"Does he always treat you like that?" Jennifer muttered.

She lowered her eyes and continued her kneading.

"You shouldn't let him, you know. It's just not on, not these days. Or is that standard practice in your party?"

Catherine glared at her. "Don't. It's my party and I won't have you badmouthing it."

"OK, OK. I'm sorry. But I hope that I saw the bad side to him tonight, not his nice, public face."

Catherine said nothing. Jennifer watched her walk away, reflecting on what she and John had discussed. This wasn't going to be easy.

32

MAY 2021. BIRMINGHAM

"Jen!" Yusuf knocked on the bathroom door. "Jen, you need to come and see this."

Jennifer was under the shower, trying to revive herself. She hadn't made it home to Birmingham until almost midnight the previous night and had a surgery in just over an hour. She wasn't sure how much confidence she'd give her constituents in her ability to help them, with her face pale and her eyes rimmed with dark circles.

She turned the water off. "What? What's up?"

Samir again?

"There's been another bomb."

"*What?*"

She hurried into the bedroom, dripping on the carpet. On TV was a flat, low building, with flames just visible on the right of the screen and smoke rising into the air. A caption rolled onto the bottom of the screen. *Breaking news. Bomb in Milan.*

"Milan," she said. "The summit."

Yusuf put a warm hand on her shoulder.

She turned to him. "Catherine's there."

He nodded, eyes on the TV.

She took a step backwards, hitting the back of her legs on the bed. "What's happened?"

"It happened about an hour ago. I was in the garden, only just saw."

She put a hand to her chest. "Oh my god." She paused, thinking back to Trask's face over Catherine's shoulder. "Have they said anything about the British delegation?"

"No, not yet."

There was a shout from downstairs; the boys, arguing over the PS4.

"I'll go," said Yusuf.

She perched on the bed, watching the screen. She flicked between channels, hoping for more information. They were all showing the same pictures.

The building was a convention centre in central Milan, where a summit was being held between European foreign ministers. The summit Catherine was attending. Fire-fighters moved around the huge building like ants between pockets of smoke.

She tossed on some clothes then hurried down to the living room. She perched on the edge of the sofa, chewing a hanging nail on her thumb.

The TV switched to an indoors shot: a long, empty table with five groups of microphones in front. The press faced it, corralled behind a slim rope. Finally one of the doors opened and a group of men filed in, accompanied by seven heavily armed security guards; one for each country represented. James Harrington, the Foreign Secretary, was there, and five of the other Foreign Secretaries. The Russian representative had been injured, and a deputy was in his place.

No sign of Catherine.

Jennifer half-listened as each representative in turn repeated the same message: this was an atrocity, an attack on a democratic and open summit, and the perpetrators should be condemned. All refused to answer questions about who those perpetrators might be, or confirm casualty figures.

The politicians rose and filed out through a door behind them. Jennifer screwed up her eyes to watch the door. As James Harrington stepped through it, there was a glimpse of a woman speaking to him. Tall with long dark hair. The lights in the press conference room made her shadowy and indistinct. But it was her.

Jennifer sat back, realising she'd been holding in tension for over an hour.

She flicked through screens on her iPad than looked up to see Samir walk in. He stood next to her in silence for a few moments, watching the screen.

"Serves them right."

Jennifer blinked.

"I beg your pardon?"

He turned to her. "Government. What do they expect with the way they treat us?"

He sat down in the armchair across from her, watching the screen. She stared at him, wondering if this was really her son.

"Samir, my friend is in there. She could have been hurt. There are other people too, people who've got nothing to do with the government. They've been hurt. Or they're missing."

He shrugged. "OK."

"OK? Is that all you can say? Innocent people are missing, possibly dead, because of a bomb going off and you think it's OK?"

He gazed at her. His eyes were dark and his cheeks flushed. He was gripping his knees with both hands.

"Mum, these bastards are kicking Muslims out of the country and calling us all terrorists. They can't really be surprised when someone hits back, can they?"

"Samir! I'll thank you not to use that kind of language!"

He shrugged. "True, though."

She stood up. "No Samir, it is not true. I don't agree with what they're doing any more than you do. But no one deserves to die because of this."

He looked down, avoiding her gaze. "I'm not so sure."

"Not so sure about what?" She tried to keep her voice even. This wasn't work, after all. This was her son.

"You disagreeing. You haven't done much to stop Trask, have you? And now you're cosying up to that woman who works for him."

She paused to take three slow breaths, feeling a tremor in her chest. *Cosying up* wasn't exactly the phrase to describe what John had asked her to do. A wave of guilt crept over her.

"I've done everything I can to stop Trask, you should know that. It's not easy in opposition. Not when Trask is so good at convincing the media and the general public that he's right."

He shrugged again. She wanted to take him by the shoulders and shake him. Instead she knelt in front of him in a vain attempt to meet his eye.

"Samir, you have to understand that I hate what Trask and his government are doing, that I'm doing everything I can to stop them. I risked everything to stop Michael when he was doing this, and now—"

"OK Mum. Calm down. I've had enough of this."

He stomped up the stairs, leaving her staring up at his

retreating back. The TV was still blaring but she was oblivious. When Yusuf came in she was fighting back tears.

"Jen? What is it? What's happened?"

He rushed towards her, looking over at the TV. She shook her head, sniffing.

"It isn't Catherine. It's Samir."

Yusuf knelt in front of her, hands on her upper arms. He stared into her face, puzzled. "Samir? What about him?"

She opened her mouth to speak but nothing came out. Where would she start? And how had her son become so bitter?

Yusuf stood up. "I'll talk to him."

Jennifer shook her head. "No. I need to deal with this."

"Sure?"

"Sure. Let me straighten my face up first."

She shuffled to the downstairs toilet, where she examined herself in the mirror. Her skin was blotchy, wrinkles creasing her forehead. When had the crows' feet become so deep? She splashed water on her face and then buried it in a towel. The house was quiet, the only sound the dim buzz of the TV in the living room.

She pulled the towel away and reached for the door, taking shallow breaths.

The quiet was disturbed by the slam of the front door. She rushed into the hall. Yusuf had his back to her, facing the door.

"Samir?" she asked.

"Yes."

She darted past him and opened the door, scanning the street. Samir was halfway down it, running.

33

MAY 2021. BIRMINGHAM

HER CHEST STIFFENED. SHE OPENED HER MOUTH TO call after him but he wasn't going to hear her.

She turned back to Yusuf who pushed past her to look out himself.

Hassan came bowling down the stairs, slamming into them to join the hug.

"Mum, Dad! Let's go out," he urged. Jennifer prepared herself to tell him what had happened, but Yusuf put a finger on her lips.

"OK, Hassan. Maybe that's a good idea," he said. "Jennifer, why don't you take Hassan out for a bit, get some fresh air." He gave her a look that said *trust me*. He was better than her at calming Samir, and they both knew it.

"What about Samir?" Hassan whined. "Is he being boring again?"

Jennifer forced a smile. "No, sweetie," she said, her voice pinched. "He's just gone out. Dad's going to wait here for him." She raised her eyebrows at Yusuf who nodded. "Then they'll come and join us."

She hustled Hassan into the car, looking up and down the street, and headed for the botanical gardens, Hassan's favourite place. She scanned the pavements on the way and kept her mobile in its holder on the dashboard, anxious for news of both Samir and Catherine.

Hassan always enjoyed the gardens, most of all the talking mynah bird in the glasshouse. He marched past it again and again, collapsing into fits of laughter every time it said hello.

Eventually he stopped marching and looked at her. She could see he was about to ask a question.

"Come on, you," Jennifer said. "Let's go outside."

"No."

Hassan ran off into the depths of the glasshouse.

"Hassan? Please Hassan, this isn't funny. Come back."

She paused, listening. She could hear the slap of his shoes against the paving slabs, receding.

"Hassan!" Jennifer called, her chest tight. "Come back, *now!*"

Hassan wasn't one to run off, and although he was eleven now, he didn't have the presence of mind to remember where he'd been. She could feel her heart racing; how could she lose two boys, in one day?

"Boo!"

Hassan jumped at her from behind, giggling. She spun round.

"Hassan! That was—"

His face crumpled and she stopped herself. "That was funny. But you gave me a scare. Don't run off again. Please."

He shrugged, his lip quivering. She sighed.

"Come on, let's get some fresh air."

As they left the glasshouse she took a deep breath, praying that by now Yusuf had tracked down Samir and that they'd have followed them to the park.

Hassan yelled Samir's name and ran off across the grass. Jennifer put her hands to her face, groaning with relief.

Yusuf was sitting on the grass with Samir, their backs to her. They hadn't spotted Hassan yet. She edged towards them, anxious. Yusuf spotted her first and threw a smile over Samir's shoulder.

Yusuf nodded at Samir, an unspoken agreement in his eyes. Samir stood up, brushing his hands on his trousers and looking down at the ground. He turned to Jennifer.

"I'm sorry, Mum," he muttered.

Jennifer felt her heart lift. She held out her arms to him and he let her give him a light hug which he returned reluctantly. She decided it was wisest to accept his apology. They could talk about why he'd run off another day.

"Thanks, Samir. I love you." She touched his cheek, ignoring his flinch. "Don't scare me like that again, huh?"

34

MAY 2021. LONDON

Jennifer looked up from her desk to spot John peering round her office door. She bit her tongue and closed her laptop.

"Hello John. What can I do for you?"

She watched him squeeze into her office. His bulk looked ridiculous in the confined space, elbows brushing against the walls. She wondered what was so urgent, or so confidential, that it had brought him up here.

The armchair was piled with files; John looked at it and then at her.

"Just put it on the floor," she sighed.

He picked the pile up and held it for a moment, casting around for a free space.

"Under the desk." How long must it have been since John had had to endure cramped conditions like this?

He deposited it at her feet and slumped into the armchair. He shifted his weight then placed an ankle on his knee.

"How are you?" he asked.

She'd arrived late this morning, taking a later train so

she could have breakfast with the boys, something she'd been doing for a few weeks, since Samir's outburst. Today it had backfired, making her start the week grouchy and irritable. Still, he didn't need to know about all of that.

"Fine. You've never been up here before."

He snorted. "Yes I have. Before your time though."

She shrugged. Maybe he'd been housed up here in his first or second term, before his promotion to the government and before her election. She didn't remember Yusuf saying anything about it, at the time. She wondered who'd seen him come up here; the Leader of the Opposition wasn't in the habit of venturing up to the eaves.

"Look, Jennifer. I know Catherine could have been hurt, but she wasn't. We still need to talk about your friendship with her."

So this was it. She thought about the last month, the conversations she'd had over the phone with Catherine. Knowing her friend was unhurt had made her warm towards her, and planted an idea in her head, a better idea than John's. And Catherine's second promotion – to the Home Office this time – had cemented it there.

John looked at her, waiting for a reply. She didn't provide one.

"Jennifer?"

"You look tired," she said, stalling.

He frowned and pulled at the skin of his cheek. It was grey and loose. "Yeah."

"What's up?"

He shook his head. "Trask. As ever."

She pushed her paperwork to one side. "What's he done?"

"Well, he's not satisfied with the bill he's already passed.

Immigration. The bill I guess a person might say you didn't stop."

She tensed. "You failed to stop it too, John."

He laughed. "Don't say that outside this room. Please. Ever."

She smiled. "Of course not. So what's he planning now? And how do *you* know what Trask is thinking?"

"Oh, I have my sources." He tapped the side of his nose. "The Milan attack has got to him. I guess it's had the same effect on him as the Home Office bomb did on us."

They were both silent for a moment.

"He's rattled," John said. "Wants to retaliate."

"How?"

"Well," he said, shuffling in his chair. "How do you cope up here, anyway?"

She laughed. "I'll be moving when they can find me a better office."

"Good. Not right, for shadow cabinet to be up here."

She shrugged. "Maybe it is. See how everyone else has to put up with it."

"You've had your stint. No need to be a martyr about it."

"No. So – Trask?"

"Hmm. OK, so none of this is official. But we do have our ears to the ground."

She wondered whose ears he was referring to specifically; certainly not his own. John Hunter and Leonard Trask were both men whose presence in a room was impossible to miss. Whenever they found themselves together, an uneasy silence descended over everyone present, until one of them decided to leave. It could take some time, as neither wanted to give the impression he was running away from the other.

"So," said John, examining his bitten fingernails. "He wants to toughen up even more on anyone they think's a terrorist, plus the people around them. To be honest I think he was planning this before, but Milan has just sped things up."

"What's that got to do with it? The Milan bombers were both Iraqi." The two men had been travelling under false Italian passports. There had been a backlash in Italy, Muslims being attacked on the street and one group of women having their hijabs ripped from their heads. There had been a countermove on social media, people worldwide declaring solidarity with Muslims, but it wasn't enough. It was only when the true nationality of the bombers was released that the tensions had died down. Jennifer had watched it in horror, remembering the night when she'd been at the centre of a stabbing just two streets from home.

John eyed her. "But who's to say that there aren't similar men in this country being recruited and brainwashed right now, plotting something similar?"

"Come on, John. You're sounding like Michael."

"I'm right, Jennifer. Recruitment is going on, and you know it."

She sighed. There was tension in her local mosque, and one of the imams had mysteriously left the city after being suspected of involvement in radicalising teenagers. Luckily it was a different mosque from the one Yusuf took the boys to.

"Doesn't he have the police working on that? Security services?"

"I don't think he trusts them to do it. Wants to start some sort of citizen army."

She stiffened. "What?"

John spread his hands. "I exaggerate, sorry. An army of citizen spies, more like."

"How on earth—?"

"It's fairly easy. Reward being a tittle-tattle. Punish being connected to suspects. Anyone who provides the police with information will receive a commendation."

"And the punishment?"

"Extend the deportation laws. Not just terrorist suspects and sympathisers, but families too. Extended families. So the granny of someone Trask's vigilante army accuses of being a terrorist sympathiser could be out on her ear."

Jennifer moved over to the window. All she could see was the roof below and a clear white sky.

She turned back to him. "So. How do you plan on fighting it?"

Fatigue passed over his face. "That's just it. I'm not sure we can."

"What do you mean, not sure? This would turn the country into a police state, with everyone spying on their neighbours. What the hell has gone wrong with the world?"

Her voice had become high pitched. She thought of Samir, of how he would react to this. She turned back to John and glared at him.

John came to stand next to Jennifer, gazing out of the window. An image sprang to her mind of the Home Office bomb, his face against the glass before it shattered. She shuddered.

After a few moment's silence broken only by the coo of pigeons on the roof, he leaned back, still looking out of the window.

"I need your experience," he said. "And the fire in your belly. I want you to find out what he's planning."

Catherine was her friend, and she was expected to spy on her, to use her. "I don't feel comfortable with this."

He glanced back at her office door. Seeing it was shut, he inhaled but continued to speak in a low murmur.

"Why are you refusing me? It's bloody rude. Why don't you want to help?"

Samir's voice rang in her head. *They don't want us here, Mum.* Then the headteacher: *a different school.* A Muslim school. A segregated school.

She put up a hand. "I do want to help. But not the way you think."

"OK."

"I've got an idea. Sit down and I'll run it past you."

35

MAY 2021. LONDON

THE HOTEL ROOM WAS AS SOULLESS AS ANY OTHER, despite the extra layers of luxury. Jennifer sat on the soft bed, feeling the mattress dip beneath her weight. Opposite her, the full width mirror reflected her anxiety back at her. Her eyes were rimmed with dark shadows and her hair was dishevelled.

This won't do, she thought, and stood up. She crossed to the mirror and licked her forefinger. She rubbed around her eye, wiping off some stray mascara, and then licked her fingers again and used them to straighten her hair. Her roots needed doing.

A quiet knock came at the door, making her jump. She pinched her cheeks, trying to will some colour into them. Then she gave herself a final look in the mirror and crossed to the door, closing the bathroom door as she passed it.

She peered through the peephole. There was only one person outside. She pulled back and opened the door, ushering her visitor in.

"Hi," she said, closing the door again. Suddenly the

incongruity of the hotel room hit her, making her wonder why she'd gone along with this.

Catherine stopped by the bed, dropping her coat onto it and placing her bag on the floor by her feet. She smiled nervously. "Hi."

Jennifer laughed. "This all feels a bit cloak and dagger," she said.

Catherine's face was hard. "Yes," she agreed. "Necessary, though."

A shiver ran through Jennifer. Was this a good idea?

Catherine turned away from her, stopping at the easy chairs in front of the window. She touched the net curtain that filled the wall, as if deciding whether to look out and then thinking better of it. After a moment she pulled one of the chairs further into the room, and then dragged a low table next to it.

Jennifer grabbed another chair, pulling it next to Catherine's. Catherine took her phone from her pocket, glanced at the screen and then turned it off. She placed it on the table between them. "Can't be too careful."

Jennifer frowned and then looked at her own phone which she'd dropped onto the bed after making a couple of calls when she arrived early. Was that wise? This was ridiculous. Two friends meeting for a chat, what was wrong with that?

Except they were in a hotel room near Heathrow Airport, miles from Westminster. She hadn't told anyone else she was coming here. Not even John. Not even Yusuf.

She looked at Catherine. "Does anyone know you're here?"

Catherine rubbed her lap. "No."

Jennifer steadied her breathing. *Calm down*, she told herself.

They both looked up at the sound of voices outside the door. Catherine stared at Jennifer, her eyes wide.

Jennifer stood and went to the door, leaning her face against the peephole. A group of people, American by the sound of it, were passing in the corridor, heading for another room. Nothing to worry about.

She turned. "It's OK," she breathed. "Just some tourists."

Catherine nodded. "Right," she said. "So, you've got me here. What d'you want?"

36

JUNE 2021. BIRMINGHAM

"Samir?"

Jennifer stopped in her tracks, car keys dangling from her hand. She was outside her constituency office, having been in to check on her post before heading out to a meeting at the local hospital.

Samir turned to her. He was at the centre of a group of boys, huddled over something that one of them shoved into a pocket.

His eyes grew wide. "Mum."

"What are you doing here? Why aren't you at school?"

He blinked rapidly. One of the other boys nudged him and sniggered. She didn't know him. Or the other one.

She stepped forwards, checking her watch. "It's ten o'clock in the morning. Why aren't you at school?"

"Free period," he muttered. One of the other boys laughed.

She cocked her head. "Samir, you're in year eleven. If you had a free period, you'd be in school, studying."

He glanced around. "They let us out."

He was lying, she knew.

The other boys had their heads down now, staring at the pavement. One of them was white, the other Asian. Who were they?

An elderly man barged past, grumbling at her for getting in the way. She scowled and watched him recede, rubbing her shoulder where he had banged into it.

She turned back to see Samir flash her a wide-eyed stare and a shrug as his friend grabbed his arm and they ran off, disappearing down the gap between two empty shops.

"Samir!" she shouted. She looked around, wondering if anyone in the office had been watching.

She hurried to the spot where he had disappeared, peering into the alleyway. But there was no one there. Just piled up rubbish and a discarded sleeping bag. She frowned and headed back to her car, her mind fogged.

J
ennifer didn't get home till five hours later, after picking Hassan up from school. Yusuf was still out and there was no sign of Samir. She opened the front curtains wide, hoping to spot him coming home. Hassan grumbled at her, annoyed that she was hovering in the living room, disturbing him.

"Mum, what are you doing?" he whined.

"Nothing, love. Do your homework."

He grunted and leaned over his work, reluctant. On a Friday night he'd rather be out with his friends, playing football. But Jennifer didn't want to leave the house to take him.

Finally she heard the door slam and she rushed to it, to be confronted by a red-faced Samir.

"You embarrassed me, Mum."

She clenched her fists. She should be accusing him, not the other way around.

"Why weren't you at school?"

"I told you. Free period."

She shook her head. "I checked your timetable. You should've been in Maths."

"Whatever," he said, pushing past her.

She grabbed his arm. "Whatever? Is that all you've got to say?"

He shrugged her off.

Behind her she could hear Hassan laughing at something on the TV. She glanced at the living room door then back at Samir. "Upstairs, now. We need to talk," she snapped.

He walked up the stairs, making slow progress. She resisted the urge to push him up.

Once in his room, Samir slumped onto the bed and picked up his phone, scrolling through it.

"Put your phone down please."

He grunted and threw it to the floor.

She looked around. His room was unnaturally tidy. The floor was clear and books were stacked in an orderly pile on his desk. The curtains were pulled open and a jacket hung neatly on the back of the door. It was almost as if he didn't live here. It certainly wasn't the same room he'd inhabited a few months ago.

She sighed. She couldn't criticise him for being tidy. But it felt wrong.

She took a few deep breaths and decided to change her approach. She edged towards the bed and eased herself onto it, leaving some distance between the two of them.

She cleared her throat. "OK," she said. "I'm not going to shout at you. I just want to find out what's been going on."

He grunted.

"Is this the first time you've skipped school, or has it happened before?"

"Dunno."

She closed her eyes for a moment. *Be patient*, she told herself. Losing her rag with him would achieve nothing.

"Who were those boys? I didn't recognise them."

"Just mates."

"Mates who play truant?"

A shrug.

"What happened to your old friends?"

"They're still my friends."

"Good."

He said nothing. She dragged a hand through her hair.

"Is there a reason for this, Samir?" She thought back to that conversation in the headteacher's office. To the fight. She'd written that letter to the school but it had achieved nothing; they had evidence that Samir had been caught fighting, and he'd already been punished. "Are you having problems at school? Have you been fighting again?"

He threw her an angry look. "No."

She shifted her weight, moving towards him. He retreated, pushing himself into the wall at the head of the bed.

"Samir, you can tell me. Have there been any more fights? Any racism?"

He looked up from his fingers, which he'd been picking at, and stared at her. "You wouldn't understand."

"Try me."

"They don't want us there, you know."

Again she thought of the headteacher, her calm rejection of Jennifer's appeal for sympathy. *You might want to consider moving Samir.*

She heard a car pull up outside. Samir looked at the window, then strode over to it and pulled the curtains closed. She watched him, wondering who this young man was who'd taken possession of her little boy.

"Have they said that to you?" she asked.

He stood over her, his face tight. "No. But I know that's what they think." He narrowed his eyes. "You know what I'm talking about, don't you?"

She ran a hand through her hair. She nodded.

"Why aren't you more angry, Mum? They're vilifying Muslims, singling us out. They hate us."

She looked at him, remembering the little boy who used to reach out his arms for a hug when she got home from Westminster. Then she thought of the conversations she'd been having with John and Catherine, about the government's plans.

"I am angry, love. And I can understand why you are. But you can't play truant. I think maybe—"

"Truant? Mum, who gives a damn about school when they're deporting Muslims? Who cares about that when there are guys at school whose families are being torn apart?"

The door opened with a high creak. They turned to it as one. She panicked, hoping Hassan hadn't been listening, then relaxed. Yusuf.

He looked between the two of them, not moving from his position at the doorway.

"Is it true, Samir?" he said. "Have you been playing truant?"

Samir blushed. "Once."

Yusuf raised an eyebrow. "Really?"

A shrug. "Twice."

"How long am I going to have to stand here before you tell me how many times?"

Samir looked up at him. "You don't get it! You, of all people, should understand. School is irrelevant! They don't want us there, anyway."

Yusuf shook his head. "What are you talking about?"

"You know. You've seen it."

Yusuf sighed. "He's got a point, Jennifer," he said. "I don't think you know how bad it is."

She stood up. "I'll say it's bad. I don't like him playing truant. I don't like him being so angry."

Yusuf put his hands on his hips, glancing at Samir. "That's not what I mean."

"Mum," Samir said, looking at Yusuf. "This is more important. I've been helping Dad at the weekends, cleaning up racist graffiti. I want to know what's going on. We should all know, so we can resist them, fight back."

"But don't you see? That's exactly what I'm worried about!" Jennifer cried, not caring if Hassan heard now. "Talking like this could get you into trouble! You go out there and start resisting, as you say, and you'll very likely end up arrested or worse."

"In every struggle there are martyrs," Samir said, his voice low and level.

"Martyrs! Don't give me that! Who told you that?"

He blushed. "No one."

"Look, Samir, all I want to do is protect you. I'm not saying you shouldn't help people. I'm proud that you want to do that. Your dad is too." She looked hopefully at Yusuf who nodded agreement. "But I don't want you putting yourself in danger. I want you to promise us you won't do anything stupid, won't break the law. I want you to stay away from those boys. And I want you to be at school, all day every day. You don't want to give them an excuse to expel you."

Samir opened his mouth but then clamped it shut after a look from Yusuf. He pushed his hands behind his back and stared at his phone on the floor.

"OK," he muttered. "I'll be careful."

"And you'll go to school. Every day. Or do we have to take you in ourselves?"

"No. No, I'll go."

Jennifer relaxed. "That's all I ask of you. You're only sixteen. It's great that you want to help Dad, but just the weekends. He's going to keep an eye out, make sure no one encourages you to do anything stupid."

"I—" interrupted Yusuf. Jennifer looked at him.

"Won't you, love?"

Yusuf sighed. "I suppose so. I don't want him getting into trouble any more than you do. But Jennifer?"

"Yes?"

"He's angry. He's scared. So am I. You should be too."

She grabbed his hand, relieved when he didn't pull away. "I know. I do, honest. And I'm scared too, scared of losing my family. We need to pull together."

Yusuf nodded but Samir grunted and headed for the bathroom, slamming the door behind him. Jennifer leaned against the wall, her heart pounding.

37

JUNE-SEPTEMBER 2021. LONDON
AND BIRMINGHAM

CATHERINE HAD ALREADY ARRIVED THIS TIME, AND WAS in the hotel lobby when Jennifer entered. Jennifer looked at her watch, flustered; she was five minutes early.

She stared at Catherine, waiting by the lifts. Should she say hello, or not?

She looked around. The lobby was quiet at this time of day, with just the occasional person heading for the restaurant or asking for directions at the front desk. A group of businessmen huddled in a corner, laughing conspiratorially.

Catherine turned and spotted her, then froze. She gave her an almost imperceptible shake of the head then moved away from the lifts, heading for the Ladies'. Jennifer breathed a sigh of relief, then rushed to the reception desk, claiming the key. She scuttled to the lifts and was in the room five minutes before Catherine knocked on the door.

"That wasn't good," said Catherine. Jennifer nodded then stuck her head out into the corridor. There was no one there. *Stop it*, she told herself. She was behaving suspiciously.

"I'll get here earlier next time," she said, following

Catherine to the window. Once again, Catherine was moving the furniture. This was a different room, on a higher floor, but the layout was the same, only mirrored.

She turned her phone off and put it in her bag then settled into her chair. It had a hard curved back and she knew she'd pay for sitting in it later. But getting comfortable on the bed didn't seem appropriate.

Catherine was leafing through a notebook. Jennifer watched, startled. "You're not writing any this down, are you?"

Catherine looked up and shook her head. "No. This is from a meeting this morning."

"Oh." Jennifer looked again at the notes, squinting. How she'd love to read them.

Catherine closed the book and Jennifer pushed down her disappointment. A plane took off outside, only partly muffled by the triple glazing.

"Does John know we're meeting?" Catherine asked.

Jennifer was ready for this, had discussed it with John. She shook her head. "No." This was part of her cover, the reason she'd given for meeting with Catherine. Two rebels, finding common cause. She hoped.

"Of course he doesn't," she continued, hating herself. "You know I don't agree with everything my party does, and I know you feel the same way about yours."

Catherine blushed. Jennifer ignored it; Catherine needed to be more comfortable with having her own opinions.

"It's not as simple as that," Catherine said.

Jennifer could smell Catherine's perfume, light and floral. Everything about her was a picture of the demure modern Conservative woman: dark skirt suit, subtle makeup, short pink nails. Jennifer wondered how much of it was real.

"I know," she said. "More than most."

A smile crossed Catherine's lips. Jennifer remembered their first meeting, the admiration for her act of rebellion. Was this the real Catherine? Were they the same, the two of them?

"Anyway," Jennifer said. "We haven't got long. What have you got that we can use?"

Catherine's eyes narrowed. "This is a two way street, I thought you said."

"Of course." She paused. "I've got information too."

"OK." She didn't sound convinced. She opened her notebook again, skimming the pages. Her writing was small and neat, with a round, looping script. Jennifer smiled, impressed that she still made handwritten notes.

Catherine bent the book back, leaving it open in her lap. "I've got something that might be helpful," she said. "Nothing too big. Not yet."

Jennifer nodded. Catherine would be worried that whatever she told Jennifer would be leaked to the press, and that it would find its way back to her. "Thanks. It's not going anywhere."

Catherine nodded and licked her lips. She picked up the notebook and started to read.

～

The following weekend, Samir and Yusuf were in the kitchen when Jennifer got home. The air was heavy with tension.

She looked between them. "What?" she asked. "What's happening?"

"Nothing," said Samir.

Yusuf frowned. "That's not quite right, is it Samir?"

Samir scowled at his dad. "You said you wouldn't tell her," he hissed.

Jennifer felt as if he'd slapped her. "What?" she gasped, rounding on Yusuf. "What're you keeping from me?"

Yusuf put a hand on her wrist but she shook it away. Her body felt hot.

"Does this happen a lot? You not telling me things?"

Yusuf's shoulders fell. "No," he said. "And it's not like that."

"I'm off," snapped Samir. "You two can have your row without me." He marched out and stamped upstairs. Jennifer grimaced; this was becoming tiring.

She turned to Yusuf, willing herself to be calm. "What's happened?" she repeated.

Yusuf slumped into a chair. "It's the school," he said. "I was going to tell you. Well actually, Samir was. That's what we agreed."

"Tell me what?"

Yusuf leaned back, closing his eyes. "There's been another – incident."

Upstairs, music boomed from Samir's room. At least he wasn't listening in.

"What sort of incident? Another fight?"

"No. An argument with a teacher."

"Oh hell. What about?"

"The new stuff they've got to do in class. British Values lessons. He said it was racist, refused to take part."

She nodded slowly. Samir was right. But refusing to engage with the school wasn't going to do him any favours. "What did the teacher say?"

"I don't know. He's been suspended again. A week."

"*A week?* He gets two days for fighting and then a week for speaking his mind?"

Yusuf nodded. "Seems that way."

She moved towards him, planning to sit down and discuss this, to agree how they were going to tackle it. But as she crossed the room, there were three sharp knocks at the front door. The kind of knocks the police would use.

She jumped and turned to it. "Who's that?"

Yusuf stood up. "How do I know?"

"Sorry."

"It's OK," he said. "I'll go. Probably one of my families."

He looked tired; his skin was blotchy and grey in places, and his clothes looked unkempt. As he brushed past her she noticed that his sweater smelt musty. This wasn't like Yusuf.

She touched his hand. "It's alright. I'll go."

She walked to the front door and pulled it open.

A flash popped in her eyes. She threw a hand up to shield herself.

Two men stood on her front step. One was holding up a phone and the other had a camera.

She squinted at them. The man with the phone grinned and pushed it at her face.

"Jennifer," he said. "Have you got anything to say about Catherine Moore?"

The flash popped again. She slammed the door in their faces.

She turned to Yusuf, leaning on the door and panting. Her mind was buzzing.

Yusuf stared at her. "What the hell?"

38

SEPTEMBER 2021. BIRMINGHAM

JENNIFER LEANED AGAINST THE DOOR, BREATHING heavily. What had Catherine done? Had there been another bomb attack? Had she told someone about their meetings?

Jennifer shook her head. Catherine would have just as much to lose as she did. More, in fact. She was pretty sure that Trask had no idea that the two of them were meeting, while John knew everything. Not that Catherine knew that, of course. She froze. Trask would know everything, too.

She pushed herself away from the door and stumbled up the stairs, barging into Samir's room.

"Mum, I don't want to—"

She put a finger to her lips. "It's not that," she said. "I just want to look out of your window."

Samir returned to his book. She slipped past him to the wall next to the window, making sure she couldn't be seen. Then she edged her face round the window frame, peering outside.

Her heart leaped into her throat. On the street and spilling onto her lawn was a pack of reporters and photographers, maybe twelve strong. She put a hand to her chest, feeling it tremble.

Samir was staring at her. "What's going on? Can I have my room back?"

She flung out a hand, beckoning to him. "Give me your phone."

He frowned but handed it over.

She jabbed at the screen, googling herself, When she found the headline she didn't know whether to laugh or cry.

'*Jennifer and Catherine: Their Secret Lesbian Affair*'.

She dropped the phone. Samir picked it up and gave her a look of disgust.

"Eww, Mum," he said.

Yusuf barged into the room. "What's happened?"

She gestured towards the window. "There's twelve of them out there."

He frowned. "Why?"

Samir handed his phone to Yusuf, who blanched. He looked at her, his expression wary.

"It's not true, is it?" His voice was uneven.

She laughed. "Of course not!" She crossed to him, making sure to avoid the window. "Don't be daft. She's not my type."

He frowned.

"I'm joking!" she said.

"It's not funny."

Yusuf was scrolling through the accompanying article on Samir's phone, hitting links to find out more. "So why are they saying this?"

She sighed. "Come downstairs," she said.

～

Jennifer wished she'd already told Yusuf about her meetings with Catherine. But now was as good a time as any.

Finally she finished, telling him what she could about the latest meeting – the fourth. She stopped talking, waiting for him to speak. Behind her, beyond the front door, she could hear the faint sound of voices and cars. More of them arriving.

Jennifer was standing in the kitchen with her back to the door and Yusuf was in a chair, his knuckles white on the table next to him. He'd been standing up when she began, facing her, but when she told him of her agreement with John to spy on Trask via Catherine, he dropped into the chair.

Now he was staring at her, licking his lips and saying nothing. He coughed.

She watched his face.

"D'you think it'll work?" he asked.

She smiled, then her face fell. "Not now, I guess."

There was a rustling sound behind her, in the hall. She flicked her head round to see that something had landed on the door mat. She glanced at Yusuf then went to the door and picked it up.

It was a folded up piece of paper, a printout of tomorrow's front page of the *Daily Mail*. Scribbled across it in blue marker pen were the words 'Care to comment?'

She let it drop to the floor. It landed face up.

She looked up the stairs, startled by a sound. Yusuf looked up from his hands, still slumped in his kitchen chair.

She stared at him, panicking. Could they have got in?

She threw him a hopeful smile then mounted the stairs

slowly, waiting to be accosted at every step. At the top, the hallway was quiet.

Then it came again: a quiet knocking, from Hassan's room. She breathed a sigh of relief and pushed the door open, expecting to find Hassan bouncing a ball against his wall. It was a new habit of his that drove her insane.

There was no one there. Of course: football practice.

She looked at the window. Something was leaning against it on the outside.

She crossed to it to get a better look, and was met by the sight of a middle aged, balding man, level with her. He held a camera in one hand and gripped the object she'd seen in the other. It was a ladder.

She shrieked and thumped on the window. He gasped and nearly fell backwards, only keeping his balance by letting his camera fall.

She yelled at him and jerked the curtains closed, her breath high and wheezy.

"What's happened? Are you OK?" Yusuf was in the doorway, his eyes wide with panic.

She nodded, then let herself sink to the floor in front of the window. The closed curtains brushed the back of her neck as she went down, making her shiver.

She wrapped her arms around her knees and buried her face in them. Yusuf sank to the floor and crawled to her. He put an arm round her.

"Why didn't you tell me?" he breathed.

"I just didn't get the chance, what with Samir and everything."

Behind her, the ladder clattered against the window. She hoped it was being lowered. She pictured the press pack down there on the lawn. The neighbours peering round their curtains, wondering what she'd brought to their quiet street. She heard another vehicle pull up outside, louder than the cars she'd heard earlier. Then there was laughter.

"Did you see the headline?" she asked Yusuf.

He nodded.

She sighed. "You know it's not true."

He squeezed her knee. "You don't have to tell me that."

She smiled. "I wonder if they're on Catherine's doorstep too."

"Hmm."

She frowned and stood up, pulling on her fingers to stretch out the tension. She fetched her phone from their bedroom and came back into Hassan's room, leaning on the doorframe. Yusuf was still on the floor.

She selected Catherine from her contacts, then paused, staring at the screen. Was this wise?

She hit dial.

No answer. She decided not to leave a message, and hung up.

Yusuf raised his eyebrows. She shrugged.

"What now?" he asked.

Another shrug.

Yusuf stood up and wrapped his arms around her. She closed her eyes, sinking into the embrace.

"What are you going to do about it?" he whispered.

"I don't know."

He stiffened. "Come on, this isn't like you. Take a battle head-on, that's what you do. They're all out there, and they're not going anywhere till you make them."

She turned to him in exasperation. *How can you be so positive?*

"So how do you suggest I do that, exactly?"

He stroked her cheek. "I don't know. But I know you,

you'll think of something. Look at how great you were when you were challenging Michael Stuart – you always found the right thing to say, to the press and in Parliament."

"Yes, and look where that got me. Do you realise that if I hadn't done all that, they wouldn't be out there now?"

Yusuf sighed, looking as distressed as Jennifer felt.

"Don't think like that. None of this is your fault. It's John's just as much as it's yours."

She leaned on him, staring ahead. There were no sounds from the window now; the ladder must have gone. She hoped.

The peace was shattered by a megaphone-enhanced voice from outside.

"Ms Sinclair!" it boomed. "Do you have a statement to make?"

Her heart was racing. Her palms were becoming wet and her face hot.

"You're going to have to do something," Yusuf said.

"I know."

She went to the bathroom and splashed water on her face. Then she changed into a clean blouse, trying to select something that would look effortless but appropriate. She put on makeup, not wanting her harassed face to appear in front of millions without some improvement, and ran a comb through her hair.

She went downstairs, staring at the door. Yusuf had closed the curtains in the living room, which was plunged into darkness.

"I'm ready," she said.

"Do you want me to come with you?"

"No. Too Mellorish. *Respectable MP flanked by her loving family*. That's not me. I got into this mess, and I'll get out of it."

He squeezed her hand. "Good luck. I'll make a gap in the curtains, watch you," he said.

"Don't let them see you."

"Of course not."

As she reached the door he was tweaking the curtain.

"Hang on a minute," she said. "Are there cameras out there?"

He twisted for a better view. "Yes. BBC and Sky."

"Well, don't look out the window like that. Watch it on TV."

He switched on the TV. It cast a surreal blue glow on the dark walls. Sure enough, a Sky reporter stood in front of their house, talking to camera, filling time until Jennifer emerged.

"Press reports this morning allege that Ms Sinclair and Miss Moore have been engaging in clandestine meetings in hotel rooms," he said. "We've got sources that verify that it's true." He smiled: *what a story*. "We can only speculate as to how their party leaders will react to this."

"Right, I'm going," Jennifer said.

39

SEPTEMBER 2021. BIRMINGHAM

JENNIFER OPENED THE DOOR QUICKLY IN A DISPLAY OF confidence, but with her free hand clenched behind her back.

A sea of faces turned in her direction. She gulped and smiled as steadily as she could. Somewhere in the tangle of thoughts, she felt relief that they'd tidied the garden the previous weekend.

She pulled the door shut behind her. A closed door would make a better backdrop than an open entrance, and she didn't want them looking inside.

She was blinded by a succession of flashbulbs. She waited for them to subside, taking the opportunity to catch her breath. Someone shouted something unintelligible from the back of the crowd.

She raised a hand and a hush descended. She risked a glance past them into the street. There were faces at the windows opposite and a man had stopped on the pavement, his dog tugging at its lead.

"Good evening, everyone," she said, projecting her

voice. "I'd like to make a short statement. I won't be taking questions."

She looked around the expectant faces, wishing now that she'd written something down. But she was better when thinking on her feet and would rather maintain eye contact.

"I am aware of the allegations that have been made about myself and Catherine Moore in today's press." She paused to lick her lips. "And I am categorically denying them."

Flashes started bursting in her eyes again, and the crowd surged forwards. She tried to ignore it.

"It's true that Catherine and I have been meeting. We've been friends since she was first elected. Our constituencies are near each other and we've often travelled to and from London together."

Another barrage of flashbulbs. She forced herself not to flinch. She closed her eyes then forced them open again.

"More recently, we have been meeting in hotel rooms, yes. I'm not denying that. The purpose of those meetings was to discuss ways in which we could work together to counteract the more extreme aspects of Leonard Trask's government."

She paused again, looking ahead. The quiet was broken by the sound of someone's phone ringing and being hastily shut off.

"I've made no secret of my horror at the extreme direction the government is taking. There are Conservative MPs who are also concerned, but don't necessarily wish to speak out. By sharing information, Catherine and I hoped that we might be able to work across parties and find some common ground." She turned her head to face the BBC camera.

Would Catherine be watching? "I still hope we can, despite this setback."

The pack surged forwards, and a questions were fired at her. She raised her hand.

"That's all I've got to say. Now I'd be grateful if my family – and my neighbours – could have a little peace and quiet. Thank you."

A man at the front shoved his microphone under her chin. "Why a hotel room? Were you sleeping together too?"

She thought of Yusuf back in the house. Of her mum, who would probably be watching. Her chest tightened.

"I know it looks unusual, meeting where we did. But we wanted to keep our meetings private so that we could be as open with each other as possible, and not attract the attention of our colleagues. We were not sleeping together. Now I want to get back to my family, and I'd be grateful if you could leave them and our neighbours in peace. Thank you for your time."

She smiled thinly and turned her back on them, slipping through the front door and shutting it behind her.

She leaned against the door, running over what she'd just said. She hoped there'd been nothing they could take out of context, no editing they could do to turn her words on their head. It was too late now; they would do with it as they liked.

She opened her eyes to see Samir sitting at the bottom of the stairs, watching her. "What's going on, Mum?"

She felt a lump form in her throat; on top of everything else Samir hated her for right now, would this be the final straw?

RACHEL MCLEAN

She took a deep breath.

"Come into the living room with me and Dad, and we'll tell you what's happened."

As he shuffled after her and perched on a sofa, the phone rang. Yusuf shot Jennifer a look.

"It'll be for you. I'll talk to Samir while you answer it. If that's OK with you?"

She smiled. "Of course."

Not pausing to think that it might be a journalist, she rushed to her desk in the dining room to answer the phone.

"Yes," she asked, breathing heavily.

"Jennifer. It's John."

She let herself relax, slumping against the desk. A friendly voice. "John. Hi."

"Quit the pleasantries. I just saw you on TV. What the fuck do you think you're doing?"

Moments passed before she could speak.

"What do you mean?"

"What do you mean, what do I mean? You just appeared on live TV making some sort of hash of a statement, without even telling me what was going on. The national media knew before I did whether what the *Mail* is saying is true or not."

"What? Of course it's not true. You know that."

"Why the hell did you go and talk to them, Jennifer? All you've done is given the story legs."

"But I wanted to set the record straight."

"Jesus Christ, Jennifer, you can be so naive sometimes."

"What?"

"What you were doing was a secret. You know that."

She swallowed. "Sorry."

"You've set us back miles. Just how stupid are you?"

She didn't need this.

240

"John, I didn't pick up the phone to be insulted. Now if you don't mind, my sons need an explanation and I have to sort out my family's dinner. Call me tomorrow if you still need to speak to me."

"No, I need you to—"

But he was gone, his voice cut off when she hung up.

She collapsed into a chair and stared at the wall. She felt cold. The media would have it in for her over the next few days or even weeks, and she'd lost the support of John. And she had no idea what Catherine was thinking, whether her career was in jeopardy too.

She leaned into the mirror by her desk, rubbing a spot of makeup under her eye. *Is John right? Am I naive?*

She was brought back to life by Hassan running in, back from football practice. She hoped Yusuf had let him in by the back door.

"Are we on TV? Cool!" he exclaimed, stopping when he saw the look on Jennifer's face. He cast his eyes to the ground and shuffled out.

"Hassan, it's OK," she called after him. "Just don't go out the front, OK? Please?"

She followed him into the living room. Yusuf and Samir had gone and Hassan was standing in the middle of the room, facing the window. The curtains were wide open and the press pack stared back at them. They grabbed their phones, desperate to catch a photo. A flash popped.

She ran back to the hall, dropping to the floor. "Hassan!" she hissed. "Crawl back in and close the curtains. Make sure they don't see you."

She watched as he crossed the room on his hands and

knees. The curtains edged closed then he stood up, looking at her hopefully. She smiled and beckoned him to her for a hug and a thank you.

Samir appeared from the kitchen. She looked at him warily, unsure of what Yusuf had told him or how he would react.

He returned her stare with a shrug and approached her. She waited; he wasn't in the habit of getting close these days. He stopped inches away, looking down at her; when did he get so tall? She looked at him, waiting. What had Yusuf told him?

"They're bastards, Mum," he said. "Don't let them get to you."

"Right. No."

He shrugged again and pushed past her, heading up to his room with a bowl of cereal. She listened as his door closed – not a slam for once – and his music started up.

40

SEPTEMBER 2021. BIRMINGHAM AND LONDON

THE NEXT DAY, JENNIFER HAD A VISIT TO A LOCAL primary school. She arrived to find the headteacher friendly but wary, as if expecting her to bite. In the hall, contributing to an assembly on democracy, she spotted the teachers giving her sidelong glances.

John had been on the early morning news, denying all knowledge of Jennifer and Catherine's meetings. She'd been expecting this, but his lies still felt like an attack. *I need your experience*, he'd said. *The fire in your belly.* That fire counted for nothing now.

At lunchtime she decided to go home. She needed the peace of the house.

She was pulling into her street when the one o'clock news came on. There was a handful of cars parked outside her house.

She sighed and parked before reaching them, pausing to watch the silent cars. She imagined the waiting journalists sitting inside, listening to the news along with her. Enjoying it.

This end of the street was quiet. An elderly woman

passed her car, laden down with two bulging shopping bags. A younger man in a suit slid past her. Jennifer dipped her head down as he passed, hoping he wasn't from the press. But he carried on his way, not even breaking stride before reaching the end of the road and turning the corner. She watched him, aware of her own strangled breathing.

The first report was about her and Catherine. John's denial had prompted speculation about Jennifer's future, and the reporters were relishing the opportunity to go over old ground. To remind listeners of her earlier treacheries.

She closed her eyes and leaned back in her seat. She needed to sleep. Maybe she could just nod off here, spend the afternoon in peace. Would anyone notice?

Of course they would. She imagined tomorrow's front page. Not just a traitor and a slut, but someone who slept in her own car.

The introduction ended with the announcement that an interview with Catherine was coming up. Jennifer's eyes shot open.

She pulled herself upright and yanked up the volume.

"Good afternoon, Minister." The interviewer's tone did nothing to conceal his delight at getting the interview.

"Afternoon," came Catherine's curt reply. Her voice was steady, upbeat even. Jennifer held her breath.

"I'll cut to the chase," continued the interviewer. Catherine made a sound: a laugh?

"Jennifer Sinclair hasn't denied that you and she have met a number of times in hotel rooms. What can you tell us about these meetings?"

"Well, I'm not denying them, for a start."

Jennifer frowned. Where was this going?

"Good. Can you tell us what the purpose of these meetings was? Ms Sinclair claims that you were sharing information."

Another laugh, this time unmistakeable. "Well, she would say that."

A pause while the reporter waited for Catherine to continue. Jennifer's knuckles were white now.

"The fact is that Jennifer Sinclair is known to be a close confidante of John Hunter's," Catherine continued. "If anyone was looking for information, it was me and not her."

"Mmm-hmm. So there wasn't a friendship between the two of you?"

Catherine took a breath. "There was, once. I wouldn't say so anymore."

Jennifer glared at the radio.

"And you deny that you were having an affair?"

"Oh goodness yes. Let me get this straight. The meetings between myself and Jennifer Sinclair were an idea of the Prime Minister's. He knew that we'd been friends, and that she had John Hunter's ear. He also knew how prone she was to betraying her own party."

Jennifer gasped. A movement near her house caught her eye. A woman had jumped out of one of the cars and was hurrying up her drive. She knocked the door. No-one answered.

Jennifer turned the key in the ignition and turned the car round, making for the office.

H er phone was ringing on the passenger seat next to her. She ignored it and ploughed on towards the office, determined to hide.

At last she parked the car and picked it up. Three calls: two unknown numbers, and John.

She grimaced.

She stared at his name on the screen, considering. She'd have to speak to him sooner or later.

She dialled, surprised when it was answered after one ring. She cleared her throat, ready to deal with his new secretary. But it was John.

"Jennifer," he said.

"John." She clenched her fists, feeling sweat glide onto her palms.

"This isn't looking good for you." His voice was dull.

"No." She bit her tongue. Best not to tell him that it would be better for her if he'd been more supportive. Not on the phone, anyway.

"We need to talk," he said. "In person."

She nodded, relieved. With John's help, she could weather this. What Catherine was saying didn't matter. It was John's friendship that counted now. She hoped it was strong enough.

"Thanks. When?"

"Monday, first thing. Party offices. Not the House."

"OK. See you then."

He grunted and hung up. She looked out of the car at the shoppers passing her, wondering what they thought of their MP. If indeed they cared.

41

SEPTEMBER 2021. LONDON

JENNIFER WAS RUNNING LATE. SHE SPRINTED ACROSS Parliament Square, cursing herself under her breath. She'd ripped the seam of her sleeve in the rush to get off her delayed train and hoped she'd find time to straighten herself up before confronting John.

Weaving through the crowds, she crashed into a woman coming the other way. She bent over to rub her shin, which had caught the woman's heel, then looked up to apologise.

"Catherine!"

She scanned the crowds; who would be watching? But the people surrounding them were mainly foreign tourists posing for selfies.

"Jennifer," Catherine gasped. She leaned towards her then pulled back, also looking around them. Sharp patches of red appeared on her cheeks.

"Catherine," Jennifer repeated. She looked back towards Big Ben. "I need to be somewhere. See you around."

Catherine gave an uncertain smile and stepped back.

As Jennifer strode away, she could feel the other woman's eyes boring into her back.

"Stop!"

She turned to see Catherine coming after her. A crowd of tourists passed between them, pausing to take a selfie. Catherine pushed through. She grabbed Jennifer's arm and lowered her voice.

"We need to talk."

"What about?" As if she needed to ask.

Catherine's eyes scanned Jennifer's face. Her forehead had a sheen of sweat and she looked more nervous than Jennifer had ever seen her. What had Trask said to her?

"It's not what you think," Catherine said. She was scanning the crowds again, her head dipped low.

Jennifer cocked her head and raised an eyebrow, saying nothing. She wondered if this was related to being 'prone to betraying her party'.

"There's something I need to tell you about."

Jennifer straightened up. "What?"

Catherine looked around. "I can't tell you here. But I have some information I think you'll want to know about."

"What information?"

An icy shudder ran down her spine. She glanced at her watch. She was nearly half an hour late for John.

"Catherine, what information?"

"I can't tell you here. Meet me later. This afternoon, at one."

"Where? Not the hotel."

Catherine described a pub to her. A pub just off Leicester Square, away from Westminster. How did she know these places?

"OK. This had better be straight up."

"Of course it is." She blushed. "I'm sorry. About what I said, on the news. It was Leonard's idea."

Jennifer grunted. Leonard's idea or not, it was Catherine who said it.

~

The party offices were quiet, with just a few voices echoing along the corridors. She listened to the sounds of the building, wondering who was watching her. What John's staff already knew.

John wasn't in yet – thank god – and she was ushered to a seat outside his office.

"I'll be in the Ladies', if he arrives," she told his assistant. She needed to compose herself.

Once inside, she scanned the toilets for other occupants and then, on finding none, slumped against the sinks. Her face in the mirror was pale, her mousy blonde hair wispy and dishevelled and her shirt crumpled. She stood back to survey herself and straighten her clothes.

She didn't want to be here. In truth, she wished she'd run after Catherine and not let her get away until she'd told her what the hell was going on. But the shock of the encounter had left her unable to think straight.

Information. What information was Catherine talking about? Was it about Trask? Was Catherine still working with her? Or was this a plot, a lie?

She leaned in to the mirror and dabbed at her eyes. An angry red blotch had appeared under one of them and her mascara had run. She licked her finger and dabbed at the skin around her eyes, only making it sting.

Finally she drew back and took a deep breath. Time to face John; Catherine would have to wait.

When she got back to his office, he still wasn't there. She sighed; his lateness had made the intended point, couldn't he just show up now? She lowered herself to the chair and pulled her phone out, anxious for distraction. Then she put it back in her pocket; she didn't want to read about herself.

John's assistant was shooting her glances from a neighbouring office. She tried to read what she could from the man's expression but it gave nothing away.

At nine am John breezed into the corridor, an hour late. He ignored Jennifer, muttering to the assistant instead. The assistant pointed her out and he looked round.

She smiled at him. He nodded in return.

"Won't keep you long, Jennifer," he said, disappearing into his office.

After another twenty minutes the assistant's phone buzzed and he waved Jennifer in.

Jennifer hadn't been in here before; she always met John in his Commons office behind the Speaker's chair. This was a medium sized, nondescript room, with modern office furniture and papers strewn across surfaces. John stood by the large, aluminium-framed window looking out on to the street. Behind him, the city was well into its morning; she could hear the buzz of traffic and occasional sound of a horn or a shout from someone passing by. Jennifer hesitated, feeling the flimsy door at her back, and smoothed her skirt.

After ignoring her for a moment he moved towards a seating area, motioning for her to sit down. She waited for him to pick a chair, then sat at right-angles to him, her back to the door. He sat back in the ugly chair and surveyed her in silence, his chin resting on his fingers. Jennifer waited for him to speak.

Instead, he leaned over the low table and rifled through a pile of anonymous brown files. He stopped at one and slapped it onto the glass surface without opening it.

"So," he said.

Jennifer raised an eyebrow. "So."

"What are you expecting from me?"

She stiffened. What *was* she expecting?

"You were in on this from the start. I know you can't admit to that – I'm not stupid. But I think I can expect your support."

"Do you?"

Stay calm, she told herself. "I do."

"Hmm."

She said nothing, waiting for more.

"Have you spoken to Yusuf?" he asked.

"Yusuf?"

He nodded.

"I don't understand," she said. "What's Yusuf got to do with this?"

He sighed. She narrowed her eyes. What wasn't he telling her?

She tried to laugh. "If you think he believes all this crap about me and Catherine having an affair—"

"No, that's not it."

She watched him, puzzled. Had *he* spoken to Yusuf? And why would he go behind her back like that? Why wouldn't Yusuf tell her?

John stood up. He pushed at the skin of his forehead. He looked tired.

"Look," he said. "There's going to be more trouble, you're going to be at the centre of it, and it won't be good for the party."

"John, this is going to blow over tomorrow. Well, it will

if you let it. All I need is your support. Not publicly, of course. But if we all keep quiet about it, it will go away."

"Oh Jennifer, I really hope so. For your sake."

"John?" She hesitated. "This trouble you're taking about, is it the Catherine thing? Or something else?"

He frowned but said nothing.

"Would— would this be Home Office related?"

His head shot up. "Who've you been talking to?"

She thought of Catherine, her body language when they had collided on Parliament Square. She had looked worried, scared even. "No one."

"So why're you—"

"Nothing, John. I'm talking nonsense."

"I bloody hope so."

She stood up to face him. "I need your support, John. Just tacit. I think we've been through enough together for me to deserve that."

"Together? We've been enemies for a lot of the time."

"John, please. That's behind us."

He grunted, then let out a long breath and rubbed his palms together. "You're right. I'm sorry. I'll keep quiet about this Catherine thing."

"Thank you."

He walked to the door and opened it. As she passed him, he put a hand on her shoulder.

"Take care, Jennifer."

She frowned. "Of course. And you."

"No. I mean it. Watch yourself."

She forced a smile and left, confused.

42

THE PUB WAS QUIET, JUST A YOUNG COUPLE HUDDLED in a corner, a man at one end of the bar and the barman absent-mindedly filling bowls with nuts.

Jennifer shuffled in, feeling conspicuous. She glanced at the man sitting at the bar; he was about her age, wearing a dark suit and a pale trench coat. Old fashioned. He didn't look at her. She told herself to stop being paranoid.

She ordered a Coke then took it to the table furthest from the pub's other customers, where she could see the door. This was a bad idea, she thought. Catherine arriving here to meet her would surely attract attention. Someone could recognise them. She considered ringing Catherine, telling her to switch to the hotel, then thought better of it.

She wrapped her fingers around her glass and thought about her conversation with John that morning. She'd never seen him behave so strangely. It added to her rising sense of panic; he'd always been solid, even when they were on opposite sides. If he was with her, that counted for something. But she had no idea if he was now, or not.

She drained her drink and reached into her bag for her

phone. *Catherine, where are you?* She looked at her watch: 1.30. It seemed like today was her day to wait.

Finally she let impatience overcome her and hit the dial button.

"Hello, Catherine Moore."

"Catherine, it's Jennifer."

"Jennifer?" A pause. "Oh, drat."

Jennifer grit her teeth. Catherine couldn't have dragged her all the way here and forgotten about her, surely?

"Where are you?"

"Oh, *hell*. I'm sorry, but I'm not going to make it. Something's come up."

Something? Not something to do with her, she hoped.

"When can you get here?"

"That's just it. I can't."

Jennifer lowered her voice. The barman was closer now, wiping tables. "Then will you tell me what's going on with Samir now please?"

There was silence.

"Catherine?"

"Hang on. I'll find somewhere quiet."

Jennifer gripped the phone while she waited.

"Right," said Catherine finally.

"So?"

"So. So." A pause. "I'm sorry. I can't tell you this. Not on the phone."

Jennifer let an angry shudder run through her. "Well, when can you tell me?"

"I don't know."

"Catherine, you can't do this. I need to know what's going on."

"I know, I know. Look, go back to your office. Go back to the House and go to your office."

"What?" This was ridiculous. "Are you going to meet me there?"

"No. I can't. Just go there. Now."

~

S he stumbled into a taxi. Traffic was heavy and it was all she could manage not to shout at the driver to hurry up. She glared out of the window at the cars, vans and people outside; vehicles crawling past and people hurrying between them.

On Whitehall she gave up and threw some notes at the driver before jumping out and dashing between the cars to the pavement. She started to run towards the Houses of Parliament.

She ran across a side road without stopping to look and almost hit a cyclist.

"Look where you're going, bitch!"

She threw a shouted *sorry!* behind her and carried on running. At last she was at the corner by Westminster tube station. She skidded into the turn, ducking between tourists and tour bus reps.

She reached the entrance to Portcullis House and slowed. She didn't want to attract attention. She hurried through, returning the guards' greetings breathlessly, and dashed to the tunnel that led to the Commons. She kept her head down and ignored the few people who turned to look at her. She sped through the covered walkway towards Westminster Hall then pushed her way inside, her footsteps loud on the stone floor. Tourists milled around in the echoing space; she sped through, keeping her head down. She darted up the steps at the far end and turned the corner towards St Stephens lobby...

...only to crash into a man coming the other way. She dropped her bag, fumbled for it then looked up. He was surrounded by a group of staff, smiling at her and licking his lips.

Leonard Trask.

"Jennifer Sinclair, well, well. In a hurry?"

She stared at him. His eyes were dancing. How much did he know?

"Excuse me," she said, and tried to find a path around his gaggle of aides. He pulled back with a flourish.

"Why of course. Mustn't keep you from whatever it is you're plotting."

She clenched her teeth – *ignore him* – and carried on, clattering her way to the lift and throwing herself inside.

~

The corridor outside Jennifer's office was empty, the only sound the occasional muffled voice or trill of a phone behind a door.

She forced herself to slow down, anxious that no-one should hear her. The last thing she needed was to stop for small talk.

At her door she paused and put her ear to the wood. Was Catherine inside, waiting for her? *Don't be stupid.* How would she get in?

She pulled her keys out of her bag and opened the door gently, ready to face whatever – or whoever – was inside.

All was quiet, but on the floor, immediately behind the door, was a piece of paper.

She lunged at it, peering out to check the corridor before closing the door and dropping her bag. She slumped

to the floor and unfolded the paper. It had no names on –
not hers, not Catherine's.

*Your son's on a list. Suspected of associating with
members of a proscribed organisation. Don't know any more.*

And then, on its own line:

Destroy this.

43

SEPTEMBER 2021. BIRMINGHAM

IT WAS GONE MIDNIGHT WHEN SHE GOT HOME, AND THE house was quiet. She crept up to the bedroom, relieved to find Yusuf awake. He was startled, not expecting her on a Monday night. She put her finger on his lips and told him about her encounter with Catherine, the note.

"Say that again," he said, his voice taut.

"You heard it. I don't want to say it again." She lowered her voice, nodding towards the closed door. "They might hear."

"Where's the note?"

"Here." She'd taken it from her bag before coming upstairs and tucked it in her palm. She unfurled it and handed it to him.

"Why didn't you call me?"

"It didn't feel safe." Was she overreacting? "Sorry."

"Bloody hell," he breathed. "They can't have any evidence, anything concrete, surely?"

Jennifer looked at him. "What do you mean? Our son isn't a terrorist."

"We both know that, of course we do. But do we know

about his friends? You know what they're like about associations now. You have to be careful who you spend time with."

"Yusuf, is there something you're not telling me? Is it those kids he played truant with?"

He said nothing.

"Yusuf? Has it happened again?"

Yusuf, as the one at home on weekdays, would know if Samir hadn't been at school. He would know when Samir was getting home, and if he was keeping to the curfew they'd imposed. But he'd have told her, if anything was wrong. He shook his head.

"No. He's stuck to the rules. But he has made some new friends lately, not from school. Just boys he met when he was out with me. Just boys— like him. A couple of girls, their sisters I think."

"How well do you know them, love?"

"I know their parents." He paused. "Most of them, anyway." He looked at her. "I didn't think anything of it. They're just local Muslim kids. What harm could he come to?"

He slumped down on the bed. Jennifer sat next to him, their thighs touching.

"We need to think about what we should do," she said. "What we say to him."

"Do?" He turned to her. "All he's done is make some friends. And bloody Catherine Moore thinks he's a terrorist."

He hugged himself, shaking.

Jennifer put a hand on his back. "We need to talk to him. Make sure he knows to be careful. And maybe we need to keep tighter checks on who he spends time with—"

He turned, his eyes swollen.

"Jennifer, does it not occur to you that the problem here isn't who our son makes friends with?"

"I know, I just—"

He shook his head. "No. You don't get it. The problem is this bloody government, turning us all into criminals. Segregating us. Maybe that's what you should be focusing on. Maybe you should be taking the fight to them. Or have you given up?"

She closed her eyes. "Not this again. Look, that isn't the issue. I'm already doing what I can to fight Trask, and you know it. But Samir's got to stay out of trouble. He's just sixteen, he might not understand what his new friends are like. I can't face work tomorrow. I'll stay home, have a chat with him."

Yusuf sighed and blew his nose into a tissue. "If you have to. But he won't like it."

~

Jennifer woke early the next morning. She'd slept fitfully, her dreams full of Samir.

She checked her alarm clock and groaned. It was five thirty. She needed more sleep but knew it wasn't going to come. She looked at Yusuf, still asleep, and eased out of bed, glancing at the boys' doors as she passed them. All was quiet.

She made herself a coffee and fired up her laptop, ploughing through emails. Her brain felt foggy. Finally she gave up and closed the screen with a sigh, checking the kitchen clock. Six am. Samir would be getting up for school in half an hour. Should she wake him, give them more time for this conversation?

This would need more than the spare five minutes he

would allow her in the midst of his morning routine. She checked the clock again and decided to give it fifteen more minutes. She leaned back in her chair and rubbed her eyes. A headache was brewing behind her temples.

Quarter of an hour later she pushed back her chair and headed for the stairs. She padded up, not wanting to wake Hassan. She stopped outside Samir's door and paused to take a couple of deep breaths.

She knocked quietly and pushed the door open, adjusting her eyes to the gloom.

"Samir," she whispered. "Wake up."

There was no response. She made her way to the bed, her hands in front of her. Samir had blackout blinds and the room was in total darkness.

Her shins hit the bed and she winced. She put a hand down, feeling for his body beneath the duvet. *Go gently,* she told herself.

Her fingers brushed the fabric. It was cold. She placed her palm on it then stiffened. The duvet was flat. She pulled back, squinting. She flicked his bedside light on and refocused on the bed. It was empty.

She turned towards the room, expecting to see him sitting at his desk, awake and doing last minute homework already. But there had been no glow from the screen when she entered. His desk was empty. No laptop and no Samir.

She scanned the room, her heart picking up pace. She stumbled to the door and threw herself towards the bathroom, falling into the door and expecting it to push back against her weight, locked.

It fell open and she almost slipped on the tiles.

She dashed to Hassan's room and looked around the half open door. He was waking, rubbing his eyes and yawning luxuriantly. There was no one else with him. She darted out, relieved that he hadn't spotted her.

Jennifer stumbled backwards into the hall and leaned against the wall, her eyes pricking. Where was he? Had he heard them last night? Maybe he'd just got up early and gone to school.

No. School wouldn't be open for hours, and it only took him twenty minutes to get there.

She clenched her fists and made for her own room, where Yusuf was snoring lightly. She put a hand on his back and pulled him into wakefulness.

He rolled over, groaning. "What is it?"

"I can't find Samir."

Yusuf registered the tone of her voice, an octave higher than normal, and jerked upright. "What?"

She shrugged. "He's not in his room. Or Hassan's. Nor downstairs."

She frowned. Maybe he had slipped downstairs, while she was in the bathroom? She squeezed Yusuf's hand then dashed downstairs, running from room to room.

"He's not here," she cried, not caring now who she woke.

Yusuf was beside her, dragging on his dressing gown. "Are you sure?"

She nodded, blinking back the fizzing behind her eyes.

"Maybe he's gone to school early."

She spun round. "It's half past six."

He dragged his fingernails through his beard. "Shit."

She felt her chest hollow out. "Did he hear us last night? Could he have heard us?"

"I don't know. I don't think so." A pause. "We were quiet – weren't we?"

She shrugged. "If he was outside our door..."

She fell into a chair, shivering. "Where is he, Yusuf?"

Yusuf stayed standing, staring at the wall. "I don't know."

"You go out with him. You know who he hangs out with. Could he have gone to one of them?"

Yusuf shook his head. "I don't know."

She glared at him then made for his room again, taking the stairs two at a time. After a couple of minutes she called him from the top of the stairs.

"His rucksack's gone. His phone, his wallet and his laptop."

Hassan came out of his room, his eyes dark pools. "Mummy? Mummy, what's happened? Where's Samir?"

"I don't know," she snapped. He started to cry.

She closed her eyes and dug her fingernails into her palm, willing herself to be patient. Yusuf came up the stairs and pushed past her, laying a hand briefly on her shoulder. He disappeared into Samir's room. There were the sounds of drawers being yanked open, doors being flung wide.

He reappeared, shaking his head. Jennifer stared at him, her breathing ragged. Hassan was leaning into her, clutching at her stomach.

Yusuf's face was grey, his muscles slack. "He— he's run away."

44

SEPTEMBER 2021. BIRMINGHAM AND LONDON

DROPPING HASSAN AT SCHOOL, JENNIFER FELT SURE the eyes of the other parents were on her. She pushed the straps of his rucksack onto his back and gave his hand a squeeze as she let him go into the school. Having him walk away from her so soon after Samir's disappearance felt like her heart was being torn out. She had spent the last couple of hours trying not to pass her anxiety onto him but couldn't keep herself from grabbing him every time he passed her and giving him a tight hug.

She glanced around the other parents as she headed back to her car, wondering if any of them knew what she was going through. Some of them had older siblings in Samir's year at secondary school; would they have talked about him, his fighting and his intention to run away?

On the drive home, she tried to focus on the road, rubbing her eyes furiously and muttering at herself to keep it together. Stopped at traffic lights, the man in the car next to her did a double take as he recognised the local MP. She stared at him, horrified, and sped off as soon as the lights changed.

At home, Yusuf was on the phone. She slid past him in the kitchen, her eyes a question mark. He shook his head and she felt herself deflate.

"Who was that?" she asked when he put his phone back in his pocket.

"One of his friends' mums." He dropped into the chair opposite. "None of them know anything. Their kids are all at school."

She rubbed her forehead. "We need to call the police."

His voice shook. "No. Not if he's under suspicion. It'll just precipitate things, give them cause to think he's done something that he hasn't."

She stood up. "But that's ridiculous. He's missing, and we have to get help."

"It's only been a few hours."

"We don't know that. What time did you last see him?"

Yusuf closed his eyes. "I've been running through yesterday evening in my head. He told me he was going to bed at nine. That's the last I saw of him." He looked up, his eyes searching her face. "I should have checked on him, but you know how he is..."

She nodded. Samir didn't like being disturbed in his room at night. A wave of nausea swept over her and she rushed to the toilet but nothing came. She leaned over it for a few moments, clutching the seat, trying to control her breathing.

She staggered back to the kitchen. "We don't leave this house until he's back," she said.

"He's probably just playing truant again. He'll creep back this afternoon after school finishes, tail between his legs."

She spun round. "I don't think he will. He's played

truant before, but he always kept up the pretence of going to school."

"Things change."

"Yes, but that's exactly it. Things *have* changed. I came home last night telling you what Catherine told me, and he overheard us. I'm sure of it. That's why he's gone."

"We can't be sure of that."

She lifted her face to glare at him. "It's a hell of a coincidence."

"Please, Jen, we need to take this calmly. I'll make a few more calls. You never know. And we wait till five. Then we'll decide what to do."

His head was cocked and his face pale. His eyes were searching her face for a response. She let herself slump against the kitchen counter. "OK."

~

By five, there was no sign of Samir. Jennifer sat in the front room, staring at the window.

She checked her watch again. Five past five. Yusuf was upstairs, distracting himself by changing beds.

She headed up the stairs. Hassan passed her, flinching as she approached.

She stooped to put her hands upon his shoulders. "Hey sweetie. You OK?"

"S'pose so. Where's Samir?"

She swallowed, pushing brightness into her voice. "He's at a friend's. Sleepover."

"It's a school night."

She bent down to him. "Maybe when you're sixteen, we'll let you have sleepovers on a school night."

He yelled approval then clattered downstairs. She shivered and went to find Yusuf.

"It's gone five," she told him.

He was tugging pillowcases over the pillows in their room; he didn't stop or turn to face her. "I know."

"I think we should call the police now."

He turned and sat on the bed. He looked worn out; his cheeks sagged and his eyes were rimmed with black circles. She sat next to him and took his hand.

"I know you're worried, but we have to find him."

"I know."

"So?"

"Not yet." He tried to her, taking his face in his hands. "Please. I'm worried what will happen to him if they arrest him."

"What makes you think they'll do that?"

"You know what Catherine told you. You know what things are like now. People suspected of being involved in terrorist groups face deportation." He paused. "Even sixteen year olds."

"But we don't know—"

"Exactly." He tightened his grip. "That's what scares me. We have to find him, Jennifer. Of course we do. But when you've seen the things I have, you stop trusting the police."

"We have to trust someone."

He stood up, grabbing another pillowcase. "But who, Jen? Who can we trust?" He paused and put his hands on his hips. "Did I tell you about Asif Malik?"

Jennifer shook her head.

"He was under suspicion. His mum came to see me. I started the process of writing letters, finding out what I could. There was nothing. At least nothing anyone would let me, his local councillor, have access to." He licked his lips. "They arrested him a week later. He was sixteen, Samir's age. And his parents haven't been able to see him. They don't know where he is. They weren't allowed to be at his trial, if there was a trial."

"What was he under suspicion of?"

"That's not the point! Why aren't you listening to me?"

"Yusuf. Samir hasn't done anything wrong. He's safer here, with us. We need to get him back. That means calling the police."

"No."

"What do you mean, no?"

"This is something we both have to consent to. I say no. It's too risky."

She let herself fall back onto the bed, her limbs heavy. "So what do you suggest we do?"

"Go see Catherine. Get her to tell you everything she knows. Then at least we know what the risk is."

She nodded, the ceiling blurring above her. "OK. I'll talk to her tomorrow." She sat up. "But once I've done that, if he's not back tomorrow night I want to call the police."

He shrugged. "That depends on what Catherine tells you."

~

"You know this place?" Jennifer asked, looking at the gin and tonics Catherine had brought from the bar. They were in the pub where Jennifer had waited last time. It was busier tonight, with five tables occupied. The barman was attentive, coming back to check on her twice before Catherine arrived. It made her uncomfortable.

Catherine nodded. "Helps to get away from the usual haunts sometimes." She pulled off her coat and sat down to face Jennifer: she was perched on the seat edge and kept tugging at her sleeve.

"What is it, Catherine? What's going on?"

Catherine glanced towards the bar. She said nothing but took a gulp of her drink.

"Tell me, please."

Catherine's eyes roamed over her face as if she was trying to make a decision. Jennifer took a sip at her drink, irritated. She pinched the bridge of her nose, feeling strung out.

Catherine let out a long breath and clenched her hands together in her lap. Her glass was empty.

"Look, I shouldn't tell you this," she said. "But it's going to affect you. You and your family."

Jennifer sat up straight. "Yes?"

"Before I tell you this, I want you to swear you won't tell a soul. I know you'll tell Yusuf, but, please, he has to not tell anyone either."

"OK. But how can I know that *you* won't?"

Catherine's shoulders slumped. "What do you mean?"

"After what you've been saying to the press, I'm not sure why I should trust you."

She pursed her lips. "I'm sorry. We both had to defend ourselves, didn't we? I didn't say anything that you didn't."

Jennifer blushed; she was right.

Catherine picked up her glass, draining the last drops. Behind her, a group of drinkers swelled as more people came into the pub; a man stepped backwards, jostling Catherine and turning to offer a laughing apology. She nodded at him then leaned in towards Jennifer, pulling at her sleeve again. "Anyway." She lowered her voice. "Look, this is just something I read in a file. I may not have all the story."

"Go on then."

"It's just that – well – if I tell you, I'll be breaking the law. You can't tell anyone."

Jennifer clenched her fists. "Tell me."

Catherine examined her hands and then picked at a hanging nail. Her other nails were as neat as ever, but that one looked as if it had been bitten.

"I have access to information," she whispered. "On suspected terrorist activity. Not everything. There's far too much MI5 is watching for me to see everything."

"Mm-hmm." Jennifer felt cold.

"Sometimes other names are in the files. Associates, followers. That sort of thing." She reached for her glass, then gave it a disappointed look. "I shouldn't be telling you this."

Jennifer nodded, her heartbeat thundering in her ears.

"I saw Samir's name. He hasn't done anything. Not as far as I can tell. But I think he's been involved with people who have."

Jennifer thought of Samir's anger, the truancies. That book. She shook her head. "But he's sixteen."

Catherine leaned in further, her voice a low murmur. "I know. But it's quite common, you know, for boys to be recruited. They're impressionable. That's the theory."

Jennifer knew this, of course. She'd talked to enough women whose sons were under suspicion. Was she one of these women now?

"But he just goes out with Yusuf. Helps people out," she said. There was a lump in her throat. Where was Samir now? Had he already been arrested?

"I'm sorry, Jennifer. I really am. But I saw his name in a

list of people associated with a group. A proscribed organisation."

Jennifer remembered John's behaviour in his party office. "Who else knows about this?"

She shook her head. "I can't discuss that. Sorry."

Jennifer stood up. "But it's ridiculous!"

Catherine looked around the pub, her eyes wide. Jennifer sat down. "My son is not a terrorist."

"You need to know that the group, the one he's involved with..." She paused.

Tell me, dammit, thought Jennifer.

"Some of them have already been arrested. It won't be long before the police catch up with the rest."

"What kind of group?"

"I can't tell you that."

"What have they done? What's Samir done?"

"Shh, please. I can't tell you that either. But as far as I can tell, I don't think *he's* actually done anything. Not yet."

Jennifer stared at her, tears welling. Catherine pulled a tissue from her bag and handed it to her, scanning the bar again.

Jennifer didn't need to be reminded of the harshness of anti-terrorist law. Samir could be detained without trial for up to six months.

She could hear her own breathing, despite the noise of the pub. It was shallow and laboured.

"Do you— do you think he's at risk of deportation?" she whispered.

There was a moment's silence. The barman passed them, making Jennifer shudder. How much had he heard?

"Do you?" Jennifer asked.

A shrug. "I don't know. He could be, or maybe an

internment facility. Or maybe nothing." She grabbed Jennifer's hand and squeezed it. "I'm so sorry about this."

Jennifer opened her mouth to tell her about Samir's disappearance then thought better of it. She nodded, her lips tight.

"I have to go. I'm sorry. I can't tell you anything else." She licked her lips, bending to Jennifer and whispering. "Good luck." Jennifer stood and they hugged each other tight, not letting go for some time.

Jennifer waited a few moments then followed Catherine to the door. She paused outside and watched as Catherine walked away along the damp pavement, glancing back then opening her umbrella before disappearing in the crowds.

Jennifer shook herself out, stifling a wail. She scanned the street urgently, hailing a taxi.

PART IV

SEPTEMBER 2021. LONDON.

45

SEPTEMBER 2021. LONDON

JENNIFER DRAGGED HERSELF BACK TO HER FLAT, wishing she could just go home and leave London forever. But she needed to take stock and plan what she and Yusuf would do next. He was at home waiting for Samir, but she could be of more help here in Westminster. Tomorrow she would speak to John, see what help he could give.

She pulled her phone out of her bag as she jumped out of the taxi. Phoning Yusuf had become something tainted with dread. Every time she felt compelled to ask him if there was any news, and every time there was none. If Samir did turn up or get in touch, he wouldn't wait to tell her.

But tonight, she would have to tell him what Catherine had told her. She looked at his name on her phone screen, formulating the words in her head. At last she took a deep breath and put the phone to her ear.

"Hi." He sounded tired. She glanced at her watch; it was nine pm.

"Hi."

"What did she say?"

Jennifer looked up and down the street. On the other side of the road a man was walking in the same direction as her, matching her pace.

"Can I call you back in five minutes?" she whispered. "I'm almost at the flat."

"OK. Is there nothing you can tell me now?"

She cupped the phone with her hand. "I just saw her. She's confirmed what she told me last time." She looked at the man again; he had picked up pace. She was being paranoid. "I'll fill you in when I get back."

"OK. Take care." Yusuf didn't like her walking to her flat at night; this wasn't the most salubrious part of London and the thought of her making her way home alone brought out his protective nature. But now they needed to divert that to Samir.

At last she reached her front door. Her keys were ready in her hand and she slipped inside, watching the man recede down the street as she closed the door.

She took the stairs two at a time and had the door to her flat open just as quickly. She flicked on a light switch and threw her coat onto the sofa.

She froze.

On the coffee table was an empty glass of milk.

She cast about wildly, turning towards the hallway.

"Hello?" she called, tentatively.

She looked back at the coffee table. The empty glass sat alone on its surface, the unmistakeable film of milk coating its inside. She never drank milk like that. And she'd loaded the dishwasher before leaving for work two days ago, last time she'd been here.

Somebody had been here.

She threw open the door to her bedroom. The bed was untouched and the lights were out. Her heart was pounding now. She went back through the living room into the kitchen and started opening cupboards.

A packet of biscuits had been opened, one she kept for the boys's visits. And a Pot Noodle had gone. She pictured her kitchen at home, the same items placed where Samir could find them.

She clenched her fists.

"Samir?" she called, her voice shaking. There was no response.

She ran to the bathroom – empty – then flung open the cupboard in the hallway. It was empty except for her Hoover, some jackets and the kids' sleeping bags. She closed the door and leaned against it. She slid down to the floor, resting her feet against the wall opposite.

How long ago had he been here? And where was he now? She staggered upright and ran to the front window in the living room, pulling the curtains aside. The street was empty save for a couple walking away from her, wrapped tightly around each other. She squinted at them then shook her head.

She turned back to the room, picked the glass up and sniffed it. It smelt fresh. She took it to the kitchen and opened the fridge again. The litre carton of milk she'd bought two days ago was almost empty. Some pizza she'd kept from a takeaway had gone.

She opened the bin lid. The box from the pizza was inside, and some tissues.

Her phone rang and she almost jumped across the room.

"Yusuf?"

"I've been waiting for you to call. Everything OK?"

"Yusuf, can you check something for me?"

He hesitated. "Of course."

"Your key to the flat. Is it there?"

"Why?"

"Just check, please."

The line went quiet and she heard movement at the other end of the line as Yusuf went to the jug on the hall table. She listened to him rattling through the assorted keys that they kept in there.

"They're gone. Did you take them?"

She brought her hand up to her mouth, her body feeling as if she'd been scooped out. "He's here. He's in London."

"What? Samir?"

She nodded. "He's been in my flat. Recently, I think."

There was a long sigh at the end of the line. "Thank god for that."

"Seriously."

"At least we know where he is."

"London is no place for a sixteen year old on his own." She pictured the young people she passed every night between Westminster and the flat; huddled against walls, perched on the pavement, hands out, begging for the means to live. She always muttered a brief apology, believing that she was helping them more by donating to homeless charities.

She gasped. Was Samir out there now, sitting in a doorway somewhere? Or was he roaming the streets, waiting until she left her flat again?

"Hang on a minute." She pocketed her phone and rushed back to the window, leaning against the glass to see the street better. A man stood outside a house opposite, looking up at the first floor windows, calling to the occupant. Further along, two women hurried away from her, heels audible through the glass. There was no one else.

She picked up her phone again. "Sorry. It just occurred to me he could be watching the flat."

"Do you think he is?"

"I've got no idea." She dropped onto the sofa, scratching at its fabric with her free hand. "Where is he, love?"

She heard muttering on the other end. "You OK?" she asked, anxious.

"Yes. Sorry." He sounded impatient. "Hassan needs me."

"Of course." She swallowed. "How is he?"

"He's OK. Asks after Samir every ten minutes but I've managed to appease him with the story we agreed."

She nodded. Before she'd left, they'd told Hassan that Samir was staying with a friend for a few days, catching up on his studies. It was unlikely but not impossible, and had elicited some scowls from his younger brother. Hopefully he would be home before they had to tell him the truth.

"Jen, what did Catherine say? Is he under suspicion?"

She recounted the details of her conversation in the unfamiliar pub. It felt like hours ago if not days. While she spoke, she paced the flat, checking every square inch again and again. Repeatedly she returned to the window and checked outside, making sure the lights were off behind her so he wouldn't see.

"Sit tight, Jen. He'll appear. Soon."

"I'm not so sure. He clearly got out before I came home."

"It could be a coincidence. Maybe he wants your help.

She shook her head. "He probably thinks he's safer in

London, more anonymous. But this is a bolthole for him, somewhere he knows he can find food and shelter." She walked back to the door and rested her hand on it. "I don't think he'll come back if he knows I'm here."

"You're wrong. He needs you."

"Maybe. But he doesn't know that. Maybe I should clear out. Then at least he'll have somewhere safe."

"I don't like that idea."

She sat on the hall floor again. The flat was in darkness now and she could hear noises from the flats around her. Somewhere, music was playing; loud rap. Beyond the wall she could hear her neighbours arguing. She squeezed her eyes shut.

"Alright," she said. "I'll stay here. God, I hope you're right Yusuf."

～

"What time is it?"

She'd been woken by her phone: Yusuf.

"Is he there now?"

"I'd have called you if he was."

"Please, don't take it out on me."

"Sorry." She dug her thumbnail into her palm. Her legs felt heavy. She made her way into the living room and lowered herself to the arm of the sofa. She perched there, staring towards the window. If he was out there, he wasn't going to let her see him.

"I think I should come down," Yusuf said.

"No. I don't think that'll help. Hassan needs you there right now. Besides, where would they go while you were dashing down here?"

"To my mum's."

She nodded her head. Hassan loved going to Granny's, and adored playing with her little dog, an elderly but friendly Yorkshire Terrier. "I know. But I don't think it would help. If we're mob handed we could just scare him away."

"What do you suggest?"

"I'll try coming back at a time he doesn't expect me. Meanwhile I need to do more to help him."

"How do you mean?"

"I haven't been thinking straight, love. I'm the bloody Shadow Home Secretary. I can stop this."

"I'm not so—"

"Yusuf, if all the hard work I've put in to get here doesn't mean I can help my son when he needs me, what's the point?"

"You know that's not why—"

"I know. But I have to help him. Even if we get him back, he's still under suspicion. He could be arrested any day."

"I know that. So does he."

She sighed. "That's why I'm so scared."

She stood up and moved to the window, staring along the street towards Waterloo.

"Yusuf, I'll call you back later."

"What?"

"Later. I promise."

She hung up, not waiting for his reply, and headed for the front door.

~

Jennifer didn't go as far as the Houses of Parliament. Instead she stopped at the hotel that faced it across the river. She made her way up the escalator to the first floor lobby inside, looking around her as surreptitiously as she could. On a Thursday afternoon, this place was full of tourists, oblivious to her.

She found a table in the far corner of the bar and sat down to wait. She pulled her phone out of her bag and tried to read through her emails – twenty had arrived since she'd left the flat – but couldn't concentrate.

At last she heard footsteps approaching and looked up. She smiled. "Catherine."

"I don't understand what's so urgent." Catherine glanced around them, but the surrounding tourists were oblivious to them. "I don't think this is a good idea."

Jennifer licked her lips. "I'm sorry. But this couldn't wait."

Catherine nodded and sat down, looking at her watch. Jennifer leaned in towards her.

"I appreciate the fact that you told me about Samir," she muttered.

Catherine nodded but said nothing.

"I know what you're risking. What it means."

Catherine nodded again, her face tight. She'd broken the Official Secrets Act to tell Jennifer about Samir, and they both knew it.

"He's in London," she whispered.

Catherine's eyes widened. "Where?"

"He's been to my flat."

"Why?"

Jennifer swallowed. "He ran away from home. In Birmingham. After he heard me telling Yusuf about your note. We didn't know where he was for three days."

"You've seen him?"

"No. He's been letting himself in while I'm out."

Catherine let out a long breath. "You really shouldn't be telling me this."

"I know." Jennifer smoothed her palms on her skirt; they were clammy. "But I need your help."

"No. I need to stay out of this."

"I don't agree."

Catherine leaned back, looking annoyed. "Don't be ridiculous. I'm a minister in the Home Office. I've already been stupid to tell you what I have. Besides, I don't have the power to stop this."

"I believe you do."

Catherine frowned. "That's madness, Jennifer. I can't possibly stop a police operation that's—"

"That's not what I mean."

"Well, what do you mean?" Catherine looked at her watch again.

"You told me he was under suspicion. You know what that meant. You're involved in this, like it or not."

Catherine frowned. She looked back towards the escalators then pulled her chair closer to Jennifer's. "Are you threatening me?"

"No. Of course not. But you cared enough to warn me. You can help me fix this. And not just for Samir."

"How, exactly? I can't just make a phone call and change—"

"That's not what I mean."

A sigh. "What, then?"

Jennifer pursed her lips. "The meetings we were having. Before all this."

"Ye-es."

"What we were trying to do. Our plan."

"Your plan, you mean."

Jennifer ignored that. "We can pick it up again. We can speed things up."

"I'm not so sure."

Jennifer eyed her. "Do you want my son to be deported?"

Catherine shook her head.

"Well then. Just listen to what I have to say."

46

SEPTEMBER 2021. LONDON

JENNIFER HURRIED BACK TO HER FLAT, ANXIOUS TO surprise Samir if she could. But the flat was empty and there were no changes from earlier.

She stared at the empty living room, her chest deflating. After a few moments standing in silence, she turned on her heel and made for the shop on the corner of her street. She kept her head down as she picked out items; instant noodles, junky breakfast cereals, Samir's favourite biscuits. She dashed back to the flat, checking her watch and cursing under her breath as she picked up pace. She dumped the groceries on the coffee table, hopeful.

There was a debate in the Chamber that she couldn't miss; a minor amendment to the Prevention of Terrorism Act. The topic was related to the next day's debate, and would serve to take the temperature of MPs. John was already in his seat when she slipped in, listening to her own Tory opposite number speaking. He frowned as she slid into the spot next to him.

"Where have you been?" he hissed.

"Sorry." She hesitated. Could she tell him about Samir? If she'd entrusted her family's secrets to Catherine, surely she could trust John. She looked at him, shaking his head furiously at the opposite benches, and decided it could wait.

She forced herself to concentrate, rifling through the speech she'd prepared with her advisor the day before. Normally she would have gone over it that morning, practised in front of the full length mirror in her bedroom. She'd have to make do without.

When the time came, she hauled herself up, squaring her shoulders. Catherine was directly opposite, avoiding her eye. She was two places along from Trask, who was looking bored more than anything. She kept glancing at him, her expression a mix of wariness and determination. Jennifer wondered what she was thinking. Without her help, Jennifer's plan was empty. Trask would prevail, the government would go from strength to strength, and her family— her family would be torn apart.

Jennifer picked her way through her statement, giving a competent if uninspiring performance. She tried to push more feeling into the words, to clear her head as she spoke. But she was too preoccupied with Samir.

As she sat down, John gave her a curt nod; she'd performed adequately. She'd have to raise her game tomorrow. And so would Catherine. She'd avoided Jennifer's eye throughout her speech; did she have the strength to do to her leader what Jennifer had done to her own, or was she finding a way to say no?

At last the debate ended with the predicted aye vote. The Chamber would be busier tomorrow, packed to its oak-panelled capacity. She needed to prepare.

She made her apologies to John, resolving to call him

later and arrange a drink in the bar so she could confide in him. Instead of heading to her office, she made straight for the flat.

She hurried under the tunnel to Portcullis House and out of the turnstiles, brushing past colleagues, visitors and tourists. She crossed Westminster Bridge and picked up her pace, heading for Waterloo and her flat beyond. She'd considered getting a taxi but then decided she could be stealthier – and probably quicker – on foot.

As she approached her street she slowed, considering the best route. She slid around the corner, staying close to the buildings, and then walked along her side, being careful to stay in the shadow of the houses, tucked in so she couldn't be seen from an upstairs window. She had to be careful not to arouse suspicion, so did her best to walk normally, and not to fall over her own feet in her desperation to find her son.

She opened the front door as quietly as she could, easing it shut behind her. She slid up the stairs, staying close to the wall. Her heart felt like it would pound its way out of her chest.

Outside her flat she paused to regain control of her breathing. If he was in there he would see her through the spy hole. But he had no other way of leaving. She looked at the door and pulled on a smile, just in case.

She turned her key and pushed the door open as naturally as she could.

"Samir?" she called, trying to sound as if she was arriving at the house in Birmingham, as if it was just another day and she was greeting her family as she always did.

The bag on the coffee table had been opened, and the packet of biscuits was missing. The cereal had been opened too, half of its contents gone. A dirty bowl sat in the sink. She tried to imagine Samir arriving here, finding the food and feeding himself. Where was he now?

She picked up her phone. Yusuf answered within two rings.

"He's been here again," she breathed. She was standing at the window, easing the curtain aside to watch the street. It was dark now and the street was quiet, with only a taxi drawing up outside the house opposite. She eyed it, hoping Samir might be inside.

"When?"

"While I was at the House. I can't work out his routine, love. He seems to know when I'm out, but I haven't seen him watching."

"Can you come home at a different time, catch him?"

"I've been trying to." She felt her voice catch.

"At least he's eating."

She nodded, wiping her nose. She sniffed. "Yes."

"That's good. Hold onto it."

"I spoke to Catherine."

"Oh. Why?"

"I asked her to pick things up again. It's our only hope."

A pause. "What did she say?"

She sniffed. "She's going along with it. So far. I'm meeting her again later. Her last chance to back down."

"You really think she'll stab him in the back?"

"I have to believe she will. She told me a few things about him, about the way he treats his ministers."

"I can imagine."

"But that won't be enough. She has to believe that what she's doing is right. She also has to believe that it won't destabilise her party."

"They're the Tories, Jen. They'll survive. Like woodlice, they are."

She thought back to her own rebellion, the way it had made things not better, but worse. Catherine would be considering that too.

"There's a chance they could replace him with someone even worse."

Yusuf snorted. "No such thing." He sighed. "We have to believe that they'll improve. That they'll roll back some of the harsher legislation. You know how many sharks Trask has got snapping at his heels. And that plenty of them think he's gone too far."

She sat down, feeling tired. Could she do this, again? "I know."

There was a crashing sound at the other end of the line followed by shouts. "I've got to go," Yusuf said.

"What's up?"

"Hassan. He's playing up. Missing Samir."

"Give him a kiss from me, will you?" Jennifer wrapped her arms around herself, missing her family. She needed the feel of Yusuf's hands on her skin, the smell of Hassan's hair after a bath.

"He'll turn up," Yusuf said. She wondered what he was going through, so far away. "Try not to worry too much. I love you."

"I love you too."

Her phone pinged and she pulled it away from her ear: Catherine. She switched calls, feeling her stomach clench. "Catherine?"

There was silence. Jennifer gripped her phone, waiting.

"Catherine? Are you there?" She took a final look along the street and drew back from the window, sliding onto the sofa. The flat was cold.

"Sorry. Yes. I've been thinking."

"Yes?" She tried to keep her voice level; Catherine was going to refuse her, of course.

"You're right, I know you are. I've been doing some research, checking some files."

Jennifer felt her chest slacken. "What did you find?"

"He's not alone." A pause. Jennifer waited. "There are dozens like him. Maybe hundreds."

"What do you mean, like him?"

"Kids who haven't done anything wrong – not anything substantive. But they're under suspicion."

Jennifer pursed her lips and let out a whistling breath. They had to stop this.

"So you agree with me that we have to do something about it? This isn't right."

She could hear Catherine's breath; it was stilted.

"Catherine?"

"I don't know."

"You don't know? You've just spent the evening digging into this, risking your job, but you still don't know?"

"Please, Jennifer. Don't talk like that. Not on the phone."

There was another pause.

"OK," Catherine said. "I'll do it."

The line went dead.

Jennifer looked out of the window, wondering again if Samir was watching. Maybe if she went out, he'd come back. She'd walk over Westminster Bridge, then back across Waterloo Bridge. Some fresh air would clear her head.

She looked around the flat as she opened the front door, wishing she knew where Samir was.

Jennifer's head spun as she walked. She rolled words around in her head; things Catherine had told her and things that she would say tomorrow, in the House. Things that they would both say.

Catherine had been doing more digging than she'd originally admitted to. She'd found files on eighty-six children between the ages of twelve and fifteen, all in the same situation as Samir. None of them had done anything wrong, but all of them were associated with people who had. She thought of the day she'd spotted him outside her constituency office, bunking off school. Could he be with those kids now? Could he be in danger?

One case had brought her up short. A twelve-year-old girl in Birmingham, just miles from her own constituency. She'd joined a chat room and got involved in conversations she shouldn't have. It made her think of Hassan. Did she police his computer activity adequately? Did Yusuf keep an eye on him when she wasn't there? And if he found himself in the midst of subversive conversations, would he have the presence of mind to leave quickly, or would he say something that could get him into trouble? He was twelve, and had the naivety and eagerness to jump to conclusions that you'd expect from someone that age. Catherine had seen a photo of the girl; she looked about ten, she said, with pigtails. Hardly a terrorist.

And these were the kind of people Leonard Trask and his party were happy to criminalise, to lock up or deport, along with their families. She shivered, and not just from the cold air as she crossed the Thames, heading back for her flat. When had this started? Was it with Trask's election, with Michael's misplaced zeal, or was it earlier than that? The bombs, the riots?

She switched her thoughts to the next day, and the speech she was going to have to sit up all night and write. This would need to be good, but not as good as Catherine's. And before either of them had their chance, she would have to tell John.

Damn. She'd promised to speak to him tonight. She looked at her watch as she rounded the corner to her street. It was nearly midnight. He'd still be up, either in his office in the House of Commons or his flat on the other side of the river. Should she call him now, or wait until daylight?

She pulled out her phone and flicked through the contacts. As she reached the front door to her building, she held her thumb over John's name.

Best to wait until she was inside. She clattered up the stairs, mulling over what she was going to tell John; there was so much. She pushed into her own flat, finally breathing again as she closed the door behind her.

She flung her coat onto the peg, not stopping to pick it up from the floor after missing. She grabbed her phone and pulled up the contacts again; John's name was waiting for her. She bumped into the coffee table and winced, cursing her lack of attention.

She looked down. The bag of groceries had been disturbed again. The noodles had been taken out, and the bag was on the floor next to her feet. On the coffee table where the bag had been was a plate, smeared with the remains of the noodles. Next to that was a half drunk glass of milk.

She dropped her phone, her heart pounding.

There was a sound behind her, the thunk of the fridge door closing. She held very still, listening. Another noise, shuffling this time.

Forcing herself to breathe, she turned slowly.

A figure emerged from the shadows of the unlit kitchen. It was tall and skinny, with lank hair hanging over a dirt-streaked face. She took a step back.

"Mum?"

47

SEPTEMBER 2021. LONDON

He looked pale and his hair was in dire need of a wash.

He stared at her, his eyes pools of blackness.

After a moment's silence she rushed to him. He stepped back. Her arms fell by her sides and she blinked back a tear.

"How are you?" she asked.

He nodded, saying nothing. There was the usual fire in his eyes but it was tinged with something that reminded him of the little boy she'd comforted after a tumble so many years ago. She itched to hold him.

"How are you? Where have you been?"

She knew he'd hate her firing questions at him. But he'd disappeared without a word, and he'd been breaking into her flat. Surely he owed her an explanation?

He still wasn't speaking. She looked him up and down. He was wearing his favourite jeans and an imitation leather jacket. Beneath it, a T-shirt. Not enough to keep him warm on the streets. Had she seen a bag or rucksack, on her way in? She tried to remember which one he'd taken from the house, but her mind was a blur.

"Thank you for coming here," she said finally. "I'm glad you're safe."

He shrugged and grabbed her arm. She reached out to touch his other shoulder with her hand but he pulled back again. He motioned towards the bedroom and pulled her towards it. She frowned at him but followed.

Inside, he closed the door and leaned against it, staring at her. His face was dirty, dark shadows orbiting his eyes. He looked older and younger at the same time.

He put a finger to his lips and crossed to her bedside table, where he fumbled with the alarm clock. The radio came on and he turned the volume up. She frowned.

"What are you doing?"

He shook his head and approached her. "Your flat'll be bugged."

"*Bugged?*"

He nodded.

"Why the hell would they bug my flat?"

He gave her one of his exasperated looks and took a step towards her. She could feel his hot breath on her cheek; he stank. "Don't be naive, Mum," he muttered.

"I'm not being naive." She hated having her own son insult her like this.

"You're the Shadow Home Secretary. Your son is suspected of being a terrorist. Of cour—"

"You're not suspected of being a terrorist."

He pursed his lips. "No?"

"No." She ran her hand through her hair. "Jesus, Samir, how much did you overhear?"

"Of you and Dad whispering about me? All of it."

She ran over the conversation in her head; the rushed account of what Catherine had told her, the speculation about what he had actually been doing.

"I don't believe it, you know," she said, fixing him with her gaze. "What they're accusing you of. I know you're not like that."

He shrugged. "You don't know me."

It was like a bullet. "Of course I know you. I'm your mum."

"Did you know I was playing truant, before you caught me?"

"No one knows that sort of thing until they—"

She considered. How much did she really know him? He spent so many hours shut up in his room, doing homework and chatting with his friends online. When he was out of the house, he was either at school or with Yusuf.

"I'm sorry, love," she said. "I've been a crap mum."

His body slackened. "No, you haven't."

She looked towards the bedroom door. Had she locked the front door? Could they be coming up the stairs now, about to arrest him?

She turned back to him and brought the back of her hand up to brush his cheek. He flinched but didn't stop her. Her hand rested on a red mark on his forehead. "You're bruised," she said. He nodded. "How?"

He shrugged. "Tried to nick some food."

Her heart felt so full of pity, and love, and remorse, that she thought she would burst. "That's when you decided to come here?"

He nodded. "I had a key."

"Dad's. I know. Were you always planning to come here?"

He shook his head. "Backup plan." He grinned, showing his white teeth, still bright.

She breathed out, thanking the heavens that he'd taken Yusuf's key.

"I need to tell Dad you're here," she said. "Tell him you're safe."

He frowned. "I'm not safe, am I?"

"You will be. I'm working on it."

"Oh shit, Mum. That never works."

"I don't know what you—"

"You think you're doing the right thing. You always do. But you don't get it. They hate us, Mum. I'll never be safe, and nor will any Muslim."

"That's not true."

"It is. I have to leave the country. I've bought a ferry ticket..."

He fished into his back pocket and brought out a slip of paper. She stared at it. "You haven't got your passport," she said, hating herself.

"It's in my rucksack."

He'd thought of everything. The rucksack must be in the living room somewhere. She wondered if he'd stolen anything other than food. She looked around the room; the duvet was crumpled and there was dirty underwear on the floor. At least he hadn't been sleeping rough, not all of the time.

"Samir, please. Give me a couple of days. I promise you that I'll make things better. I've got a plan. And don't take that ferry. They'll check your passport. They'll arrest you."

"Maybe."

"At least let me call Dad." Perhaps Yusuf could convince him. She pulled her phone out of her jacket pocket.

He threw his hand out to grab it. "No."

"What?"

"Use a phone box."

"*What?*" He was behaving as if they were in a spy movie.

"OK," she muttered. "But you stay here while I call him. Right?"

He said nothing.

"Please, Samir. If you leave now and they're watching, they'll see you."

He narrowed his eyes. She hated herself, manipulating his paranoia like this.

"I'll be ten minutes," she said.

~

Jennifer closed the front door to the street and paused, catching her breath. Her palms were clammy and her legs felt like jelly. She resisted the temptation to look up at her own front window and instead scanned the street.

It was quiet, just one group of people walking away from her about a hundred yards off, and a few cars passing.

She squinted and refocused, looking into the shadows; the gaps between buildings, the recessed doorways where someone might be watching her. No one.

Then she looked up at the houses opposite, the lamp posts in front of them. Two of them had CCTV cameras. A jolt ran down her body. How long did she have before they came for him?

She checked her watch – one minute already. At the end of the street was a phone box. She hurried towards it, anxious not to run.

She yanked the door open, wondering how she would pay for the call. It had been years, maybe decades since she'd done this, shoving coins in while calling her mum from University. Surely she wouldn't need the correct change?

She looked into the phone box. There was no phone. It was a wifi hotspot, nothing else. She cursed under her breath. All phone boxes in central London had been converted to hotspots years ago, and painted black instead of the iconic red. Did none of them have phones anymore?

She threw herself back out to the street and headed for Waterloo. There had to be phones at the station.

Sure enough, there were. The station was quiet at this time of night, the occasional person hurrying home after a late night working or weaving their drunken way through the space. She rubbed her arms, wishing she'd stopped to put on a coat.

Bingo. There was a pay-phone against a wall. She hurried towards it, feeling in her bag for her purse.

Yusuf answered on the first ring. She didn't pause for greetings, letting the words tumble out of her.

"He's here, he's in my flat. I'm at a phone box, he thinks my phone's tapped and the flat's bugged. He wants to leave the country."

She stopped, panting. She looked around the station concourse. Two women passed, clutching each other's arms and laughing together. They didn't look at her.

Yusuf's voice was full of concern. "Is he safe? Is he hurt?"

"He's got a bit of a bruise on his forehead, but he's OK. I can't talk long, I'm worried he'll disappear."

"Is he with you?"

"No. At the flat."

She leaned her forehead against the plastic dome that surrounded the payphone, felling its cold against her skin.

"He's a state, love. Completely paranoid. I don't know how to get him to calm down. We can't let him leave the country."

"Maybe he's right."

"Right? About buggering off to France?"

"No. About being watched. Think about who you are. Who he is."

He was right. How long did she have, before Samir was arrested and she was forced to resign in disgrace? Long enough to do what she needed to?

"I'm coming down," Yusuf said.

"No. Hassan needs you. Tell him Samir's with me. Make something up. A visit, a school trip or something. I don't know."

"I want to talk to him. He'll listen to me."

She bristled at the implied accusation. "That's what I thought, too, but how? He's right about not using his mobile. I don't even know if he's got it anymore." Two station staff walked past, one pushing a cleaning cart. The other tipped her a greeting. She nodded back, then turned towards the phone and cupped the receiver with her hand. "Please. I'm going to sort it out," she whispered.

"You think you can trust Catherine? Even if she does what she promised, I don't see how that will help Samir. And she's Catherine."

Jennifer ignored the veiled insult. "It will. I promise. Look at the news. Tomorrow's debate. Watch it."

She checked her watch. Twelve minutes since she left. "I've got to get back to him."

"OK. Call me, in the morning. I still want to come down."

"I'll try. Please, give me until tomorrow. Then I'll try to bring him home. Kiss Hassan for me."

Anxious to get back to Samir, she hung up and half ran back to the flat, not pausing to see if she was followed. This plan had to work.

∼

S he let herself into the flat quietly, terrified that he would have gone. But his rucksack was still on the floor by the front door. She bent down to grab it, then decided to allow him his privacy.

There was no sign of him in the living room or kitchen. She opened the door to the bedroom, which was still in darkness. He was slumped on the bed, his feet still on the floor. Asleep.

She put her hand to her chest. She crept towards him and lifted his legs onto the bed, slipping off his trainers. They were worn and dirty. She pulled the other half of the duvet over him, kissed her fingers and placed them gently on his forehead. He stirred but didn't wake. She pulled back and leaned against the wall, watching him. He mumbled in his sleep, occasionally throwing an arm out. She held her breath.

Silent tears tracked down her cheeks as she watched her son sleep for the first time in years. All the times she'd watched over him rolled through her head, the childhood illnesses, the holidays where they'd all had to share a room. He was a heavy sleeper, difficult to wake and grumpy in the mornings. Hopefully he would sleep well beneath her soft duvet.

She backed out of the room, wiping her cheeks, and went to the cupboard in the hallway. The sleeping bags reminded her of the times Samir and Hassan had slept on the floor here when they were younger. She thought of the

night before Hassan's tenth birthday. The night before the
Waterloo and Spaghetti Junction bombs, when everything
had changed.

She spread the sleeping bag on the sofa and arranged
the pillows as best she could. She slipped off her shoes and
skirt and got into the sleeping bag, knowing that she
wouldn't sleep much.

She was woken by Samir's hand jostling her shoulder.

"Wake up, Mum. It's eight o'clock."

She put a hand up to her face. The room was in darkness, the curtains still closed. Samir had showered and put
on clean clothes. She smiled; even on the run, he was still
Samir.

There was a mug of coffee on the table next to her.
Samir nodded towards it. "I wasn't sure if you took sugar."

She shook her head. Had her sixteen year old son never
made her a cup of coffee? "Thanks."

She drank it greedily, glad that it had cooled a little,
then sat up, the sleeping bag still wrapped around her. She
was aware that she had no skirt on.

"I'm going to the bathroom," she announced. "I've got
nothing on below the waist except my pants."

"Eww, Mum." He turned away and shuffled into the
kitchen, tidying up the mess from last night. She watched
him for a moment, relieved that he seemed to have come to
his senses. Then a ping from her phone jolted her back to
life and she leapt up. She needed to hurry.

When she returned he was sitting in front of kids' TV
with a full bowl of cereal.

She watched him. Leaving him here like this, when he
was threatening to get that ferry, scared her. But if her plan
worked, if things came together today, he'd be able to come
home. He wouldn't have to hide.

"I've got to go to work, love," she said. "I'll be back as soon as I can. Sit tight and wait for me."

He put the bowl down and turned. "Just for today."

"Yes. Then you can go back home."

He stood up. "No, Mum. Don't you get it? I need to get away. If they arrest me they'll deport us all."

"No, they won't. They don't do—"

"How do you know what they do?"

"Samir, I'm the Shadow Home Secretary. I know."

He shrugged. "Maybe."

"Please," she said. "It'll all be different after today. We can go home. You can talk to Dad."

"It won't make any difference."

She'd run out of answers. If she left now, would he wait? She couldn't stay here, not today.

"I've been thinking about it," he said. "They'll deport me to Pakistan. Because of Granny and Grandad."

"But they don't live—"

"That doesn't matter. They were born there." His forehead creased. "What do you think will happen to me there, Mum? Will I be welcomed into the bosom of some distant relatives, or will I be a target for other groups? People you *really* don't want me ending up with."

His voice was trembling; this was the first time she'd seen how scared he was. Last night he had been edgy, and determined, if more responsive to her than he had in years. But today he was a frightened child. He looked towards the window and she followed his gaze.

"It won't come to that," she said.

He sniffed. "You think that. But I don't believe you. I need to get away. My ticket is for tomorrow."

She put a hand on the back of the sofa for balance. He couldn't use that ticket. Even if he wasn't stopped as soon as he tried to leave Britain, how would she ever find him again? "Just wait here. Today. Wait for me."

He said nothing.

"I have to go, Samir. Please, wait for me. Watch the news, this afternoon. Then you'll understand."

He shrugged. Her phone pinged again. Fear mixing with anticipation, she went to the door and opened it. She could still see him in the kitchen.

"I'm sorry, love," she said.

He turned. "Me too."

She reached for the spare keys in their bowl; Yusuf's keys, the ones Samir had stolen. She closed the door quietly then turned the key to the deadbolt. She hated herself for imprisoning her own son. But she had to keep him safe. She crept down the stairs, hoping he wouldn't try to leave.

AT THREE O'CLOCK IT WAS TIME FOR THE DEBATE. Jennifer had spent the morning trying to make contact with John; calling his office, even hanging about outside it. But he was nowhere to be found, and his PA was cagey.

She had to warn him. She decided to get to the Chamber early, and take him to one side. She arrived at two thirty and stationed herself in the corridor behind the Speaker's chair after poking her head around the door to the Chamber and checking he wasn't there already.

MPs filed past her, some chatting, others more serious. Maggie passed with two other women, both known rebels.

She let Maggie cover her in a hug.

"Hi Maggie."

"Hiya. How's things?"

Maggie gripped her shoulder, her long fingernails digging in. Jennifer shrugged, wondering what Maggie would think of what she was about to do.

Maggie searched her face for a few moments then, seeing no response, squeezed her shoulder and carried on towards the Chamber. Jennifer watched her, envying her clarity of conscience.

John was with two other members of the Shadow Cabinet when he arrived. She caught his eye and waited, shifting from foot to foot. She glanced at her watch. *Come on.*

Finally he was free of them. He approached her, a friendly frown on his face. "Everything OK?"

She shook her head. "I need to talk to you."

She looked around then pulled him into the Chamber and the small space behind the Speaker's chair. This was where MPs came when they wanted to talk outside the earshot of colleagues during debates, or they didn't want to be picked up by the cameras. He frowned at her, puzzled.

"It'll be quick," she said.

Colleagues thronged past them, hurrying to grab a decent seat. The chamber would be as crowded as for PMQs or Budget day. They were going to get a show, she thought to herself.

She leaned in towards John. "I need to tell you something."

He looked at his watch. "If this is about your son—"

She fell back, winded. "What do you know about Samir?"

He cocked his head. "I didn't say which son."

"Please. Tell me what you know about Samir."

John's face turned grey. "I'm sorry. I shouldn't have said that. It's nothing. Nothing."

"It's not nothing, if you're asking me about it. What do you know?"

Colin Hayes ran past them, slamming into Jennifer. "Sorry!" he muttered. He turned to give them a curious look before he headed further into the Chamber.

She turned back to John.

"This can wait," he said. "We need to get into the Chamber."

She stared at him. He was right; there would be nothing he could tell her that Catherine hadn't already. Not that he knew that.

"I already know," she said.

"What? What do you know?"

"He's under suspicion. Association with a proscribed organisation."

"You know? Has he been arrested, then?"

"No." She thought of Samir, sitting in her flat. Watching TV. She hoped. "Someone told me."

His eyes narrowed. "Who?"

She tightened her jaw. "I can't tell you."

He wiped his forehead, which was damp. "Hell. Sorry, Jennifer." He looked back towards the Chamber. "We need to get in there."

"I still need to tell you something."

"What? Make it quick."

"This debate. There's going to be a surprise."

John's eyes widened. "What kind of surprise?"

She glanced around, and lowered her voice further. "Catherine Moore is going to make a speech. Putting the knife in to Trask."

"What? But she's a poodle."

"Not today."

"You think she's going to do a— do a— a *you*?"

She smiled. "Yes."

He shook his head. "You've got the wrong end of the stick. There's no way she'll do that. I know she's your friend, but..."

He hesitated, looking at her. He'd realised who'd told

her about Samir. But he said nothing.

"You just need to be prepared," she said. "This could be big."

He snorted. "We'll believe that when we see it. Let's just bloody well get in there, eh?"

❧

The Chamber was humming. MPs thronged the space between the opposing benches, conversation rising to the ornate ceiling. John worked his way through the crowd, answering questions, shaking hands, slapping backs. Jennifer pulled on her bravest face and tried to emulate him. Maybe it would distract her.

He made it to the front bench before her, sitting down and looking up at Deborah Mills, Shadow Education Secretary, who was laughing at something he had said. Jennifer threw her a quick hello and she moved aside, allowing Jennifer to slip in next to their boss. This was a Home Office debate, after all.

Deborah touched her on the shoulder. "Good luck."

Jennifer thanked her, pushing away the notion that she knew what was coming. This was just a friendly encouragement, that was all. She smiled and thanked her again. She needed all the support she could get.

She shuffled into her seat – it was tight – and delved into her bag for a notebook. She'd written notes for this debate a week ago, planned the main points she would be making. But that was before Catherine had told her about Samir. Before Samir had run away. And before Catherine had agreed to help her. She jotted some hasty notes in the margins, crossing out most of her original plans. Could she wing this? Thinking on her feet was her forte, but she was tired and couldn't stop thinking about Samir back in the flat. It would be getting dark soon and he wouldn't want to turn the lights on. She imagined him, the blue light from the TV flickering in his eyes as he watched her. She felt hollow.

She pulled her shoulders back and leaned forwards to stretch her arms, grasping her fingers together behind her back. She shook her head from side to side as surreptitiously as she could.

John gave her a sideways glance. "You OK?"

She nodded. He looked down at the scribbled notes in her hand.

"Have you got a speech prepared?" He sounded worried.

She looked at him then smiled. "Of course. Just some last minute edits, that's all."

He squinted down at the notebook in her lap. She pulled it towards her.

"This is a Home Office debate, Jennifer. I'm relying on you."

"I'll be fine." Her heart had picked up pace. He had to trust her.

He grabbed the notebook from her and she swiped at it.

"This is crap," he said, rifling through the pages.

She snatched it back. "Don't. It'll be fine."

He leaned in, bringing his head closer to hers. "Are you sure? First you tell me Samir's under suspicion, then this nonsense about Catherine Moore, and now you haven't prepared."

She dug her fingernails into her palm. They needed clipping. "I'll be fine."

He shook his head. "No. I'm benching you."

"What?"

"If somebody's got to wing this, it'll be me. I'll respond

to the Government."

She looked around them. Who was listening? "You can't—"

"I can. And I am. If you want to put your hand up and see if you get called, then fine. But I'm speaking for the Opposition."

"John. You owe this to me."

He turned to face her, his eyes flashing. "When it comes to Parliamentary debate, I don't owe you anything. You're a member of my shadow front bench, and I expect certain standards."

"Look. I've got these notes, at least. That's more than you've got."

"Sorry. I've made my decision."

She slumped against the wooden bench, staring ahead. The Government benches opposite were a blur of movement and noise.

"Jennifer? Are you OK?"

Deborah was standing in front of her. Jennifer widened her eyes. "I'm fine." She straightened up, glancing at John, who was ignoring her. "Sorry. Just thinking. I'm fine."

Deborah nodded and took her place again beyond John. Jennifer blinked, focusing on the Government front bench. She looked for Catherine. Where was she? Had she got a seat at the front? Surely as a Home Office minister, she would be there, alongside Trask and Peter Hillman, the Home Secretary. But the benches were full, and there was no sign of her.

Jennifer's phone buzzed in her pocket. She pulled it out, hesitant.

It was a text from Samir. She flicked it open, forcing herself to breathe.

Mum. I'm sorry. S.

49

SEPTEMBER 2021. LONDON

SHE STARED AT THE MESSAGE, TRYING TO WORK OUT what it meant. Was he apologising for what he had already done, or something he was about to do? Was this just a reiteration of the conversation they had had earlier?

John was looking over her shoulder. "Everything OK?"

"Yes. Just Samir."

"Apologising."

She pulled her phone to her chest, irritated. "Yes."

"Where is he?"

She stiffened. "At school. On his way home. I guess." She could hear John's breathing next to her ear. She should trust him with the truth; he'd known Samir since he was a baby. But he was her boss. And he had responsibilities.

Her phone buzzed: Samir again.

Love you.

She frowned. He'd never told her he loved her in a text; he hardly ever said it in the flesh anymore. Something wasn't right.

She looked at her watch. The Government would be making a statement first, then John, and then it was the turn of backbenchers and junior ministers. But if she left and came back again, the Speaker wouldn't call her. She had to be here from the beginning.

"If he's saying he's sorry, that's good isn't it?" John said.

John's children – two girls, delightful and little trouble to him as far as she could tell – had long since grown up. Did he have any idea what she was going through, or had his wife dealt with all of this?

"Yes," she muttered, looking up and past her phone. Catherine was opposite her, picking her way across the second bench back. She murmured apologies to people who stood to let her through, smiling graciously and shaking the occasional hand. She was wearing a pale grey skirt suit and looked composed and professional. Jennifer pictured how she looked herself. Her eyes, she knew, were puffy and red from lack of sleep, and she was hunched from the effect of sleeping on the sofa. She looked ten years older than Catherine, not three.

Catherine sat down and scanned the Opposition benches. Her gaze flicked quickly over Jennifer, not making contact. Jennifer frowned.

Her phone, loose in her hand, buzzed again. John shifted in his seat and she turned it away from him, bringing it up to her face.

It was Yusuf. *I know you wanted me to stay home but I felt so helpless. I'm at Euston. On my way to the flat. H is with my mum.*

She screwed up her face and gripped the phone. Anger at his impetuousness fought with relief that he was here. Samir would listen to Yusuf, she was sure.

She tapped her feet on the floor, trying to decide on her response. As she raised her finger to the screen, the Speaker stood and called for order.

The noise died down, MPs falling into their seats and wriggling to fit into the tight space. There were people standing at the end of the Chamber, by the doors. She looked up at the Strangers' Gallery; it was full. She smiled.

The Speaker raised an arm and called for order again, and a hush fell over the benches.

The Speaker cleared his throat. "The Right Honourable Member for Yeovil has a statement for the House."

Opposite her and next to Trask, the Home Secretary stood up and bustled to the dispatch box. He was a short, rotund man who gave the impression of a life of rich food and too much wine. His cheeks glowed red under the spotlights and his bald head gleamed.

He arranged his papers in front of him then leaned back, clasping his hands in front of him and looking around the Chamber.

"My Honourable Friends will be aware that there is a significant threat to the security of this country, despite the measures taken by this Government to counter it."

Behind her, the muttering started, rising to a grumble. She thought of Michael Stuart, now no longer an MP. If he was still here, would he have crossed the floor by now?

Jennifer pulled at her shirt; it was sticking to her skin, making her stomach itch.

"What's up with you?" John whispered.

"Nothing. Just hot."

John's skin was coated in sweat and dark patches had appeared on his shirt. When the Chamber was full like this, it was a furnace.

"I need you to focus," he grunted.

She eyed him. He was ignoring her now, watching Hillman with his arms folded across his chest, a patronising smirk playing on his lips. She grimaced and looked back down at her phone, glad now that Yusuf was working with her, helping their son. They would sort this out, between them. And from now on, she would be a better parent. As good a parent as Yusuf.

Hillman continued. He was announcing measures to increase powers of citizen's arrest, to strengthen Trask's civilian army. It was a measure that horrified everyone on her own benches, and a fair few on the Government side too. But Trask had the majority, and his Whips were notorious bullies, worse even than Michael's.

She closed her eyes and tried to focus. She needed to speak straight after Catherine, to back her up. Maybe that would work better than her going first.

Her phone buzzed again. Yusuf. *En route, be there soon. Hope it goes well. I'm listening online.*

She grasped her phone, thankful for Yusuf's tenacity. He and Samir would watch this together, and Samir would believe he was going to be safe, that he didn't need to run away again.

Great. Call you when it's done, she fired back.

She closed her eyes, feeling her mind clear. It was all there now; the points she needed to make, the order she needed to arrange them in. She ran through the words in her head, aware that her lips were moving slightly. Not caring. She smiled and opened her eyes again, ready.

Hillman had sat down and the Speaker was calling for order. Opposite her, MPs and ministers were patting him on the back, some wholeheartedly, others less so. Catherine was talking to a neighbour, not showing any reaction. Good.

John stood up, smoothing his jacket down as he headed

for the dispatch box. His hair was pointed with damp at the back of his neck, and his skin was patched red. Just the heat, she hoped. She wondered if he'd been sitting next to her doing the exact same thing as her, planning his speech.

Her phone buzzed again. Yusuf.

At the flat. Door busted. Samir's not here.

50

SEPTEMBER 2021. LONDON

JENNIFER STARED AT HER PHONE. SHE COULDN'T MOVE. Her legs felt like lead and her hands were shaking.

She forced her thumb to move and flicked back to the texts Samir had sent. *Mum. I'm sorry. Love you.* A farewell message?

Are his things there? His rucksack? she sent back to Yusuf.

No.

She looked across at Catherine, torn. If she left now, would Catherine do this without her?

I have to stay here, she sent to Yusuf. *Be as quick as I can.*

OK. I'll go looking for him.

She pictured Yusuf running along the street, searching vainly for Samir. It reminded her of the day of the Milan bomb, when Samir had run out of the house. Yusuf had waited for him, trusting him to come back. And he had.

She felt cold. On that occasion, he was reacting to an argument with her. Not to the threat of arrest, and deportation.

John had paused and the Speaker was talking, his voice hard.

"I would like to remind honourable members of the rules around the use of electronic devices in this Chamber."

Jennifer felt herself blush and slammed her phone into her lap. No one looked at her; there were too many others committing the same crime. Phones were allowed, but only if they weren't used 'in breach of Parliamentary decorum'. Sending texts counted as a breach.

John looked round at her and frowned. She shrugged an apology and bent down to slip her phone into her handbag. She had to leave Yusuf to do what he needed to do, and focus on what she needed to do.

The Speaker sat down and John puffed out his chest, continuing with his ad-libbed speech. He was doing a good job; he was a natural at this, with over twenty years of experience. And he'd been briefed, by Jennifer amongst others. At least she wasn't completely useless to him.

Dread washed over her. She was powerless, sitting here. Whatever she managed today would be for nothing if Samir disappeared.

A commotion was growing around her. Phones were buzzing, pagers bleeping. MPs fumbled in their pockets or reached into briefcases and bags. One by one they gasped and looked around the Chamber, seeking out prey.

Opposite her, Trask put his own phone on his knee and raised his eyes to meet hers. He smiled.

Someone behind whispered her name. She shot her head round. A woman stared at her, her mouth round.

The Speaker stood and barked out an admonishment. A few MPs put their phones down, but not all.

Her flesh was crawling. People were staring at her, whispering and muttering. She looked across at Catherine, who was finally meeting her eye. Her neck was a deep red. John had turned back towards his own benches and looked exasperated.

Trying to ignore the eyes on her, Jennifer leaned over and eased her phone out of her bag. She cradled it in her hands. Was there a message from John's offices, something everyone had received? But that wouldn't explain the Government reacting too. And it wouldn't explain everyone staring at her.

She looked at the benches behind her. Maggie was two rows back, giving her a maternal smile. A pitying smile. It was worse than all Leonard Trask's smirks, all John's impatience.

She turned back to the front. The Speaker was on his feet again, urging the Chamber to quieten down. He looked confused. He was probably the only person there without a phone.

Fingers numb, she pulled open the BBC app, only succeeding on the third attempt.

She stared at it, her chest tight. The noise around her rose, and someone behind her put their hand on her shoulder. She shrugged it off. "I'm so sorry," she heard, followed by, "not surprised."

She stared at the headline, and the photos above it. One was of her; the photo from her MP website, smiling tentatively at the camera. The other was blurred, amateur. She squinted, recognising the street outside her flat. A young man was being pushed into a police car, a hand on top of his head. It was Samir.

The headline was unmistakeable. She read it four times before the words gained their proper shape. Then she felt a chill run down her spine.

MP's son arrested for suspected terrorist activity.

Around her the voices rose, enveloping her in a wall of noise.

51

SEPTEMBER 2021. LONDON

"ORDER!" THE SPEAKER'S FACE WAS ALMOST PURPLE.

Jennifer stared at him, waiting for the instruction to leave. An official approached him and muttered something in his ear. He started then looked across at the Opposition benches, searching for her. She breathed heavily while waiting for his eye to meet hers.

He looked at her for a few moments, their eyes locked. Then he gave a tiny shake of his head and sat down, banging his gavel on the desk in front of him.

John shuffled backwards and sat down next to her.

"Have you finished?" she breathed.

"No. But I don't want to follow *that*." He nodded at her phone.

She stiffened, wishing he could be more supportive. "I need your help, John. Samir's done nothing wrong."

He shook his head, sighing. Then he grasped her hand, pulling away almost immediately. "I know."

It was an admission of confidence, but not a promise of help. She looked across at Catherine, whose gaze flicked away from hers. She balled her fists on her knees and willed herself to breathe steadily.

"I have to go," she told John.

"I understand."

She rose to leave. Catherine was watching her. She looked shocked, and scared. Jennifer looked at her, wishing they could talk. Was a text too risky? She surveyed the MPs around Catherine. Yes, it was.

She sat down again. "I'll wait. Hopefully he'll call me next," she said, motioning towards the Speaker. John nodded.

Her phone buzzed in her hand. Yusuf again.

He's been arrested.

I know, she sent back.

Wait there. I'm coming to you.

No. You need to find him.

We do this together. Wait for me. Xx.

She slid down in her seat, her eyes going back to Catherine. She was flicking through papers, muttering under her breath. She pulled a pen from an inside pocket and started writing on the sheet she held in her hand, making sweeping marks and scribbling furiously. Jennifer stared, her mouth falling open. Was she changing her speech?

John nudged her. "Are you OK?" he whispered. "You look pale."

She widened her eyes, trying to focus. "I'm fine."

"Sure? You should leave. Find him."

"Yusuf's coming. I'll go then."

John's gaze shifted up to the Strangers' Gallery. It had started to empty. Jennifer watched as journalists hurried out, desperate to follow up the story. Was this debate even going to continue?

The Speaker was calling for order again. Jennifer sighed and rubbed her forehead. It was as damp as John's.

"I call the Prime Minister."

She looked up. Trask?

In front of her, Trask drew himself up and slid to the dispatch box. His MPs watched in silence. Hillman looked annoyed. Catherine stared at him, her skin grey. Jennifer pulled herself upright.

Trask looked around the Chamber then fixed his gaze on Jennifer, saying nothing. He then turned away from her, looking towards the Speaker.

"Mr Speaker," he said. "I think this House should know that certain Members are directly affected by the measures which we are debating today."

There was a collective intake of breath. Jennifer felt John stiffen beside her. A hand landed heavily on the back of her bench. She tensed.

Still Trask didn't look at her. He swept his gaze across the Opposition benches, keeping it raised above the front bench. "These powers which we are discussing today are a vital measure to protect us from people who would do this country harm. People whom it can be difficult for the authorities to identify, and apprehend."

She stared at Trask, unblinking. John glanced at her, his face expressionless.

Trask licked his lips, turning to look at his own backbenchers. "I know we agree in my party that all those who engage in terrorist activity, or who are terrorist sympathisers, need to have the full force of the law brought to bear on them."

He spun round and looked directly at Jennifer. "No matter how exalted their family or other connections."

She clenched her fists. Behind her, the shouting began. Cries of "Shame!" and "Innocent till proven guilty!" She breathed in, relieved that her colleagues were supporting her. Then she heard a "hear, hear" behind her.

Trask looked back at the Speaker. "I apologise, Mr Speaker. I digress a little and I don't mean to breach Parliamentary protocol."

The Speaker eyed him but said nothing.

"But," Trask continued, "I do believe it is important for us all to note that the sooner we apprehend the unsavoury characters in our society, the ones who want to threaten our communities and our security, the sooner we will be able to keep everyone in this country safe."

It wasn't his best rhetoric. But it was well aimed. Jennifer glared at him, then glanced at Catherine, who was frowning.

The Speaker stood up and the shouts died down.

"The Right Honourable gentleman should apologise for his remarks. I am hesitant to accuse him of a breach of etiquette, but would urge him to consider his words carefully."

Trask gave a small bow and stood up again. He looked at Jennifer, and then at John. "I apologise for my remarks. I did not mean to insult any individual member of this House," he said. He sat down, ignoring the pats on the back from his colleagues and smiling at Jennifer.

~

T he Chamber was quiet. John stared ahead, not meeting Jennifer's eye. What was he thinking? Was he remembering her treachery, two years ago? *I had a fair bit of respect for the stand you took*, he'd told her, afterwards. Safely afterwards. She glared at him. He really wasn't the same man Yusuf had worked for. The man who'd sat at the kitchen table of her and Yusuf's first house, cracking jokes and sharing political anger.

After what felt like an age, hands started to go up. Jennifer watched Catherine, waiting for her to raise hers. Instead, she was watching Trask. She looked ill.

Come on Catherine, thought Jennifer. *You can do it.*

The Speaker called an MP from the government backbenches and Jennifer's phone buzzed.

I'm in the gallery. Look up.

She looked up at the Strangers' Gallery; Yusuf was at one end, next to the entrance. He looked flushed and his coat was askew. He gave her a small wave but didn't smile.

Come with me, he texted. *Got to find him.*

She took a deep breath, staring across at Catherine. The backbencher had sat down and the Speaker was searching for the next.

I have to wait. Have to speak.

She won't do it. You have to leave.

She swallowed. He was right. She muttered an apology to John as she rose in her seat.

Then she heard it. The Speaker was calling Catherine.

She looked across the Chamber. Catherine was rising slowly. Jennifer slammed down into her seat, her heart pounding.

52

SEPTEMBER 2021. LONDON

CATHERINE GLANCED AT JENNIFER THEN QUICKLY looked away, her gaze travelling to Trask. He was whispering with the Home Secretary next to him, oblivious of what was – or wasn't – about to happen.

There were a few quiet mutters, some shushing and then the Chamber was quiet. Catherine looked down at her notes then bent to put them on the seat behind her. She clasped her hands in front of her and held her head high.

John turned to Jennifer, raising his eyebrows. She gave him a nod and allowed herself a smile.

Catherine drew breath.

"Thank you, Mr Speaker. I'm pleased to be able to speak in this debate today, and to share my own experience, which I believe is relevant to the subject we are discussing."

Jennifer remembered the tales Catherine had told her, the horror stories. This was how they'd agreed she would begin her speech. She watched Catherine, waiting for their eyes to meet again so she could give her an encouraging nod.

"My department receives regular information about people who have breached the anti-terror laws. Now I'm sure this House will understand that I'm unable to share the details of this, but I would like to give you a feel for what I've seen, what I've read, and what I've heard."

There were murmurs behind Jennifer. John nodded and gripped his knee. Trask stopped whispering and turned, craning his neck to look at Catherine. She continued.

"I am regularly shocked by the type of person who comes under scrutiny. The demographics of the people who our security services are investigating can be quite an eye-opener."

Catherine paused and looked across at the Opposition benches. Her gaze landed on John, who was talking to Deborah. She didn't look at Jennifer.

"There are young men and women who have become involved in groups and organisations that seek to do damage to this country and to put our citizens at risk. These young people – some just teenagers – are naive and impressionable and don't always know what they're getting into."

Trask had turned back to the front, frowning. Jennifer allowed herself a shiver of anticipation.

"It can be incredibly hard, sometimes impossible, to trace these people. There are probably many more out there than we are aware of. Maybe ten times as many, maybe more. Hundreds if not thousands of impressionable young people being recruited by terror organisations."

Jennifer felt her breathing slow.

"This legislation which we are debating today will make it easier to identify these people, and others like them, of all ages. The authorities struggle to gain information about the activity of our potential attackers, which limits the number of people apprehended. This new power of citizen's arrest will mean that family, friends and community members, people who have access to information and knowledge of activities that we can't possible trace, will be able to identify and apprehend these people before their activities become a real threat."

There were a couple of shouts from Jennifer's side, but quiet opposite. Trask began to smile.

"I believe," Catherine continued, her eyes on the Speaker, "that anyone who has expressed an interest in and sympathy towards prohibited groups has the potential to present a very real threat to public safety at a later date."

Jennifer stiffened, remembering everything Catherine had said when planning her speech. What about those young, impressionable minds, those teenagers who didn't know what they were getting into? Who would be unjustly criminalised if apprehended and arrested under these new laws?

She could feel eyes flitting between Catherine and herself. Samir was exactly the person Catherine was talking about, and they all knew it.

"I therefore welcome the proposed legislation," Catherine continued. "It will enable us to identify and apprehend potential terrorists much earlier on, and nip their activity in the bud."

Catherine sat down to applause from her own benches. Behind Jennifer, MPs were on their feet, waving papers and yelling. She closed her eyes, hating the fact that Yusuf was watching this.

She stood up, and stepped forward, over the red line in front of the Opposition benches. MPs weren't allowed to cross this line during debates. The Chamber quietened.

The Speaker rose. "Can I ask the Right Honourable member to return to her seat please."

She ignored him and stared at Catherine, her nostrils flaring. Finally Catherine met her eye. Her gaze was steady.

Jennifer raised an arm. The Speaker said something she couldn't make out amid renewed shouting.

She took another step forward; she was almost at the middle of the Chamber now, well outside the permitted zone.

She stared at Catherine, shaking her head. Catherine reddened. Trask looked round at her, raising a bemused eyebrow. The Speaker stood up.

Fire licked at her limbs. She looked up at Yusuf, who was standing, watching her as he backed towards the door.

She shook her head. The shouting intensified.

"The Right Honourable member needs to withdraw to her own benches!" cried the Speaker.

She looked back at John; he glared at her.

She turned to the Speaker. "I apologise," she said, and turned for the door.

53

SEPTEMBER 2021. LONDON

JENNIFER LOOKED UP AT THE STRANGERS' GALLERY, where Yusuf was making for the stairs. He was right; Catherine wasn't her friend. She was a Tory, and would always be loyal to her own party.

She looked back at Catherine, who was staring back at her, her head high. She looked proud, and satisfied. Everything they had talked about, everything Catherine had said about those kids, teenagers like Samir, had it been lies all along? Did Catherine really believe that Samir deserved what was coming to him?

She looked towards the doors. She longed to run out, but had to maintain her dignity. She started walking. In front of her was a wall of people, the crowds who hadn't been able to get a seat for this debate. They stared at her.

"Will members please clear a path for the Honourable Member to leave!" the Speaker called.

Slowly, their eyes on her, the people at the front of the crowd began to part, the mass of MPs splitting on party lines. Her own side and Catherine's.

She muttered a thank you and started to make her way

through them. It was like walking through an ocean. Voices rose up on both sides.

She cast a glance back into the Chamber. John was staring at her, looking like nothing so much as a disappointed father. She scowled at him. A few rows behind, Maggie was shooting her sympathetic looks. Was this what it had come to? Her only supporter was a notorious rebel?

At last she reached the doors. Invisible hands on the other side pulled them open. She blinked as the light from St Stephens Lobby attacked her eyes.

The lobby was full. Members who hadn't made it to the debate, intrigued members of the public, and the press.

The press. What looked like hundreds of them swarmed forwards, pressing against each other in their desperation to get at her. Cameras were pointed in her direction, and flashes zinged in her eyes.

She tried to look past them, to find Yusuf. There was no sign of him. He would be to her right, towards the Strangers' Gallery. Trapped on the other side of the crowd.

She dove into the crowd, covering her face with her hand. "Excuse me," she said, as clearly as she could.

She pushed towards the gallery, scanning the faces. Where was he?

She stopped as a hand fell on her shoulder and felt herself relax.

❧

Jennifer leaned backwards, letting the hand take some of her weight. Now Yusuf was here, and they could face this together. She didn't care about Catherine anymore, or John, or Leonard Trask. She didn't care that she'd made a fool of herself in the Chamber, and that all her colleagues despised her. She didn't care about her ruined career.

All that mattered was getting Samir released. And doing it hand in hand with her husband.

A voice came from behind her. "Jennifer Sinclair?" It was a woman's voice, unfamiliar.

She frowned. Where was Yusuf?

She turned. The hand didn't belong to her husband but to the owner of the voice, a short woman wearing a cheap suit and faded overcoat. She looked up at Jennifer, her eyes blank.

"Yes," Jennifer replied. This woman would be a journalist. She had to get away; now wasn't the time to answer questions. But why had she asked her name?

The woman fished into the inside pocket of her coat. Jennifer waited for a phone, or a microphone. She started to push against the woman's hand. She had to find Yusuf.

The woman held a dark object up in front of Jennifer's face. Jennifer focused on it. It was square and battered. Not a phone. It was a police warrant badge.

She sighed with relief. "Are you here to take me to my son?"

The woman shook her head.

Jennifer frowned. "Where's my husband?"

"Jennifer Sinclair, I'm—"

"Please, tell me where Samir and Yusuf are. I can help you."

The crowd pressed in against them. Out of the corner of her eye she saw that the doors to the Chamber had opened again and people were spilling out. She had to get away from here.

She drew herself up to her full height to tower over the woman, who was looking at the crowd, irritated. "I'll help in any way you need me to. Just let me speak to my husband first." She was going to make it OK. Somehow.

The woman tightened her grip on Jennifer's shoulder.

"Jennifer Sinclair, I'm arresting you on suspicion of hiding a suspected terrorist."

54

SEPTEMBER 2021. LONDON

HER CELL IN THE BOWELS OF NEW SCOTLAND YARD was damp, with a fluorescent light flickering on the ceiling. She had no idea how long she'd been here.

The door opened.

"Stay there."

A uniformed officer stepped inside, not making eye contact. He instructed her to turn round and put her hands behind her back. She felt the cold steel of handcuffs snap over her wrists.

In the doorway, the woman from earlier was waiting. Detective Inspector Johnson.

"Thanks, Cooper," she said to the sergeant. She eyed Jennifer. "Come with me."

She led Jennifer out the way they had come in, along a series of corridors, into a lift and up to the daylight. Jennifer knew this building, had been here for its official opening when she was Prisons Minister. John had officiated, beaming at the modernity of the Met's new building.

Even after a few hours, she was relieved to be outside. They were at the back of the building; she could see the river beyond trees and hear traffic on Whitehall. Less than half a mile away, business was continuing in the Houses of Parliament.

"Where are you taking me?" she demanded. "Will I see my family?"

The detective licked her lips; they were thin, adorned with pale pink lipstick. Her cheeks were pale with high red spots where the autumn air was getting to the skin. "We're taking you to the Magistrates' Court. Your solicitor will be waiting for you."

She felt her heart pick up pace. She had used her phone call – still allowed, despite the anti-terror laws – to ring Edward, her solicitor for many years. He had been calm but not as reassuring as she would like.

She still didn't know where Yusuf was, or Samir. She could only assume that Hassan was safe with her in-laws.

Another man bundled her into the back of a van, led her to a tiny cell inside, and slammed the door shut. Footsteps clapped along the tarmac followed by doors opening and closing at the front of the van.

The sarcophagus-like cell was higher than it was wide, with scratches on the metal walls where previous occupants had tried to leave their mark. A minuscule square window let in some light at roof level but it was obscured so she couldn't look out. The cell smelt of vomit mixed with bleach. She pulled herself in as tight and still as possible, willing her stomach to behave, and waited. After about half an hour, the van slowed, turning some tight bends and coming to a stop.

Her stomach started to settle. Again doors opened and closed up front.

She watched the door to her cell, listening to the muffled sounds of voices outside. Finally the door opened and two uniformed police hauled her out. She stumbled to the ground, almost losing her footing, and tried to gain a sense of where she was.

They were behind a tall, modern building, slim windows adorning its walls. She'd been here too, when she was a minister. Westminster Magistrates' Court.

Would Yusuf be here?

She was led along a warren of corridors and into a small room with two chairs and a tiny table. A policewoman pushed her into one of the chairs, and told her to wait. She did as she was told.

As the policewoman left, Edward hurried in. She stood up, startled and relieved. She had to fight an urge to kiss him.

"Edward! What's happening? Where's Yusuf? Where's Samir?"

His face was impassive, betraying neither good news nor bad. He gave her a tight smile and nodded at the chair. She sat down and he took a seat opposite her at the grey formica-topped table. Outside she heard voices, muffled shouts and then silence.

"Don't worry," he said. He was unshaved and looked as if he hadn't slept. His thin grey hair was ragged, making him look five years older than the last time she'd seen him. "They're OK. Yusuf is here, and Samir. Hassan's at home."

She stared at him, subdued by his matter-of-factness. He opened his hefty briefcase and pulled out a file.

"Now. I need to explain to you what's going to happen here today."

Jennifer nodded. She knew already, or believed she did. She tried to push away her anxiety and let him take over, lead her through the drill.

"When you're in there," he finished, "let me do the talking. And Samantha, your barrister. She's upstairs, preparing."

"But—"

He eyed her. "I mean it, Jennifer. Don't say anything. You're my client now and not my friend. You've got to listen to me."

"At least tell me what's happened to Yusuf."

"They arrested him, but let him go without charge. He got to the flat after Samir left, so he wasn't involved."

"Involved in what?"

"In hiding him."

"I didn't hide him. I just let him lie low for a—"

"Jennifer. You knew he was under suspicion."

"They don't know that."

"Are you telling me you didn't know he was under suspicion? I can't lie in court."

She shook her head. "No. But how did they know?"

He shrugged. "I guess we'll find out. But it's not much of a leap. Samir ran away. He came here. The police were about to arrest him. They already had his girlfriend."

"Girlfriend?"

Edward nodded.

"Don't be silly. Samir doesn't have a girlfriend."

Edward looked down at his hands.

Jennifer tugged at his fist, impatient. "They've got it wrong," she said. "He doesn't have a girlfriend." Thoughts rattled through her head. "Is that all they've got on him? This girlfriend?"

He looked up. "She was a member of a proscribed group. They arrested her over a month ago."

"No. I'm sure of it. I know he was secretive. He played truant." She clenched her fists. "But there's no girlfriend."

He sighed and took a folder out of his briefcase. "I'm sorry, Jennifer."

He opened the folder and pulled out a sheet of paper. He placed it on the table between them. It was blank.

She frowned at it. He turned it over.

The photograph was black and white, clearly taken with a telephoto lens. It was of a young Asian couple engaged in a passionate kiss. The boy was Samir. The girl she didn't know.

She sat back. Was this where he had been, all those times he had come home late? "Who is she?"

He put the photograph away. "Her name is Meena Ashgar. At least, that's the name they've given me. She was part of this group they're accusing him of being involved in. She was one of the ringleaders."

"That doesn't prove anything."

"It wasn't just that. He went to meetings. He helped put out leaflets. They've got his computer."

"He was just an angry teenager. How does that equate to being a terrorist?"

"I'm sorry."

He stood up, glancing at his watch. "You're going to be first in. They want to get it over with, clear the court afterwards. They'll be coming for you in twenty minutes."

She slumped into her chair.

"I'm not pleading guilty."

He sighed. "If we can get a not guilty verdict for Samir, then we'll appeal your conviction, but you'll get a more lenient sentence in the first place if you plead guilty." He leaned back, stretching his fingers. Jennifer heard a click. "We can't convince anyone you didn't hide him. They've got CCTV footage of your flat."

"I was just protecting my son."

"I know. I understand, honestly I do. But in the eyes of the law, you were hiding someone who you knew to be under suspicion of membership of a proscribed group. Please, do as I say. This'll make it easier for Samir."

"What will happen to him?"

"He's lucky. If he'd been charged with membership and not just association, then he'd be subject to internment. Part of the Prevention of Terrorism Act. It was amended last year."

"I know," she told him, "I voted against it." But her voice was quiet, not the one she'd used to argue against that bill in the Commons.

He looked at her over his file. "I know."

Of course he did. "Anything else I need to know?"

"No. Just let me do my thing. When the magistrate asks for your plea, say Guilty. That's it."

She closed her eyes.

"Remember what I said, Jennifer. Stick to the minimum. Only answer direct questions. Let me and Samantha do the talking."

She nodded, holding back tears as he left her to wait.

~

A policewoman took her arm and led her along dark, echoing corridors. She wondered where Samir was. She wouldn't see him today; his hearing would be later on.

The policewoman gave her a light push in the small of the back and she stumbled through a door into the court room. She squinted up at the ceiling. High above, framed by the bodies around her, fluorescent lights cast a harsh yellow glow. The policewoman pushed her towards the dock, then removed the handcuffs and told Jennifer to place her hands on the rail in front of her.

Jennifer stared at her hands, willing them to be still. Behind her the public gallery was buzzing. She swallowed; Edward had warned her that the press were here. She raised her eyes and took in the desks and benches in front of her, beyond the glass. Edward sat at one of them with another man and a woman – her barrister.

She risked a glance behind her. The gallery was full. She recognised some of its inhabitants: journalists, as well as – her heart jumped – Yusuf, right at the front and blinking at her from a gaunt face. He stood stiffly, his eyes hooded from lack of sleep. They locked eyes for a few moments and then he put a hand to his face, wiping his eyes.

She put a hand on her chest in an effort to calm herself. The room was blurring, grey dots appearing in front of her eyes. After a moment the dots cleared and her thoughts sharpened again. The high ceilings and benches reminded her of the all the rooms like this she'd been in over the years; council chambers, committee rooms, even a court or two. Not forgetting the Commons Chamber. It didn't stop her feeling intimidated.

The magistrate looked up from his high desk at the front and over her, raising an eyebrow. "Can I ask for quiet in the public gallery please."

Yusuf looked at her again, his eyes full. She thought of Samir – where was he? – and Hassan, who they'd lied to. Would he ever trust her again? She tried to smile at Yusuf but couldn't do it. She turned back to the front.

"Ms Sinclair, please give the court your name and address."

Jennifer did so, thinking of the house, empty without her family in it.

"Please sit down."

Jennifer sat, clasping her hands together in her lap to make them behave.

An exchange followed between the magistrate and lawyers. She was to be refused bail.

The magistrate asked her to stand again. His gaze was businesslike but not harsh. Just another day's work.

"What is your plea?"

She glanced at Edward. "Guilty."

The magistrate nodded. "Jennifer Sinclair, you have pleaded guilty to harbouring a suspected terrorist."

She opened her mouth to protest but caught Edward's frown and stopped herself.

"I'm referring your case to the Crown Court for sentencing, but in the meantime you will be remanded in custody at Bronzefield Prison."

Bronzefield. Where Hayley Price had died. Jennifer felt her legs weaken.

~

In seconds she was out of the room and moving down the corridor, the policewoman's firm hand pushing her back towards the cells. She wouldn't see Edward again today; he had to help Samir now.

She shivered.

As she approached the staircase to the cells, a door slammed behind her, echoing down the corridor. Followed by footsteps.

"Jen!"

She span, pushing away the policewoman's hand. The handcuffs dug into her wrists and she gulped back a cry.

She stumbled into the policewoman, who tried to pull her back round. She resisted.

"Yusuf! How are you? Are you OK?"

He nodded, smiling. Tears were rolling down his face.

The policewoman's grip tightened on Jennifer's shoulder. She pulled against it, trying to get closer to Yusuf.

"What's happening to Samir?" she called. "Have they let you see him?"

He shook his head. The policewoman tightened her grip on the handcuffs. Jennifer didn't care.

"We'll get him back," Yusuf called. "We'll sort it. He hasn't done anything wrong."

She nodded and swallowed. It wasn't as simple as that.

He looked angry, as if he knew what she was thinking. "We will, Jen," he said. "I'll start it, then we'll get you out and we'll do everything we can to get him back. Together."

She smiled at him. *I hope so.*

The policewoman had been joined by a colleague and they were guiding Jennifer back towards the cells. Her feet skittered against the polished floor. Yusuf shot an angry look at the officers, then turned back to her.

"I love you, Jen!"

She was pulled into a room and the door was closed. The policewoman guided her to a chair. She opened her mouth but only a croak came out. She slumped into the chair, staring at the door. Could they make it right? Could they get Samir off? Or would she be in prison for a long time?

She clenched her fists. They would fight this. She had friends out there, powerful people who would help her. She would get her family back, and nothing, not even a prison sentence, would stop her.

NOTE FROM THE AUTHOR

Did you enjoy this book?

You did, didn't you? That's why you're still here, reading on after the book has ended.

Please leave a review for the book on Amazon and Goodreads. It'll help give the book what they call 'social proof' and find new readers.

And read on for details of the next two books...

Thanks,

Rachel McLean

DIVIDE AND RULE - PART TWO IN THE
DIVISION BELL TRILOGY

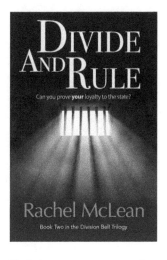

Jennifer Sinclair's fight to save her political career, her family and her freedom has failed. Traumatised by prison violence, she agrees to transfer to the mysterious British Values Centre.

Rita Gurumurthy has betrayed her country and failed the children in her care. Unlike Jennifer, she has no choice, but finds herself in the centre against her will.

Both women are expected to conform, to prove their loyalty to the state and to betray everything they hold dear. One attempts to comply, while the other rebels. Will either succeed in regaining her freedom?

Divide and Rule is 1984 for the 21st century - a chilling thriller examining the ruthless measures the state will take to ensure obedience, and the impact on two women.

Publication October 2018.

DIVIDED WE STAND - PART THREE IN
THE DIVISION BELL TRILOGY

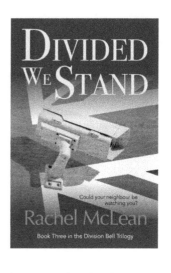

Britain is a country under surveillance. Neighbours spy on neighbours. Schools enforce loyalty to the state. And children are encouraged to inform on their parents.

Jennifer Sinclair has earned her freedom but returns home to find everything changed.

Rita Gurumurthy has failed to prove her loyalty. When a sympathetic guard helps her escape she becomes a fugitive.

To reunite her family and win freedom for her son and her friend, Jennifer must challenge her old friend, the new Prime Minister Catherine Moore. Will Jennifer have to reveal the secret only she knows, and risk plunging the country into turmoil?

Divided We Stand is a gripping thriller exploring an alternative and chilling version of Britain.

Publication November 2018.

JOIN MY BOOK CLUB

To read the opening chapters of the next two books in advance, plus a series of short stories featuring the characters from the books, join my book club at rachelmclean.-com/bookclub.

You'll get weekly emails with stories, character notes, musings on my research and lots more. And if they ever manage to work out a way to send cake by email, that may be on the cards...

Happy reading!
Rachel.

ACKNOWLEDGMENTS

I first started writing this book 15 years ago, after attending a business writing course and learning a technique that I knew would help me plan a novel. It's been through many iterations then and a lot of people have helped coax it to a publishable state.

Rob Ashton of Emphasis was responsible for that course which was the original impetus.

Sally O-J went through a very early (and terrible) draft and gave me invaluable advice on the things I needed to do to improve it (there were plenty).

Sue Hayman MP very kindly read a later draft and highlighted inaccuracies in the Westminster setting as well as giving me suggestions for locations only MPs know about. Any errors are mine, not hers.

Members of Birmingham Writers Group gave me feedback on various drafts and excerpts and told me about an embarrassing repeated typo. Special thanks to Martin (who gave me an idea that prompted the sequel), Heide and Iain.

My book group were the very first people to read it all the way through and give their feedback - which I'm sure was way more glowing than it deserved at that point. Thanks to Toni, Ruth, Liz, Teresa, Louise, Jenny and Jane.

My editor Dexter Petley gave me invaluable advice on letting the story breathe and improving my characterisation.

And finally thanks to my family, not least my mum Carol, whose political convictions inspired me to become involved in politics and whose unwavering encouragement was the impetus I needed to start writing a novel. I wish she could see this being published.

Lightning Source UK Ltd.
Milton Keynes UK
UKHW01f0210150918
328902UK00001B/28/P